CONRADOLOGY

CONRADOLOGY

EDITED BY BECKY HARRISON &
MAGDA RACZYŃSKA

First published in Great Britain in 2017 by Comma Press.
www.commapress.co.uk

This book has been co-commissioned by Comma Press and
the Polish Cultural Institute in London.

The opinions of the authors and editors are not necessarily those of the publisher.
A CIP catalogue record of this book is available from the British Library.

ISBN 1910974331
ISBN-13 9781910974339

This publication has been supported by the ©POLAND Translation Program, the
Polish Cultural Institute in London, and the British Council.

The publisher gratefully acknowledges the support of Arts Council England.

Supported using public funding by
**ARTS COUNCIL
ENGLAND**

Printed and bound in England by Clays Ltd.

Contents

NON-FICTION

Foreword

Robert Hampson

THE MAN WHO WAS to become known to the world as the novelist Joseph Conrad was born 160 years ago, on 3 December 1857, in Berdichev in Ukraine. Józef Teodor Konrad Korzeniowski was the son of Apollo and Ewa Korzeniowski, who, in May 1862, were sentenced to exile as a result of their political activities in support of Polish independence. At this time, Poland did not exist as a country: it had been divided up between Austria, Prussia and Russia. Berdichev was under Tsarist rule, but was one of Poland's border regions with a complex population of Polish land-owners, German settlers, Ruthenian peasants, Cossacks and a substantial Jewish community. Apollo and Ewa Korzeniowski were dedicated to the liberation of their country, and both gave their life to this cause. Ewa died in April 1865 and Apollo died in May 1869. After a childhood spent among political exiles in Vologda and Chernikiv, Conrad had a few years schooling in Kraków before, in 1874, at the age of sixteen, he left Poland for Marseilles and the beginning of his sea-career.

From 1874 until 1893, Conrad was to work as a sailor, first in French ships and later in the British Merchant Marine. During these years, he gradually worked his way up the rungs of the profession, although he only once had command of a sea-going ship: the *Otago*, which he captained from January 1888 to March 1889, taking over in Bangkok and resigning from the ship in Port Adelaide, Australia. During his years as a sailor, he voyaged to the West Indies, spent much time in the Indian Ocean and the China Seas, and, most famously, signed up to captain a steamer on the Congo. These experiences provided him with material for important parts of his life as a writer. His experience of command on board the *Otago* prompted two stories, *The Shadow-Line* and 'The Secret Sharer'; his experiences in Africa produced two important stories, 'An Outpost of Progress' and *Heart of Darkness*; while his glimpse of South America provided one of the stimuli for his masterpiece, *Nostromo*, the great twentieth-century novel of neo-colonialism. It was his experiences as first mate of the *Vidar*, however, which led directly to his first novel. This Arab-owned steamer made regular voyages between Singapore and small ports on the east coast of Borneo and the west coast of Celebes. At one of these, Conrad met the man who was to be the model for Kaspar Almayer, the protagonist of his first novel, *Almayer's Folly*.

Over the next thirty years, Conrad was to produce the novels and short stories which made his name: 'Typhoon', *Lord Jim, Nostromo, The Secret Agent, Under Western Eyes*. From the start, his work met with critical acclaim. However, it was only with the publication of *Chance* in 1914 that he gained popular success. Doubleday, who published *Chance* in America – and had a collected edition of Conrad's work in hand – undertook a massive advertising campaign: the success of that campaign in promoting Conrad's works established Conrad's reputation in America. Thereafter, all his novels – *Victory, The Rover, The Arrow of Gold, Suspense* – were best-sellers in the United States, and a generation of American writers, including F. Scott Fitzgerald and William Faulkner, were influenced by his work.

Conrad was very quickly established as a world writer. During his lifetime, his work was taken up by André Gide and his circle. Gide was immersed in Conrad's works: he dedicated his *Travels in the Congo* to Conrad's memory, while his novel *The Counterfeiters* was influenced by *Under Western Eyes*. In

Germany, Conrad's work was championed by Thomas Mann, and, more recently, has influenced works as diverse as Lothar-Günther Büchheim's *The Boat*, where U-boat experiences are read through the generational dynamics of *Victory*, and Christa Wolf's *Accident*, where Chernobyl and brain surgery are approached in a narrative shaped by *Heart of Darkness*. Conrad's work has also had a complex role in post-colonial writing. The Guyanese writer Wilson Harris argued that Conrad's fiction opened a door for post-colonial writers. The South African writer Lewis Nkosi and the Kenyan writer Matthew Buyu both undertook doctoral research on Conrad. Ngugi wa Thiongo's novels, *A Grain of Wheat* and *Petals of Blood*, are readings of *Under Western Eyes* and *Victory* respectively. The Trinidadian writer V. S. Naipaul was similarly immersed in Conrad's works: he felt that Conrad had been everywhere before him, and this is evident in a novel like *A Bend in The River*. Gabriel Garcia Màrquez, in *One Hundred Years of Solitude*, responds to Conrad's portrayal of South America in *Nostromo*, as does Juan Gabriel Vàsquez in his more recent novel *The Secret History of Costaguana*. Similarly, the Australian Randolph Stow's *The Visitants* is *Heart of Darkness* transferred to the Trobriand Islands and his later novel *Tourmaline* shows various debts to *Lord Jim*, not least in its narrative method.

Conrad continues to have an impact on contemporary writers. David Dabydeen's *The Intended* flags up its connection to *Heart of Darkness* with its title. W. G. Sebald devoted a section of *The Rings of Saturn* to an account of Conrad's early life. Iain Sinclair has had a long and complicated engagement with Conrad from his first novel, *Downriver*, with its Conradian endpapers, through to *Dining on Stones*. Nor has Conrad's legacy been restricted to literature. The author and artist Tom McCarthy has had a long fascination with Conrad – at one point co-creating an installation based on the Greenwich bombing that features in *The Secret Agent*. And there have been numerous dramatisations of Conrad's fiction since the

1916 stage adaptation of *Victory*. Equally, there has been a long history of film adaptations from the silent film versions of *Victory* and *Lord Jim* through to the recent French adaptation of 'The Return', the Malay adaptation of *Almayer's Folly* and Peter Fudakowski's version of 'The Secret Sharer'. The most famous film adaptations, of course, are Hitchcock's *Sabotage* (based on *The Secret Agent*) and Coppola's *Apocalypse Now*. Indeed, *Apocalypse Now* has been responsible for renewed popular interest in Conrad. This has been most evident in the world of graphic novels, with a number of publications (in Britain, France and Italy) exploring *Heart of Darkness* and Conrad's own Congo experiences.

Conrad's sophisticated handling of narrative technique, from his first novel onwards, continues to engage writers and readers. His interest in psychology has also appealed to both critics and readers: early criticism focussed on his explorations within the self (from *Almayer's Folly* through to 'The Secret Sharer'); more recent criticism has picked up on his attention to trauma (from *Lord Jim* through to the succession of traumatised young women in his later fiction). The thematic concerns of his fiction are also strikingly relevant to the political climate of today. *Heart of Darkness*, probably his best-known work, was a pioneering exposé of colonialism and empire, which became a key text in late twentieth-century post-colonial studies. *Nostromo* has proved to be a prescient work on neo-colonialism and globalisation; his London novel *The Secret Agent* is similarly timely with its address to refugees, terrorism and the policing of both; *Chance* begins with share promotion and financial fraud; while his Russian novel *Under Western Eyes* returns to the topic of political violence and political refugees. Conrad's fiction is the product of an historically-informed and politically-engaged imagination. The thorough-going scepticism that informs his work proves an effective instrument of political analysis, which he uses on the rhetoric of empire as a 'civilising mission', and on political rhetoric more generally. At the same time, his critique of the competing nationalisms that produced World War I led him to explicit support for a transnational united Europe as the best hope for the future.

This book brings together new responses to Conrad's legacy from Polish and British authors, as well as from writers further afield, to mark what in his home country has been declared the Year of Joseph Conrad. The fictions and non-fictions produced in response to this commission pick up on many of Conrad's abiding concerns. Paul Theroux's 'Navigational Hazard', for example, not only reflects Conrad's reputation as a writer of the sea, but, more specifically, recalls Conrad's early Malay maritime experiences and the fiction that grew out of them in a story that plays with the classic Conradian themes of loyalty and betrayal. Sarah Schofield's 'Expectant Management' responds to one of those maritime stories, 'The Secret Sharer', and directs its psychological exploration of 'first command' towards a very different kind of 'secret sharing'. Kamila Shamsie's 'A Game of Chess' reworks *The Secret Agent* to address contemporary issues around the secret state and terrorism; while Agnieszka Dale's 'Legoland' shows what it is like to be a Pole in post-Brexit England. Similarly, Jan Krasnowolski's reflections on his grandfather's literary connections with Conrad are a testament to the cross-generational affection for the writer in his homeland.

Conrad's legacy hasn't always been plain sailing, however. One of the most influential responses to Conrad in recent times was Chinua Achebe's 1975 Amherst lecture in which he criticised the American academy's teaching of *Heart of Darkness*, which foregrounded psychology and downplayed its themes of colonialism and the book's representation of race. Defenders of Conrad rallied and argued that Achebe's powerful but ultimately unfair reading had wilfully ignored the gap between

Conrad himself and his fictional narrator, Marlow. But in the ever-contentious arena of post-colonialism, this criticism hasn't entirely disappeared. Wojciech Orliński, in his futuristic response to *Heart of Darkness*, 'Conrad Street', subtly engages with it, through his own use of an unreliable narrator: here, a 'pilgrim' returning to the disease-ravaged Poland of his youth echoes a version of Achebe's view. But even to Orliński's narrator it's clear that, if there is any racism in the book, it is Marlow's, rather than the narrator's, let alone the author's. As someone who had experienced firsthand how King Leopold's companies operated in the Congo, and then gone on to write *Nostromo*, Conrad was clearly aware of 'corporate exploitation' than Conrad. And as Richard Niland demonstrates in his essay 'Conrad, Capital, and Globalisation', Conrad's understanding of 'long waves of economic, political, and historical development' informed his fictions throughout his life.

In the light of all this, the challenge to the writers gathered here is more than simply to explore Conrad's life and fictions from a contemporary perspective. To work in a truly Conradian manner, they must bring to bear upon their contemporary subjects the level of scrutiny to which he subjected his own experiences and the deeply-informed vision by which he measured the events and issues of his day. The resulting stories and essays – from the futuristic to the personal, from the experiential to the philosophical – offer new versions of Conrad, whose own fiction remains as richly suggestive as ever – and whose relevance, as an analyst of the globalised world we inhabit, has never been greater.

Navigational Hazard

Paul Theroux

ONE OF THE RITUALS, strictly observed by most of the expats at the University of Singapore when I taught there in the Sixties, was to meet in the Staff Club after classes, drink beer at one of the long tables and, when one of the dozen or so drinkers left, disparage him, mocking what he had just said to the others. Willie Willetts took exception to this disloyalty – he was the curator of the university art museum, an expert in Chinese pottery and Khmer celadons. He described his recreations as, 'Reading, thinking, and drinking.'

'You know I'm not umbrageous, and I'm all for having a good grouse,' Willetts used to say, 'but this is distinctly unfair.' He was only in his fifties, but I was 26, so he seemed old to me. 'You notice Harry Montvale never gangs up on anyone.'

Montvale was Willie's friend and neighbour, older than he, a commanding presence when he visited the Staff Club. Among the pale, perspiring, out-of-shape lecturers and professors, gabbling in this daily sundowner, Montvale stood out: tall, sinewy, with an intimidating gaze, and noted for his silences. He was neat in the way he dressed, scrupulous in avoiding gossip, and with a stern sense of justice. Although he was diligent in paying for his round, he had – so Willie told me – nothing but a small Royal Navy pension and was just scraping by, in a small house on upper Bukit Timah Road, a recent widower. I was to remember all this after I learned his story.

'Harry is a master navigator,' Willetts said.

'I was just a skipper,' Montvale said, smiling in impatience, uncomfortable with Willetts' praise. 'Mainly in the waters hereabouts – Straits Settlements. Charters, cruising, some fishing clients. I know the Borneo ports pretty well.'

'I was thinking of getting a boat to Kota Kinabalu.'

'I knew it as Jesselton – North Borneo. The MV *Keningau* sails there every fortnight. Let me know when you go. There's something I want you to verify for me.'

A month or so later, after I booked my passage on the *Keningau*, I met Willetts and Montvale at the Staff Club. I suggested that we sit apart from the other expats, because I didn't want anyone to know my plans. They would mock me for taking a ship rather than a plane, they would speculate on what I'd do in Borneo, the futility of it, when I could be in the Staff Club drinking beer and denigrating a colleague.

But Harry Montvale was encouraging. 'You'll see some ports,' he said.' Labuan Island, for certain. But it's in Jesselton that I want you to keep your eyes peeled. When you approach the harbour mouth look for a tall pole indicating a navigational hazard. It will be in a place where there are no obvious rocks, where the water is deep – an odd place across from a rather grand Chinese godown. I'd be interested in knowing whether it's still there.'

I took the trip and loved it. The *Keningau*'s skipper, Captain Meyrick, invited me to eat with him and his wife. I had a pleasant cabin. I read Naipaul's *Mr. Biswas*. I played whist with a Malay rubber planter and a Chinese woman who lived in KK – as they called Kinabalu. The winning hand was always slammed down, the player calling out, 'Tumpang!' The night we spent at the dock in Labuan the monsoon rain was so loud, beating on the deck, I could not make out what the planter was saying. When it let up he told me that a baby boy had been born on the third-class deck. We went there and saw the infant, swaddled with its mother, among a sweating crowd of Tamil rubber tappers, en route to a plantation.

'Call him Kenny,' the Malay planter said. 'After this ship.'

The next day, I went to the bridge as we approached KK.

'I'm looking for a navigational hazard,' I said.

'That pole,' Captain Meyrick said, pointing and seeming to wave it away, as he steered the ship around it. 'Very inconvenient, especially in the dark. Especially *there*.'

The pole was, as Montvale had said, at the approach of the channel, in front of the Chinese warehouse he mentioned, the godown. The tall pole was black with age and below the tidemark thick with greenish barnacles, a metal plate attached to the top like a road sign, the paint peeled but the warning visible in three languages: *Danger*, *Bahaya* and, unexpectedly, a waffle-like Chinese character.

'I'm glad it's still there,' Montvale said to me in a grateful tone at the Staff Club, when I returned, and with a sigh he attempted to disguise with the back of his hand he added, 'Thank you. You've given me something.'

'Tell him the story,' Willets said. 'Paul's a writer. He'll appreciate it.'

After some prodding, and insisting that we change our seats so that none of the expat drinkers could hear, Montvale said, 'I was skipper of the *Selamat*. It was owned by a towkay here in Singapore, Chung Fatt Heng. He was ten years my junior but he made his first million in his twenties, just out of college, some kind of cigarette scheme, avoiding taxes on them, and then selling them at a profit in a Malay state where they were heavily taxed.'

'I've heard of that – lots of people do it,' I said.

'Not to the extent that Fatt Heng did it. It was huge. He was moving shipping containers full of cigarette cartons. Think of the complexity.'

'Just smuggling,' I said.

'What I mean is, think of all the people involved – all the trust needed. Fatt Heng was a man who somehow inspired loyalty.'

'Why are you smiling?' I asked.

'Because loyalty is earned through righteousness.'

As a yacht skipper, Montvale was impressed with such loyalty, since a vessel negotiating mangrove coasts and hidden reefs required the crew to follow orders and be watchful. Montvale said he'd done two tours in the Royal Navy, and had been based in Singapore at the barracks in Sembawang named the HMS *Terror*. On his discharge, wishing to stay in the East, he'd interviewed for master of the yacht *Selamat*, and gotten the job. The pay was good, he could live on board, and Fatt Heng seldom used the yacht. He took Fatt Heng's friends and clients on cruises, but mainly he sailed with guests who'd paid for the privilege. The *Selamat* was chartered by the week or, now and then, extensive month-long cruises along the Malaysian coast. To live on this yacht, island hopping in the South China Sea, was to Montvale the life he'd dreamed of. These were the routes that Joseph Conrad had sailed, but he remembered how he laughed when he'd mentioned to Toni how a Conrad run in these waters was often a voyage of betrayal. 'And what do we have on board? Holiday makers, bird-watchers, and sometimes gunny sacks of copra or bales of rubber. No betrayals!'

The *Selamat* was a ninety-four-foot yacht, ketch rigged – that is, double masted – with a seventeen-foot beam, a classic wooden boat, and 'well bred', built in the Philippines of oak and teak and mahogany. At the centre of the saloon, a carved oak dining table, with a sofa and chairs for six people. The yacht could sleep six, plus the crew, which included a gourmet chef, Montvale's wife, Antoinette – Toni. On the rare occasions when Fatt Heng was on board, Montvale and his wife slept in the Stern Cabin. But the rest of the time, which was most of the time, they occupied the Owner's Cabin in the bow – plenty of room, a head, a shower, a small galley.

The *Selamat* was their home, their luck, their world; and when a Singaporean businessmen, Bill Kelley, asked Montvale whether he would work for him, skippering his yacht, *The Sláinte*, and named a high salary, Montvale was torn, to the extent that he shared the information with Fatt Heng.

'I made my fortune taking risks,' Fatt Heng said. 'So I understand your dilemma. I'd be tempted myself. I know *The Sláinte* – a nice boat.'

Speaking slowly, Fatt Heng was seated cross-legged on a low bench that had once been an opium couch. Fleshy and inert, and with the facial moles that the Chinese think of as lucky, and sometimes as a warning, he reminded Montvale of the figure the Chinese call Joss, a plump benign deity that is propitiated with incense and fruit. He seemed to be encouraging Montvale to take the job.

'I could use the extra money, sir,' Montvale said. 'Toni and I want to buy a boat of our own at some point, and live on board as we do here.'

'Think of what you're saving by living on board my *Selamat*,' Fatt Heng said.

That was not the answer Montvale had been expecting. He had thought that Fatt Heng would offer him more money.

Fatt Heng said, 'I like using the boat for guests, and there's some profit in it. But I'm a towkay at heart, happy in my godown. You probably notice that I get seasick. What use is a boat to a man who gets seasick?'

'It pays its way,' Montvale said. 'It's a business.'

'Water business,' Fatt Heng said, dismissively, tugging his legs under him. 'I'm a Sabah boy myself. I grew up on my father's coconut plantation in Sandakan. But I'm sentimental. Probably that's why I keep the boat. And you're a loyal employee.'

'It's been a pleasure, sir.'

'Glad to hear it. Now you say that Bill Kelley offered you a job. But what if I made a counter offer?'

Montvale named the amount that Kelley had mentioned.

Fatt Heng flicked his fat fingers, waving the number aside.

'Not money,' he said. 'Money is a simple thing. Look what I've made. I am offering you your freedom and your future.' His moles folded into his smile as he peered closely at Montvale, and went on, 'I like letting my friends cruise with you. The charters are okay. I guess I'm breaking even. You know the cost of fuel, of repairing the sails, painting and upkeep. It adds up. But, in eight or ten years, I'll be moving on to something else. Need something new, lah!'

'I'll still be young,' Montvale said.

'Yah. The timing's right. At that point I'll give you the boat.'

'Give me the boat?' Montvale repeated. The offer surprised him, and in his momentary confusion he was unable to understand fully the implications. But Fatt Heng was still talking.

'I had a Saudi client,' he was saying. 'He wanted to invest in Penang, where I had some interests. He brought me to Saudi Arabia to finish the deal. One of the sheiks with him was fiddling with his worry beads. In this case they were made of emeralds. I knew that from across the room – the bluish green, the way they shimmered. He was in white, looking like a priest, looking like all the others in the board room, the robes, the sandals, the thing on his head.'

'It's called a keffiyeh,' Montvale said. 'I sailed in the Gulf when I was in the Royal Navy. I bought one. It's secured by an igal.'

'I am speaking of the worry beads. My partner, Jin Bee was dazzled by them. After the meeting we gathered in the courtyard for tea, and smoking the hubble-bubble, just men together. Jin Bee says, "Those beads are fantastic."'

Fatt Heng swung his legs off the bench, rose from his seat,

imitating the sheik, and gestured to Montvale, saying, 'Take.'

Montvale squinted at Fatt Heng's assertive gesture, though he remained rigid.

'That's what the sheik said. Without any hesitation, he handed the emerald beads to Jin Bee, and he insisted that he keep them. That was the custom. You praise something, they give it to you, no questions. And the sheik did it without flinching, though the beads must have cost in the tens of thousands.'

'I've heard of that happening, though I've never seen it.'

'It should have been an awkward moment, but it wasn't. It was a lesson to me.' Fatt Heng returned to the bench and, nodding sagely, said, 'I want to be that sheik. Not attached to what I own, so that my things possess me. But to be free of them, and fair.'

The towkay's smooth face conveyed certainty. In the constellation of tiny moles, Montvale saw luck and wealth.

'Stay with me for ten years and the *e* will be yours. You can think about it.'

'I don't need to think about it,' Montvale said. 'This is the answer to my prayers.'

They shook hands on it. Montvale went back to the *Selamat* and told Toni the news. She said, 'That's wonderful, but don't you think you should get it in writing?'

When Montvale mentioned a written agreement, Fatt Heng laughed. 'You don't trust me!' and Montvale, embarrassed, backed off.

'In ten years I'll be fifty eight,' he told Toni. 'We'll cruise around the world. Maybe do some charters for money.'

So their future was assured.

Montvale was fastidious about maintenance, and in the past Fatt Heng had always paid. But Fatt Heng was not so prompt now, and sometimes did not reply to a request to fund the repairs. With the confidence that the *Selamat* would be his in ten years, Montvale used his own money to refit and repair the yacht. He considered it his even now, years before the hand-over. Fatt Heng showed up less and less. One year he did not appear at all, and – claiming seasickness – he never sailed. The money from the charters went directly to his agent, who paid Montvale his monthly salary.

Every year, Montvale was offered a job skippering a yacht – bigger yachts, more money; he always declined, citing loyalty to Fatt Heng, though he never disclosed that he was remaining on the *Selamat*, because in a few years it would be his.

And often, when the agent was slow to come up with his salary, or Montvale felt a task was urgent, he went on using his own money to replace a sail or a cleat, or to repair a spar or rigging. He bought a new tender in Malacca, a strip built rowboat, painted red. When his urgent memo *'Keel bolts need replacing'* went unanswered by Fatt Heng he spent the last of his money that month on installing new ones. Looking around the yacht he could count the repairs he'd made, allowing him to conclude that by degrees he was making the yacht his own. In his fastidious way, he kept a file of receipts, documenting every repair.

When the *Selamat* was in dry-dock for any length of time, as it had to be for some refitting, Montvale and Toni rented a car and drove to Johore, or to Fraser's Hill or the Cameron Highlands, and sometimes to Penang. It was there, in George Town, that he learned that, having made conquests in land sales, manufacturing, and hotels, Fatt Heng had moved his office and residence from Batu Ferringhi to Jesselton in North Borneo. Montvale recalled Fatt Heng saying, 'I'm a Sabah boy myself,' and his mention of growing up on a coconut plantation. But Montvale suspected that removing himself to distant Jesselton was his way of keeping out of reach of the authorities in Kuala Lumpur.

Montvale had not needed to do much research to discover the latest of Fatt Heng's successes in business. His name was always in the *Straits Times*, the news of his latest deals in mining and oil exploration. Montvale marvelled at how Fatt Heng had the loyalty of so many, and thought of him as like a captain of the line, commanding a great schooner that ventured across these seas, with a vast crew, and one man in charge. He sometimes sailed to Jesselton and anchored where Fatt Heng's godown faced the channel.

Always, at the end of one of the holidays necessitated by repairs, Montvale was reminded of how little he owned ashore – nothing, really, no house, no car, not even much in the way of savings, because of his paying for the yacht's upkeep and repairs. But when they relaunched the *Selamat* and boarded it they were able to say *we're home*. Trustworthy himself, he was trusting of others, and he had the reassurance that the yacht would soon be his.

Nine years into the agreement, after one of the seasonal refits, Montvale and Toni turned in their rental car and prepared to board the yacht, at a mooring in Singapore. A stranger stood on deck at the top of the gangway – Chinese, unsmiling, his arms at his sides.

'You are?'

'I am Jin Bee.'

Jin Bee of the emerald worry beads. He handed Montvale an envelope, saying, 'For you.'

Fatt Heng's distinctive dragon chop was on the envelope. The letter inside was brief: '*I am selling the boat. New owner is Jin Bee. He will accompany you to Jesselton.*'

Montvale felt sick, weak, empty, but all Jin Been said was, 'You must talk to the towkay,' and showed him a deed of ownership, and the papers proving that the yacht was registered in his name.

The run to Jesselton was sombre, but the winds were fair, and they arrived in the harbour after three days. Leaving Toni on board, Montvale rowed his tender into port and found Fatt Heng in his godown on the harbour, looking content behind a wide desk.

Before Montvale could speak, Fatt Heng raised his hand like a policeman stopping traffic, and said 'I changed my mind.'

'But you promised.'

'Show me the proof. Show me the paper I signed.'

'I trusted your word,' Montvale said. And he took the file of receipts from his briefcase. 'Look. These are the dockets for all the repairs I've made.'

Fatt Heng was unimpressed by the faded yellowed papers that had the look of old laundry chits.

'I used my own money,' Montvale said, and when he saw Fatt Heng smile at his helplessness, he said, 'I insist on being repaid.'

'That's your pigeon,' Fatt Heng said.

'If you don't compensate me I'll undo them – shackles, spars, a new jib sail, new tender, bolts, everything.'

'You can have them back. Jin Bee will replace them. He has money. The boat is his.'

'Put that in writing,' Montvale said.

It took the rest of the morning for Montvale to prepare the document, which he did with the help of a Malay solicitor in Jesselton, who was amused by Montvale defying the eminent towkay, Chung Fatt Heng, listing every can of paint, every screw, spar, sail and bolt on the agreement, with the price of each, and the acknowledgement that Montvale was within his rights to repossess them.

'Not really much money,' Fatt Heng said, signing the document, stamping his dragon chop beside his name. But as he did, bringing the chop down hard, his wide sleeve flapped and a bracelet of green stones dinged on the desk. Lifting his forearm, Fatt Heng made the emerald bracelet slip into his sleeve, and he frowned as the witnesses added their signatures. Dismissing Montvale, he said, 'Jin Bee will supervise.'

But it was days of work, and Jin Bee retired to the Owner's Cabin, while Montvale, assisted by Toni, removed the fittings, the jib sail, the spar and a bucket of shackles. The yacht looked skeletal as Montvale steered it into the channel at the harbour entrance and dropped anchor, before Fatt Heng's godown.

'You might need this,' he said to Jin Bee, handing him a life jacket.

Then he went below, and began to remove the keel bolts. After two were loosened, water began to spurt into the hull. He managed to extract one of them, but the hull was filling fast. He was in the tender, rowing towards the mangroves – Jin Bee frantically splashing behind him – as the *Selamat* sank in four fathoms of water, only seven feet of its tallest mast still visible when the yacht became stuck in the muddy bottom.

'True story,' Willetts said. 'You saw the hazard.'

But Montvale was peering at the bar chit. He tapped it, saying, 'Vimto Soybean Milk. We didn't order that. Must be some mistake,' and called out to the waiter.

A Game of Chess

Kamila Shamsie

THE FOOTAGE FROM THE security camera clearly showed the face of the terrorist's accomplice, a face that could be found in the social circles of both the Home Secretary and Police Commissioner. This is not to say the Home Secretary and Police Commissioner, whose antipathy towards each other was well-known, moved in the same social circles. The Home Secretary had been at the head of the student protests of '68 and continued to feel most at home among radicals and anti-imperialists, particularly those who, like him, had decided to destroy the system from within and were now highly placed figures within the government and media. That they now sought to change rather than destroy the system was not a sign of political compromise but of maturity. The Commissioner had taken a very different path, ideological and otherwise, to her present position. A child of working-class migrants, she viewed her scholarships to public school and later Cambridge as proof of a functioning meritocracy that she was determined to defend and uphold. Naturally, she was feted by a certain segment of those who had inherited their own privileges and were therefore deeply invested in the idea that rewards came to those who deserved them.

The face of the terrorist's accomplice was really the face of two men. The identical twins, Yousuf and Nasser Ismail, both British born-and-bred, who went to visit their uncle in Pakistan in 2002 to try and repair a long-standing family feud, as per the instructions of their dying grandmother. This uncle handed them to bounty-hunters along the Pak-Afghan border who, in turn, passed them on to the Americans in exchange for a substantial reward, claiming the twins had flown out from London to support the Taliban. Although a cousin in Pakistan contacted the British High Commission in Islamabad with the true story soon after this, the twins still spent three years in Guantanamo before the efforts of the British Government, in response to a media campaign across both the leftwing and rightwing press, brought them home.

The twins were twenty-one when captured; twenty-four when released. Yousuf emerged from Guantanamo, benevolent and grateful; Nasser, suspicious and angry. Both of them were happy to drink wine or shake hands with women, and looked good on camera. Soon Yousuf was a fixture in the homes of those who later adopted the Police Commissioner, particularly one Lady L_____, who said Yousuf was a modern-day prophet, and consulted him on everything from how to vote ('with your conscience' he said) to where her grandson should go to school ('his local state school,' he said, which she held up as proof of his ironic humour which no one but Lady L_____ was subtle enough to understand). It took a little longer for the Home Secretary's comrades to welcome Nasser into their ranks, because first it had to be argued about and lead to irreparable rifts, but eventually he took his place among those who remained post-rift. Though he seldom spoke, the scars on his wrists from being tied in a stress-position for endless hours meant that on the rare occasions he raised his hand to indicate he had something to say, the floor was ceded to him. If the content of his sentences was lacking, his symbolic value was unparalleled, and there was no member of the group who hadn't won an argument in wider circles simply by invoking 'my friend, Nasser, who was at Guantanamo'.

The Police Commissioner was the first to see the video which clearly showed an Ismail twin being handed an envelope from the terrorist just before he set off on his final mission, which fortunately killed no one but himself. This envelope was identified as the one containing the long rambling letter which the terrorist wrote to his estranged wife, and which she said she found pushed under her door when she was leaving for work the next morning. The terrorist himself was a former Guantanamo inmate who had been imprisoned a year before the twins were released.

First the Commissioner spoke to one of her most trusted officers and sent him to Nasser Ismail's home; then she failed to take the incoming calls from the Home Secretary, who she knew would have seen the video by then. It isn't that she was ignoring him; that would be unprofessional. She simply didn't have time to speak to him if she was to arrive punctually at the black-tie charity gala, which was raising funds for the families of police officers killed in the previous year's terrorist attack – an attack to which both the Commissioner and the Home Secretary owed their professional elevation.

Nothing about her was quite expensive enough for the gala, she knew, as she walked across the philanthropist's garden, larger than most parks, and wondered where the smoker's corner was. But there was Lady L____, and the Commissioner who usually waited to be summoned by her was able to gesture her over, brimming with news that Lady L____ would want to hear, and for which she would be grateful. They walked away from the other guests and stood by the spotlit lily pond, the Commissioner relating all in low urgent tones interrupted only by Lady L____'s repeated cries of 'No! But go on…'

'It is as if one twin has all the genes for goodness and the other has all the genes for wickedness,' Lady L____ said, when the Commissioner was finished – her scientific training proving weaker than her love for novels with improbable plots.

'But which is which, that's the question,' said the Home Secretary, his voice such a surprise that it almost knocked the Commissioner into the lily pond. He clinked his flute of champagne with Lady L_____'s in that familiar manner meant to remind the Commissioner which one of them had been born into this world and would never be an outcast regardless of politics.

'Come, come,' said Lady L_____, not without affection. 'Your man is the one full of rage who won't condemn violence.'

'If you tell me you condemn violence I won't believe it,' said the Home Secretary. 'I remember Christmas 1972.'

'Oh you wicked person,' she laughed. 'But the point is, my Yousuf is a saint, an absolute saint. By comparison to everyone else, and certainly by comparison to his devil of a brother.'

'Wolf in sheep's clothing,' said the Home Secretary. 'Whereas my man…'

'Is the terrorist some of us have always known him to be,' said the Commissioner. 'Perhaps you haven't heard?'

'Heard what? Something you should have told the Home Secretary rather than imparting it to my old friend here.'

'I've kept more state secrets than you've had cups of tea,' said Lady L_____. 'But do you really not know?'

'Of course I tried calling you repeatedly,' said the Commissioner. 'But I was unable to get through.'

'What a curious thing, given call waiting.'

'It really is. Technology. Never as reliable as you want it to be. I'm afraid you won't like the news. One of my men went over to Nasser Ismail's – just to question him, of course – and found incriminating evidence there. It's beyond doubt – he's the one in the video. I can't of course go into details in the presence of a –' she smiled at Lady L_____ to ensure no offence was taken – 'civilian'.

The Home Secretary took a long sip of champagne. Then he shrugged. 'Whatever the evidence it proves only that he was framed.'

'Now you're going to say he was framed by his brother,' said Lady L_____.

The Home Secretary looked at the Commissioner. 'That's one possibility,' he said, his manner casual enough that only the Commissioner who knew her own guilt heard the accusation in it. 'Anyway, who framed him is for the Commissioner to work out. I'm just here to say it couldn't have been him in that video because at the moment it was filmed, Nasser Ismail was with me.'

'Good god,' said Lady L＿＿＿.

'You've always been too trusting, Binks,' the Home Secretary said. Then, to the Commissioner: 'You'd better send someone to arrest Yousuf Ismail. And we'll certainly want to look into who is responsible for planting the evidence. A pleasure as ever.' He leaned forward to kiss the Commissioner's cheek, his lips very close to her ear when he whispered 'Check-mate.'

'It's only check,' she whispered back.

In a very different part of London, Yousuf Ismail cooked dinner for his brother who had been released from police custody on the authority of the Home Secretary, while Nasser Ismail showered and changed into a pair of his brother's track pants and t-shirt. A few minutes later, while they were eating, identically dressed, there was a rap on the door and the police came to arrest Yousuf Ismail.

'I'm Yousuf Ismail,' said Yousuf Ismail.

'No, I'm Yousuf Ismail,' said Nasser Ismail.

The Commissioner had the misfortune of being in earshot of the Prime Minister when the call came to tell her what was going on. Although she said very little at her end, his preternaturally acute hearing – considered by some the primary explanation for his leadership of his party – picked up enough to warrant him asking for further details. When she told him what had transpired at the Ismail house, he summoned the Home Secretary from across the garden and made it clear that he expected this matter sorted out by the two people in front of him, speedily and without embarrassment to the government. It was well known that the PM had no love lost for his Home Secretary, who had been forced upon him by his coalition partners. It was equally well known that he thought the Commissioner had been appointed as a sop to political correctness.

'Game on,' said the Home Secretary on the drive over to the safe house where the twins had been taken.

'What game are we playing now that there are four players?'

'Still chess, still two players. Two of the pawns are tripping over each other as we move them around, that's all.'

When they entered the safe house the twins stood up, and both nodded with equal familiarity at the Home Secretary and Commissioner. The geniality of Yousuf and the rage of Nasser were both buried beneath identical expressions of concern for each other.

'I thought the two of you weren't on speaking terms,' the Home Secretary said.

'The womb –'

'And the torture chamber –'

'Bind us.'

'Oh god, it's an apocalyptic Tweedledum and Tweedledee,' said the Commissioner, extracting a cigarette from her clutch bag.

'Got another one in there?' asked the Home Secretary.

'Whichever one of us met with him hadn't seen him since Guantanamo.'

'He wrote to both of us, asked to meet.'

'You don't refuse to meet someone who you've known in conditions like that, even if you never liked him.'

'One of us went along, the other stayed with our mother.'

'She wasn't well.'

'It was a short meeting –'

They carried on, speaking in turn, establishing a story of

innocence. A man had gone to see someone he'd known under the most trying of circumstances. They talked about the weather and football and returning to everyday life after their ordeals. Perhaps there was a test in the questions, perhaps if the answers had been different the other would have said something about what he had planned. But he said nothing of the sort, only that he was leaving town in a hurry and could he ask a favour – there was a letter, an important letter that needed to be hand delivered. It seemed strange but there was no particular reason to refuse. And that was it, that was all.

The Home Secretary and Commissioner weren't listening. They smoked their cigarettes and appraised each other. Each saw an adversary who wouldn't back down. The Home Secretary considered the damage that could be done if the Commissioner decided – and she would – to investigate the alibi he'd so hastily provided for Nasser. The Commissioner considered the Home Secretary's wide circle of supporters and friends, and the cost of angering them by launching an attack on him. They both considered how it would weaken their own position if the PM fired their adversary and brought in a replacement who he actually liked and trusted.

The twins kept on talking, pleading their case, as if their innocence or guilt was of any relevance whatsoever.

Conrad Street

Wojciech Orliński

Translated by Eliza Marciniak

THE AEROPLANE DESCENDED BELOW the clouds and the familiar Mazovian plains appeared in the window. I leaned my head against the glass. I had left Poland seven years earlier, on one of the last refugee transports. I'd been putting it off, but when it became clear that the border would soon close, there was no sense in waiting any longer.

What had kept me in Warsaw was an irrational hope. Perhaps all middle-class urbanites would like to believe that their own city is eternal, that it will outlast them and that their children and grandchildren and future generations will go on enjoying it.

I saw the destruction of Warsaw with my own eyes, so I'll never think that way again about any city. Not Berlin, to which we were evacuated; not London, where I ultimately ended up; not Rome, where I'd boarded the plane earlier that day, using the only connection to Warsaw accessible to civilians.

This is also irrational: just because Warsaw no longer exists doesn't mean that one day London will cease to exist. But people aren't rational.

They took us away by train. That day I was also looking out the window. What sticks in my memory most are the cars. Corpses weren't usually lying about in the streets; the disease didn't kill quite so quickly. At first people felt sleepy and weak;

21

they'd go and sit down somewhere to rest. By instinct, they sought shelter inside – at home, at work, in a café.

The exceptions were those whom death had caught behind the wheel. They died in accidents or pulled up onto the hard shoulder thinking they just needed a quick nap – a nap from which they would never awake.

The streets were full of crashed cars and others parked at weird angles. Nobody came to remove them in the months following the breakout of the epidemic. Judging by what I saw from the plane window, nobody would ever remove them now.

On our descent to the airport in Modlin, we flew over the outskirts of Warsaw. When I lived in Conrad Street, I'd ride my bicycle out to those places. I could remember their names – Kazuń, Czosnów, Łomianki – but even back then I wouldn't have recognised them from the air, never mind now, after so many years.

It was obvious at a glance that there was more green than there used to be. Kampinos Forest was in the process of devouring the suburban gardens. It wouldn't be long before it would reclaim everything it had lost centuries earlier – meaning all of Warsaw, really.

The sight was almost idyllic – except for the cars. Even from this height, the disorder on the little suburban streets and on the motorway to Gdańsk was clearly visible. The wrecks were strewn about untidily, as if a child had got bored of playing with its toys.

The other pilgrims on the plane were also looking out the windows in silence. Not all of them were Poles; at the airport and during the flight I had caught snippets of conversations in English, Italian and Spanish. Clearly the landscape below didn't have the same emotional significance for everybody as it did for me, but death has its own universal language, understood by all.

We landed at Modlin. I would have preferred Okęcie, like everyone else, but the Holy Brotherhood, the Santa Hermandad, had closed that airport until further notice. The official reason given was technical issues, but it probably had more to do with the fact that Okęcie was too close to areas controlled by the insurgents.

We walked down the steps onto the tarmac. The first thing I saw was the ruin of the modern terminal: they hadn't bothered demolishing it or even blocking it off. I had thought we'd be picked up by a shuttle bus, but instead we were greeted by a few sad-looking Latin Americans dressed in Santa Hermandad uniforms. They gestured towards a makeshift barrack block with the emblem of the Brotherhood and a sign in Polish, Latin and Spanish that read, *'PILGRIMS, WELCOME TO THE LAND OF SAINT ADALBERT'*.

We set off towards it in single file, carrying our luggage. Inside the barrack, customs agents of the Brotherhood, more Latin Americans, were waiting for us. Each had his own desk, surrounded by a low partition, which reminded me of the cubicles in the open-plan editorial offices where I'd worked before the epidemic. In each agent's cubicle there was a crucifix, an emblem of the Brotherhood and a portrait of Pope Francis III. I could still remember the shock caused by the election of the first Francis, who in his time didn't need a number attached to his name. A non-European pope – how unthinkable! But after the plague had decimated the Church in Europe, the presence of even one or two cardinals from the old continent at the conclave would cause a sensation. The Catholic Church had become a Latin American church. One day, the inexorable rules of demographics would make it an African church, but for the time being the Latin Americans were in charge, to such an extent that the Vatican had been ironically nicknamed 'Ciudad Vaticano'.

My turn came after about a quarter of an hour. One of the customs officers yelled 'Next!' in Polish and waved me over to his cubicle. When he saw in my travel papers that I'd come from London, he switched to English. I didn't mind.

This was my first time, but I'd been advised how to behave during the inspection. Without waiting to be asked to unpack, I opened my travel bag and took out a pouch containing twenty-two Krugerrands. I placed them on the desk in even piles, so that the agent could easily see there were twenty plus two.

'I'd like to declare twenty gold coins,' I said. The agent ceremoniously wrote this down on the form and gestured for me to put them away. I dropped twenty coins back into the pouch and slipped it inside my bag. Two coins remained on the desk. The customs official covered them casually with a cardboard folder.

'If you've brought any electronic equipment, it's in your best interest to include it on the declaration,' he said. 'Otherwise you might have trouble taking it back with you.'

'I'm not planning on taking anything back,' I replied truthfully. He nodded as if what I'd said was patently obvious and stamped my travel papers.

'Welcome to the land of Saint Adalbert!' he said cheerfully and handed them back to me.

Outside the barrack, a bus painted in the colours of the Santa Hermandad was already waiting. It took us to the Pilgrims' House not far from the airport. I had a good two hours before I was to meet my contact, so I went to my assigned room to freshen up. I was conscious of the fact that these were the last hours I'd spend in the comforts of civilisation for a very long time, perhaps for ever.

As I turned on the shower tap labelled 'agua caliente', I realised I'd never been inside a building constructed after the plague. Even in cities with relatively few casualties, such as Berlin or London, the epidemic had wreaked havoc on the real estate market. It wasn't worth building anything new in Europe, and neither furniture nor bathroom fittings were manufactured here anymore. Judging from the labels in my room, the Brotherhood had to import everything from Latin America.

Because of that, everything in my room smelled fresh. I had already forgotten that smell!

I had also forgotten another smell, or rather a stink. In the restaurant on the ground floor, where I'd arranged my meeting, the air was grey with cigarette, pipe and cigar smoke. European prohibitions didn't apply in the area controlled by the Santa Hermandad.

I was holding a copy of Joseph Conrad's *Heart of Darkness*. That's what I had agreed with my contact so that he'd recognise me. It had been my idea – since the aim of my journey was Conrad Street.

I had read the book only once before, as required reading in secondary school. On the plane I decided to refresh my memory. Perhaps the world had changed that much since my school days, or perhaps it was me who had changed, but it was only now that Marlow's racism hit me. For him, the evil of colonialism seemed to boil down to the fact that in Africa white people lost their civilisational superiority and came to resemble their surroundings.

The idea that the root of the problem was corporate exploitation, to which both black-skinned slaves and their white-skinned masters fell victim, obviously to different degrees, as did the protagonist, sent by his company on a pointless mission, never seemed to have crossed the author's mind. Yet from the corporation's point of view, they were all just entries in the costs column – costs which must be continually reduced.

It made for amusing reading, now that the plague had annihilated that entire world, together with the so-called white race. There was no more 'white man's burden' because there was no more 'white man' – or at least not in the sense that Conrad had understood the term.

Scientists were still arguing over what had actually happened, but they'd managed to come up with a nice scientific name: haplospecific coma virus, or HSCV. This virus was deadly only to those who had inherited, from both parents, genes found exclusively in the so-called Caucasian race. The rest of the population, meaning all the people still alive, were passive carriers.

The first cases occurred in Eastern Europe, which in the 21st century retained relative ethnic homogeneity. It was here that the plague had caused the greatest devastation. In Paris, New York or London, the streets were full of people of different skin colours, with genes from all over the world. More people survived there, whereas in Warsaw or Budapest almost everyone perished, apart from mongrels like me.

I ordered a coffee at the bar and picked the least smoky place to sit down. I placed the *Heart of Darkness* on the table so that it could be clearly seen from a distance.

That wasn't necessary, as my contact had been observing me for some time. He was a young, handsome Latin American dressed in the uniform of the Santa Hermandad. He'd been standing at the bar with a glass of red wine.

He introduced himself as Jorge and started talking to me in Spanish. I interrupted him in English.

'I got my Spanish surname from my father, a Cuban diplomat, but I'm Polish.'

'Polish?' he said with surprise. 'There's no such country on the map any more. You live in London, so you're British.'

I didn't feel like arguing about politics, especially since I wasn't meeting him for pleasure. And of course he was wrong – I hadn't taken British citizenship and I was travelling on a Nansen passport, like previous generations of stateless Poles. But nothing suggested that Jorge had meant to offend me, since he continued the conversation as if nothing happened.

'Before we strike a deal, we have to establish one thing. What do you know about Warsaw?'

'Apart from the fact that I lived in this city for the first forty years of my life?' I replied, amused by the question.

'It's not the same Warsaw any more,' said Jorge with a

solemnity befitting a member of a holy order. 'I'm not sure how well you understand that there's no going back to those days.'

'Why are we even talking about this? I thought this was a simple transaction. I pay you the agreed amount and you take me to the agreed location. We've already discussed everything online.'

'No, not everything – and I've made a point of stressing that,' Jorge replied. 'The transaction we're talking about is illegal. It could get us both into real trouble. From my point of view it's very simple, but let me go over it again just in case: you pay me ten Krugerrands and I take you to the church of Mary Help of Christians. Now, could you please give me some idea of what you intend to do?'

'Let's not complicate things,' I said. 'I simply want to pay you to smuggle me to that location. Isn't that perfectly clear?'

'But there's one key question. How are you planning to get back?'

'Does it matter? I fully understand that we've arranged a one-way ticket and I agree to that.'

Jorge sighed.

'That's why I asked you earlier what you know about Warsaw. The present-day, extinct Warsaw – the city of ghosts that has replaced the Warsaw of your memories. This is a very dangerous place.'

'I'm aware of that.'

'I'm not so sure. Because I've seen many travellers like you, driven by some bizarre sentimental attachment – wanting to spend one more night in their old house or whatever – and then having to struggle to get to one of our stations, begging to be rescued. The obvious question that arises is how that person got there in the first place – who smuggled them out beyond the green zone. Clearly, it would be very awkward for me if I became the subject of an enquiry.'

'I can assure you that I won't come running back begging to be rescued.'

'And that is precisely what troubles me, because it means you're either disregarding the risks or you've got some other way of dealing with them.'

'With all due respect, Brother Jorge, that's for me to worry about.'

'No. I'm involved as well. Yes, I'm committing a sin and betraying the trust of the Brotherhood by smuggling you beyond the green zone, but I've also sworn to protect and watch over the safety of pilgrims travelling in Saint Adalbert's land. After all, that's why the Brotherhood was formed — to protect pilgrims, like its medieval predecessor. Even those who have strayed off the path.'

'This particular traveller is paying you to stop protecting him.'

'And that's why it's so important for me to make sure you know what that means. First of all, I hope you realise that, once you're beyond the green zone, one threat that is deadly — and I'm not exaggerating, absolutely deadly — is the animals. Warsaw's dogs have grown wild and acquired a taste for human flesh, since that's mainly what they lived on in the first few months after the outbreak. Now they have other things to eat, because other animals have returned — animals to whom this land once belonged: hares, deer, wild boar and so forth. There are wolves in the forest now, but the city is still ruled by dogs.'

'I spent the first year after the outbreak in Warsaw. You don't need to explain any of this to me,' I interrupted him.

'Fine, so we can agree that outside the green zone you're probably not going to survive until sunset because wild dogs will tear you to pieces before then. They attack in packs, you know. It's not like you can grab a stick and fend them off. I'm afraid of them myself, even though I carry a gun, which I very much hope you don't because that would take us to a whole different level of illegality. After sunset your chances of survival are even lower — they'll track you down wherever you are.'

'Well, if they tear me to pieces, then I certainly won't make it to one of your stations, will I?'

'But since that doesn't terrify you, you must have another method. Which worries me even more and brings me to another question: what do you know about Amer Al-Tawil?'

I smiled because this time he was bang on. Amer and I had known each other for nearly forty years.

Perhaps it was an overstatement to say that we knew each other. We were of the same age, had lived in the same housing development and gone to the same primary school – although we were in different classes – and then we had ended up at the same secondary school, again in different classes.

That was during the last decade of the People's Republic, when it was rare to see foreigners in Warsaw, never mind foreigners with a different skin colour. As the only two non-white boys in our year, we were, in a sense, doomed to knowing each other. I was half-Cuban and he was half-Arab, but beyond that we were of course brought up as Poles, since his father was as keen on going back to Iraq as mine was on going back to Cuba.

We were never very close. I preferred to be surrounded by Poles, and I suspect he did too. Besides, apart from our otherness, we had nothing in common – I listened to punk, he listened to pop; I was a bookworm, he was an amateur athlete.

After the political system changed, I stayed in our neighbourhood and he moved away. We didn't see each other again. And then, out of the blue, just a month ago, he got in touch with me online. He had found me in London, where for many years I had been unsuccessfully trying to find myself.

I had a job and a life of sorts, but like many others of my generation I felt an incurable nostalgia for the world that had vanished in the plague. I knew that my Warsaw didn't exist any more – Brother Jorge didn't have to make me realise that. After all, I had seen the destruction of the city with my own eyes. But when Amer invited me to come, giving me precise instructions on what to do and whose palm to grease with how much, I made my decision over the course of one sleepless night. After the plague had claimed all my Polish friends and acquaintances, Amer became the only 'childhood friend' I had left. And I supposed that's exactly what I was to him, even though in our childhood we had tended to steer clear of each other.

So how could I answer the question I'd just been asked, regarding what I knew about Amer Al-Tawil?

'Never heard of him,' I said with a smile, looking Jorge straight in the eye.

'In that case, I'm sorry, but I can't help you.' Jorge rose from the table.

I was expecting this response. Amer had warned me that when members of the Santa Hermandad find out that they're about to do business with someone who's technically their enemy, they want to pull out of the deal. At that point, one should simply double the fee, which is exactly what I did.

'Twenty Krugerrands,' I replied.

'Twenty? Veinte?' Jorge confirmed in English and Spanish. I nodded both times and added 'dwadzieścia' in Polish for good measure.

He sat back down. I smiled – some things never change, even after an apocalypse.

'Since I'm the paying client here, Brother Jorge, I think things should be the other way around,' I said. 'It's you who should tell me what you know about Amer Al-Tawil. After all, I'm just a lost pilgrim in the land of Saint Adalbert. A knight should counsel the distressed, isn't that so?'

'All right, though I suspect you know more than we do. From our point of view, Amer Al-Tawil is the most dangerous of all the insurgents. *Los insurgentes*,' he added in Spanish.

'Shouldn't you call them *bandidos*?' I said.

'Please don't make us out to be Nazis,' Jorge snarled. 'That's what the insurgents call us, you know. They've appropriated the symbolism of the previous Warsaw uprising. But we haven't come here to kill anyone. We're here to protect people.'

As a result of my years spent in London, I had only one type of comeback to this.

'But of course,' I smiled mockingly.

Jorge pretended not to notice my sarcasm – or perhaps he really didn't notice it. In any case, he continued his sermon without a moment's hesitation.

'The majority of the insurgents operate within organised structures, primarily in the areas of Ursynów and Mokotów. What they're doing is against the law, but at least one can come to an understanding with them. Amer is acting on his own initiative. He's found a few dozen followers and captured the old Tsarist forts of Wawrzyszew, Babice and Groty. Do these names mean anything to you?' he suddenly paused to ask.

What could I say in reply? Correct his pronunciation? Tell him that it was not 'War-zee-soe' but 'Vav-zhi-shev' and not 'Bab-eye-see' but 'Bah-beet-seh'? When I was a kid, I used to ride my bike all over those forts, and later on I'd go there to drink cheap wine with my mates, and sometimes even with girls. I knew where you could cool down a bottle in the moat and where you might get punched by the local hoodies. All that knowledge pertained to a world that was lost for ever. Instead of sharing it with Jorge, I answered, 'Please enlighten me.'

'They're part of a ring of defences built by the Russians at the end of the 19th century in anticipation of the First World War. In the end, the Russians didn't end up using them; they left Warsaw without a fight. Later on, the Polish army set up storehouses there. Al-Tawil managed to occupy them and also seized weapons from other army units. His group has more arms than all the other insurgents in Warsaw put together.'

'I guess that's good in these post-apocalyptic times?'

'That wasn't an apocalypse; it was an HSCV epidemic,' Brother Jorge corrected me, as if that made any difference. 'It doesn't justify breaking the law. Nobody's allowed to even set foot in the ruins of Warsaw without our permission, never mind playing at being partisans. We want to avoid bloodshed, but our patience is limited. You're planning to meet with Al-Tawil, aren't you?'

I didn't reply. It was a rhetorical question anyway. Brother Jorge paused to take a sip of his wine and continued.

'I'll take that as a yes. Please tell him that we know he's cleaned up the runway at Bemowo airport and started experimenting with drones. We can't permit him to do that. We won't mess about with storming his forts. We'll bomb everything from the air, so that there's nothing left of Bemowo and Wawrzyszew.

'An excellent way to avoid bloodshed,' I muttered.

'First and foremost, we want to avoid shedding our own blood. We Christians call this the principle of *ordo caritatis*.' Brother Jorge smiled coldly. 'Will you pass on the warning to him?'

'I don't know if I'll find him. Wawrzyszew, Chomiczówka, Bemowo – these are huge neighbourhoods. Hundreds of thousands of people lived there before the annihilation.'

'I'll take that as a yes too,' Brother Jorge said. 'So now that we've settled the key questions, let's turn to the technical details...' And, indeed, for the rest of the evening he proceeded to talk me though the ins and out of the journey to the church of Mary Help of Christians at 7 Conrad Street, as if it were an ordinary tourist trip.

After we parted, I ate supper by myself. Even though it was probably my last night in a decent bed, I couldn't fall asleep. I kept thinking about Brother Jorge.

These sorts of people were referred to as 'Renaissance men'. The point wasn't their all-round abilities; it was an analogy – a forced one, in my opinion – to the Black Death of the fourteenth century. Apparently, without the Black Death, the Middle Ages would never have ended because the old elites wouldn't have been replaced.

These 'Renaissance men' viewed the present in a similar light. For my generation, the entire world had collapsed, and in that they saw their opportunity. It was clear that Jorge felt completely at ease as a corrupt functionary of an armed organisation which was a de facto occupying army. It didn't trouble him at all, and in his own mind he was no doubt a righteous man who was busy establishing peace and order in the ruins of Warsaw, while now and again turning a blind eye to a handful of gold coins.

The whole world was now in the hands of such people. That's why I didn't have to think long when Amer's email arrived. If that is what the Renaissance looked like, I preferred to perish with the Middle Ages.

After breakfast, we got on a coach. The windows were painted over, so I had no idea which way we were going. Religious songs poured out of the speakers. Out of boredom, I looked through the leaflets in the seat pocket – a map of the shrines open to pilgrims in the 'land of Saint Adalbert', a multilingual brochure on the history of the Santa Hermandad, simple infographics showing where you could worship what relics of which saint (Brother Albert and John Paul II here, Saint Jerzy and Maksymilian Kolbe over there) and a pamphlet on how to move around Warsaw's 'green zone'.

From this last, I learned that everybody was safe within the zone, but under no circumstances should you approach a guard at a checkpoint on your own initiative. It was essential to wait until they waved you over. That didn't really matter to me, however, since the plan was for Brother Jorge to take me though the checkpoint.

The coach dropped us off at Wilson Square. I hardly recognised it. Once upon a time, this had been the heart of Żoliborz. Now it was a gigantic parking area for coaches carrying pilgrims and for embraers, which were used by the Santa Hermandad to get around the city. A Brazilian company well known for manufacturing planes had produced a prototype of the embraer rover before the outbreak, and this turned out to be its lifeline, because in the aftermath the demand for planes fell drastically. These new rovers, designed initially for moving around the Brazilian interior, proved to be perfect for post-apocalyptic Eastern Europe.

An embraer was shaped like a cigar, with a cabin for the driver and five passengers, poised on top of six legs. It walked like a sort of six-legged spider, lifting its cabin up as high as two metres off the ground – enough to be able to walk over smashed-up cars and other obstacles on the road. I had never travelled in anything of the sort, but before the plague I'd been fascinated by hi-tech gadgets and part of me was glad that I'd say goodbye to the civilised world in the most cutting-edge vehicle it had on offer.

As agreed, Brother Jorge was waiting for me in front of the church of Saint Stanisław Kostka. He was dressed in civilian clothes. For whatever reason, he greeted me with the Latin 'Salve!' and without another word gestured towards his embraer. I followed.

I had already noticed on the plane that a large percentage of the 'pilgrims' were coming here on business. Occupied Warsaw was a paradise for smugglers, plunderers and speculators. The difference between them and me was that the only thing I wanted to smuggle in was myself, and my destination – as I took from our conversation the previous evening – was an area that even the Brotherhood's patrols preferred to avoid. That made me a particularly dangerous criminal according to the new laws governing the city.

Brother Jorge's embraer was parked among the trees by the church. Or rather I should say it was resting there, since these vehicles resembled animals more than machines. The cabin was sitting directly on the ground to make it easier to board. The embraer looked a bit like a dog keeping watch – if you can imagine a huge, six-legged metal dog.

When we approached, the doors on both sides opened

34

automatically. They lifted up, like those of a 1980s DeLorean. Now it looked as if the six-legged dog also had wings.

I sat in the passenger seat and fastened my seatbelt. Brother Jorge took the driver's seat and touched the lit-up steering panel a few times. The doors dropped down, the cigar raised itself up and we set off towards the nearest checkpoint. Thanks to the automatic stability control, there was no swaying at all: it felt as if we were gliding two metres above the ground.

The uniformed guard saluted us from his guardhouse, which was surrounded by sandbags, and the armoured gate slid open. Through the panoramic window, I could now admire the new Warsaw, beyond the pilgrims' green zone.

We were in Krasiński Street – that much I could still remember of the city's geography. As per the plan laid out a hundred years earlier, a green strip ran down the centre, now covered by tall birch trees. The dead windows of abandoned buildings gazed at us from both sides. The embraer stepped gracefully over cars left behind in the middle of the road by dying drivers.

At the intersection with Popiełuszko Street, there were more cars than elsewhere. I guessed that a tram must have hit a bus here, and then cars and a lorry piled up on top. The vehicles were heavily corroded and overgrown with greenery.

Brother Jorge must have seen my expression as I took it all in. It was the only time he spoke during the whole journey.

'There are places that look even worse. The ring road is maybe the worst of all.'

I nodded. I had heard on the radio about the pile-up on the ring road when it happened. That was two days after the outbreak. At first, the tone of the news reports was almost jokey: a sleeping epidemic – ha ha, maybe we should party a bit less. Then we heard about the first casualties, and then about the gigantic pile-up on the ring road, and after that – this was the most frightening of all – the Polish radio stations simply stopped transmitting. My cable connection went too and, with it, the internet.

The last news reports advised people not to go out – so I didn't. It was only when I picked up the BBC on an old shortwave radio that I found out the epidemic wasn't lethal to everyone – that it affected only certain 'haplospecific groups'. It took me a while to figure out that this politically correct euphemism meant 'the Caucasian race' and that I was safe thanks to my Cuban genes.

The embraer brought us to Broniewski Street. We left Żoliborz, where pre-war middle-class mansion blocks lined the road with their dignified frontages, and entered the world of large estates built in the 1960s according to the utopian visions of Le Corbusier. He had dreamt about skyscrapers set among gardens; here were ruins lost in a birch wood growing rapidly all around us.

Thankfully, I didn't have to see the ring road: it crossed Broniewski Street on a flyover. The embraer lowered its cabin and walked under the viaduct, like a camel passing through a gate of ancient Jerusalem.

At the end of Broniewski Street, we turned into Reymont Street – crossing from poetry to prose – which led us to Conrad Street. When Poland regained its independence, at the end of the First World War, three new roads were named after nineteenth-century Romantic poets – Mickiewicz, Słowacki and Krasiński – who had prophesied that independence. These roads converged at Wilson Square, named after the president to whom Poland owed that independence.

Broniewski Street, built later, during the communist era, was named after the poet who had prophesied the egalitarian People's Poland, where everybody would live in identical flats in identical blocks. And when Warsaw expanded to the north in the 1970s, it was trendy to emphasise our links with the West – to which we were opening up and which readily offered us loans. That's why the last street in this series was named after Joseph Conrad. After the fall of communism, streets were named after generals or priests; they were no longer named after writers.

The church of Mary Help of Christians was an architectural eyesore from the 1990s. The communist authorities hadn't made a provision for it in their plans, so the faithful found an unused plot of land at the corner of Reymont and Conrad – a nationalist and a cosmopolitan. Would they have liked each other if they had met in real life?

The Brotherhood had surrounded the church with a steel fence, of the same sort I'd already seen in Wilson Square. In addition, a low razor-wire barrier ran a few metres in front of it. When the embraer stopped just before the barrier, I read one of the multilingual signs warning about the presence of an automatic security system: '*DANGER OF DEATH. PELIGRO MORTAL*.' The warnings were clearly true, as evinced by the bodies of animals who hadn't read the signs.

This was the end of my journey. Brother Jorge looked at me expectantly. It took me a moment to realise that he was waiting for his fee. I handed him the pouch with the coins. Without counting them, he opened the passenger door.

'This is your last chance,' he said. 'I'm going to enter the church grounds and inspect the security system. I have to somehow justify this sortie in my report. Once the gate closes behind me, you'll be left on this side, and we'll never see each other again.'

'That's fine with me,' I said as I picked up my bag and jumped out of the embraer. The door closed. A moment later, the armoured gate to the church grounds opened and the embraer marched inside with stately steps.

I stood alone on the cracked asphalt, through which the shoots of young trees were poking everywhere. Within a few years, the whole street would be swallowed up by a new forest, which was already growing all around me on what used to be lawns. Despite this, I still recognised my old neighbourhood: I knew exactly where the buses once terminated, where the market was, and the doctor's surgery. The outlines of abandoned buildings, towering above the thickets, were enough for me to get my bearings.

I started walking towards the end of the bus route. After all, for many years that was the natural beginning and end of my journeys. I didn't manage to reach it, however. As the silhouette of the church disappeared behind the trees, I started to make out three people dressed in Polish army uniforms emerging from among the birches in front of me. There was a woman and two male auxiliaries – it was instantly obvious that she was the one in command.

They looked like an anthropological cross-section of the Warsaw residents who'd survived the HSCV epidemic. The woman, judging by her looks, was of Arab descent. One of her soldiers was half black while the other was East Asian. Adding in my mixed Latin American background, we made quite a set. I smiled, even though the others' expressions were dead serious.

'Amer is dead. He died this morning,' the woman said in Polish, without any introductions or greetings. 'He wanted you to be his successor. Do you agree?'

In hindsight, I think I should have guessed Amer's reasons for inviting me here, but in the end it was this woman – Amer's widow, as I later learned – who had to tell me.

I nodded. Could I have refused?

'Let's go then,' she said, and the three of them disappeared into the bushes.

I followed.

Expectant Management

Sarah Schofield

On your right side, the black and white screen flickers images from within your abdomen. The room is dim and you lie still as the sonographer repositions the scanner. The woman breathes slowly in and out as she examines the screen. Then she rests her fingers lightly on your arm and looks at you as if measuring your fitness.

'Is there someone you can call, Jess,' she says, 'to be with you?'

You stand in the corridor waiting to see the midwife.

The ground seems to liquefy so you sit on the edge of a plastic chair and grip the frame.

A short time later, outside, the air is still and heavy. You walk. You take out your phone to call your mother like you'd promised to do after the scan. You listen to the Spanish dial tone and when your mum answers, you repeat the medical language the midwife has just used. There is a long silence on the other end.

'It's called expectant management, Mum. Seeing if it will sort itself, without intervention.'

There is another pause and you wonder if it's just the delay on the phone line. But then your mum says, 'Oh. Jess. I'm sorry, love.'

'I'll take a couple of days off. I'll be fine.'

Your mother sighs. 'Do you want me to...?'

'It's okay.'

'Did they say why? Like, was it something you ate, or...?'

'Apparently it just happens. I wasn't my fault, Mum.'

'I wasn't saying...' She lets out a long breath. 'Iron. You need iron... leafy greens like kale. Spinach.'

White pain blossoms in your abdomen and you stop walking.

'Liver's good, too.'

You cannot speak.

'I know it's hard...' your mother continues. You can hear the cicadas chirping on her veranda. 'But there was probably something not right with the... So...'

You press your palm into your stomach.

'And you did say, didn't you... you weren't sure. What with your new job, and Aaron being away.'

Back at the new apartment, you lean against the furniture while the band of white pain tightens. You inhale slowly. Press your forehead against the glass door that opens onto the seafront balcony. You text Aaron. When you go to the bathroom there is blood. A lot of blood.

The apartment floor is cluttered with half unpacked boxes and there isn't room for you to stride out in the way you feel urged to.

You pace along the seafront. The large maternity pad the hospital gave you chafes your thighs. The swell surges with the wave of each contraction. You are half a mile from the apartment when you cannot go any further and you press yourself into the rails on the sea wall. You think of the painkiller prescription the midwife gave you, that you'd crumpled into your bag, never anticipating needing it. You focus on the silvering grey horizon to distract yourself from the thick hot sensation of your body coming apart. You imagine striking out through the waves. Clean, crisp. Your body working hard, a lithe machine, against the water.

Early next day, you sit behind your desk at work, a Therma-wrap around your lower back and a wad of maternity pads in your bag. The caretaker Mr Dyer leans over you holding out a sheet of paper. You would like to stand but do not want to risk moving.

'I've listed them in order of urgency. I know there's no money.' He watches you for a reaction. 'But the school is falling apart.'

'Do what you have to. We'll worry about budgets later.'

His eyebrows shoot up and you realise this was the wrong play. He wanted a fight.

'We do as much as we can ourselves. Fix things inhouse if possible. Okay?'

He sniffs and glances at the framed photographs you have arranged on your filing cabinet – a picture of Aaron and you embracing at the end of a triathlon, hair still slick from the swim. Another; Aaron in his combats squinting into sunshine.

'Had much experience?' he says. 'With kids like ours?'

Over the next hour the ache rolls outwards across your back. Feeling hot and nauseous you take two more paracetamol and click through your emails. Funding requests, pupil referrals, urgent deadlines: the kind of inbox you'd normally relish, actioning each like a game of Wack-a-Mole. You squeeze your fingers to your temples. You watch the milky sun rising over the schoolyard.

In the staffroom teachers are making coffee and chatting. You attempt to close the door behind you but it won't stay shut. You try two, three times, but the door keeps creaking open again. The staff members' intimate conversations tail off and you feel eyes turning.

'Here.' A woman steps forward. She is heavily pregnant and you flush and look away. 'You have to...' The pregnant woman pushes the door sharply above the handle and it clicks into place.

'Right. Thanks.' You look down at the agenda in your hand. When you think you can trust your voice you say, 'Okay, we've got a lot to get through.'

It is early evening and the school corridors are quiet. You turn from your computer. You go to the caretaker's office and locate a screwdriver. You kneel by the staffroom door and fiddle with the faulty latch.

In your pocket your mobile rings. Aaron. 'I've been trying to ring you all day. Are you okay?'

'The cramps are easing. I think it's pretty much over...'

'Jess. I –'

'Please. I'm at work.' You stab at the lock mechanism with the screwdriver.

'I'm going to apply for leave. I could be home in a few days.'

You swallow. 'Really – don't. I feel fine.'

'You shouldn't even be at work. You should be signed off for at least a week to –'

'I can't and I'm better being busy so...' Your eyes prickle and you stand and go into your office and close the door.

'Jess.' You hear his voice break. 'I just can't believe it's happened.'

'It happens all the time. We have to get on with it.'

There is a pause on the phone line. Then he says, 'You have told them, at work, haven't you?'

'I need to keep a professional distance. It would make things really difficult.'

'You need to tell someone – to talk...'

'I'm dealing with it inhouse. And I am fine.' Your throat closes round your words.

'You don't always have to be so...'

'What?'

You hear a small noise outside your office. A moment later a pink envelope appears under the door.

Back at the apartment, you apply a new heat wrap and sit on the sofa with your laptop asleep on your knee. You open your work diary and the pink envelope containing the invitation to Stella's lunch-hour baby shower drops out. You hold it for a few seconds then push it to the back of your diary.

You stare at your inbox until your eyes begin to glaze and then open a new tab and scroll numbly through Facebook. An old school friend has posted a baby scan image. You compose a comment and then delete it.

You return to your inbox. Three more emails have come in. They are headed 'Urgent Safeguarding Issue', 'More Strike Action' and 'Update Request' the last one from the local education authority. The room is suddenly very hot, and you struggle to focus on the screen.

Clutching your laptop you stride out onto the balcony gasping for air. The sea breeze is abrasive and you close your eyes as it tingles across your skin. The sound of the waves meeting the shore is soothing and you imagine what it would be like to have nothing to tether you, no responsibility to anyone tomorrow. You rest the laptop on the edge of the balcony. It seesaws on the narrow ledge and you loosen your grip fractionally. The weight of the laptop tilts then, a moment later, it slips from between your fingers. You keep your eyes closed and there is an expectant pause before it smashes onto the pavement. You feel a momentary thrill, looking over the balcony to the broken laptop below, lying in the gutter like mechanical road kill. Then you look at your hands, trembling, recklessly weightless, and you stuff them in your pockets. Your heart races and it is like starting from a dream. You shudder and look far out to the lonely horizon. You reason with yourself. It's only a laptop. It's mostly backed up. You can buy a new one.

When you look back down, there is someone leaning over the laptop, bending so that they appear headless. The figure straightens and looks up at you.

When you get down to the street the person is still there; an older woman, perhaps in her seventies. Broad and round like a cottage loaf. She has coarse white hair that sits shapelessly on her head and the whisper of a moustache on her lip. She wears a calf length coat over a blue flowered dress. She observes you gather together the laptop, then follows you back into the building. She grips the banister, methodically climbing the stairs. You leave her to it. You sit down at the dining table with the laptop pieces and you listen and wait. A couple of minutes later she comes in and sits on the sofa. You try to piece the laptop back together and the woman watches.

The old woman is still there a few days later. She potters silently, smoking cigarettes that smell like burnt toffee. Gauloise, you think, knowing you're drawing this from old films and dramas you have seen. You feel slightly disappointed that your imagination couldn't have created someone more outlandish or dynamic. 'I could have invented someone attractive,' you think at her as she passes you and raises an eyebrow.

The older woman sits on the balcony and knits something lumpy on a huge pair of needles. She unravels and re-knits the thing over and over.

Her moustache is sometimes covered in a layer of bleaching cream. She is Breton. You don't know how you know this but you do. 'You must have come from somewhere,' you think the words at her and she smiles knowingly. 'But you don't have to stay long. I'm fine on my own.' The woman has a bottle beside her and it is always two thirds full. You think it is probably Eau de Vie.

Saturday. A parcel arrives from your mother. A large beef prime rib. It is cold and moist inside the polystyrene container. The label stuck to the side of the box says *Nicer than liver. Love*

M x. You sit heavily on the sofa and the woman sits beside you. A gap yawns open in your abdomen where the pain once was and you hug the cool beef rib against it. You shut your eyes. When you wake, the meat is warm from the heat of your body. There is an iron tang in the air. There is a bloody stain on the sofa.

You explore the town together. The older woman pauses at a bookshop window. 'We can go in if you want.' You look at the woman's cigarette. 'But you can't smoke that in there.'

Inside the shop, you go to the children's section at the back of the store. You pick up a plastic bath book with ducks on the front. You flick back and forth through it.

You find the woman in the biography section with a book held close to her face. You look at the cover; *Gertrude Ederle Swims the Channel.* A sepia photograph shows a woman chin deep in choppy water, swimming cap drawn over a determined brow, her arm raised mid stroke. The Breton woman reaches into her pocket, takes out a cigarette.

'Nope, really you can't.' You grab her by the sleeve.

The woman puffs on it the whole way home.

Aaron calls. 'I love you,' he says. 'Are you okay?'

'I'm fine.' You root in your bag for your cigarettes. Your fingers brush against the baby book. You close the bag and spark the lighter.

'I wish I was there.' Aaron lets out a breath. 'You need to talk, Jess. To me or... someone.'

You inhale hard.

'What are you doing?' Aaron says.

'Nothing.'

He is silent for a moment. 'It's tough for me too, you know.'

The line crackles.

You slide the phone from your ear and turn it off.

You are wrapping up the baby book. The old woman glares at you from the sofa, tugging at her wool to unravel the knitting.

'I know you don't want me to go,' you say. 'But I'm good at compartmentalising. That thing where you're supposed to keep dairy and meat separate in the fridge; I'm good at that kind of thing.' You tear the sticky tape with your teeth.

'I can't not go, can I? How would that look?'

The woman is tight lipped as she winds the wool into a ball around her hand.

'I know, I could have thought up an excuse. But it will do good to show up and be social – get the staff on side. That's how I work.'

The woman's fingertips are turning white.

'We won't stay long.' You drop the wrapped book into your work bag. 'I promise.'

The prep room is airless and crowded. Stella's department colleagues are pinning pink bunting to the notice board. There's a tray of pink cupcakes.

Stella smiles and comes over to you where you stand in the doorway holding the gift like a sparkly shield.

'Thanks for coming... I know this probably isn't your thing.'

The Head of Department holds out a tray of pink fizzy drinks. 'Thanks...' Natalie, you think she is called. By this point at your previous school you knew everyone by name. You lift a glass and take a gulp. The Breton woman stands beside her topping up each glass with Eau de Vie.

'Listen up, ladies!' says Natalie. 'Everyone has an ice cube in their glass with a jelly baby frozen inside. The first lady to release the jelly baby from her ice cube has to shout, "I'm having a baby!"'

You peer into your glass. You scoop out the jelly baby ice cube and squeeze it in your fist.

You perch on a chair beside three teaching assistants. One

woman is describing the third degree tears she experienced during delivery. 'You've all this to come,' she says to you and the women laugh. The jelly baby is goo inside your clamped palm. You excuse yourself and shove your way through jostling children to the staff toilet and sit in a cubicle with a wad of tissue pressed against your mouth. The Breton woman is in the cubicle with you, arms crossed against her bosom.

'I know... you don't have to say it,' you mutter.

The final bell sounds as you accelerate out of the school car park. You stop at the supermarket and run in. You pick up the largest piece of brie and two bottles of red wine.

On the way out, you pass a stand displaying cards for Mother's Day. You stop and stare at it and the bright cards gaze back, the curly fonts yell saccharine love to a club you never even wanted to join. You imagine the sensation of kicking at the flimsy cardboard base; how it would take it, meekly heeling over. You tap at the stand with your toe. You pick the cards out one by one and drop them like petals onto the floor where they skip and slide in their plastic wrappers.

Someone is shouting from the far end of the supermarket. The bottles in your bag bang against your shin as you run.

You sit and drink on the living room floor.

'It's just reminded me actually... I haven't got a card for my mum.' You bite a chunk out of the brie. 'Do you think it would arrive in time? What's the date today?'

The woman frowns.

'It's funny really, because you think everything is going just fine, and then you suddenly realise...'

The woman nods and kicks the tangle of wool and needles under the coffee table.

'And I'm still bleeding. Still. I don't think I can go in tomorrow.'

The woman lifts the bottle and takes long thirsty gulps.

'Steady on.' You look at each other and you laugh and you can't stop. You press your face into the sofa as the tears roll down your face.

Your phone vibrates. Aaron. You stuff it down the side of the cushion.

Later, you heave the old woman down the hall to your bedroom. You spread across the bed like a starfish.

You wake fully clothed on top of the duvet. It is early. Quiet. You stare in the mirror at your tannin stained mouth. And you feel a giddy urge to push your body. Push it in the way you have diligently avoided doing for the last few weeks.

You are at the gym pounding at full speed on the treadmill when you realise you are not energised but merely teetering on the cusp of drunk. The first prickles of nausea overcome you and you stagger off the back of the treadmill and towards the exit. You make it behind the entrance before vomiting onto the concrete. You cough and spit. When you finally catch your breath and look up you see that this side of the building has windows that face into the pool. One solitary swimmer methodically breast strokes up the swimming lane. Grey hairs curl from under her white rubber flowered swimming cap. The whiskers of her moustache dip in and out of the water.

You sit on the edge of the sofa and flick through the channels. There is a documentary on about making a wildlife programme. The woman slumps down beside you. In the programme actors in a studio are recording seabird noises.

The director says, 'This time can we go more plaintive?'

The actor nods and clears her throat.

'It's nesting season. And you've lost sight of your chick.'

The Breton woman slips her hand into yours.

The Indian man on the phone is trying to help you.

'Yes, madam. You are experiencing computer difficulties

and I want to help you fix your problem.'

You are smoking a cigarette on the balcony. 'I thought you were my husband. That's the only reason I answered. He's deployed overseas.'

'I will help you, madam.'

'I don't know how.' You take a long drag. 'How will you help me?'

'So I am telling you there's a problem with your computer. I can see on my system there is an issue with your Windows,' the man says. 'If you will please now go to your computer and click on the Windows icon, I can help you resolve this problem, madam.'

You clench the cigarette between your lips and slide the door open. You raise an eyebrow at the Breton woman who sits on the sofa with a tangle of wool. You both look to the pile of laptop bits on the table.

'Madam? Do what I am saying and we can fix your problem.'

'I doubt we can,' you say.

'But I see you have a problem, madam,' the man says.

You look at the phone in your hand. The Breton woman sniggers into her fist.

'Madam? Do you see the start icon?'

You coo the bereft seabird call gently into the phone. It echoes back.

'Madam?'

You make the noise again, louder, with more emphasis.

'Madam? Click now the Windows icon.'

You squawk. Then you try a different bird noise; drawn out, sorrowful. You repeat it over and over. The Breton woman rocks on the sofa. Your throat is raw.

The phone purrs its dial tone.

'Look,' you cough. 'There're spots on my throat.'

The Breton woman gazes into your mouth.

'I'll let them know I won't be in for a few more days.'

The phone rings and you hand it to the older woman, who tosses it into the washing machine and slams the door. Every so often it goes off, rattling against the drum, until later that evening you register the absence of the sound.

'Battery's gone,' you say and the Breton woman nods.

The apartment buzzer goes. You hide under the table. The Breton woman bites down on her knitting and wraps her arms around you.

The bed in the scan suite is high. The Breton woman is lying on it when you follow the sonographer into the room. She rolls over on her back and flings one arm across her eyes, her face hidden. You stare at her wondering how she made it up there unaided.

'Hop on the bed. It's an internal exam... is that okay?' She touches you lightly on the shoulder. 'It shouldn't hurt, just a bit uncomfortable.'

You nod and when you look back at the bed the woman has gone.

Later, the midwife looks over the results. 'It's coming away nicely,' she says. 'Is someone looking after you, while you're getting back to normal?'

The Breton woman is waiting in the hospital lobby. You stride past her and she follows. You bite down, holding the sob in your throat until you are both in the car. You scrub the tears away with your sleeve.

'I'm fine. I'm really fine,' you shout. 'Just go away.'

The woman reaches out and you shrug her off. 'I don't need this... this is not me. I don't fall apart over a baby.'

The woman purses her lips.

'I mean, for fuck's sake. It never even had a heart beat.'

The old woman is leaning over a map spread across the table. Her bosom rests on France and a cigarette smoulders between her fingers. She regards the distance between Dover and Calais. Ash scatters across the blue.

'It's 21 miles,' you say.

The woman narrows her eyes.

'That's quite a long way.' You look at the expanse of empty blue. 'To swim it alone, I mean.'

Another meat parcel arrives from your mother. You read the label. *Is your phone out of order? Find enclosed, Wagu beef. The man said they massage the cows. Hope you're doing well. Love M xx*

You should be in work. You smoke in the living room.

'Aaron's coming home soon.'

The woman lies on her stomach on the coffee table practicing breaststroke. She scissors her short legs out behind her. The shapeless skirt balloons up with every kick.

'Did you hear me? Aaron's home soon on leave. So you'll have to go.'

The woman rolls off the table and stomps through to the kitchen. You squeeze your eyes closed and rub your temples.

There is a hospital drama on the television. You and the woman sit side by side. A woman on the programme is giving birth loudly.

'Breathe,' the midwife is saying. 'Push! Push! Push!'

The Breton woman tries to unpeel your fingers from the TV remote. You snatch it out of reach.

You recharge your phone and scroll through the work emails. You flag fifty-three of them as urgent. The Chair of the Governors has emailed. 'We're aware of your recent illness but we need some clarification of when you might be fit to return to work.'

You pour yourself a glass of wine.

You iron a blouse, a cigarette clamped between your lips. You glance at your watch.

'I've got to go in.'

The woman picks her teeth with a knitting needle. You cannot see the wool anywhere.

'Did you finish your...?'

The woman gazes out of the window towards the sea.

When you return the apartment is quiet. You stand on the balcony. The afternoon sun glitters in spikes across the sea. You get out a packet of cigarettes.

'Stella's had the baby.' You wonder where the Breton woman is. 'She's called her Ella.' Your throat stops. And she is beside you. You look out together.

'I mean, really?' You sniff. 'There're a thousand names I would choose before that one.'

The woman turns and looks at you and raises an eyebrow. Close up, you see she has eyes exactly like your own. You feel heady, like you're staring into a double mirror, seeing forwards and backwards all at once and you are flooded with an emotion you cannot quite name. But you let yourself feel it. And the woman is asking you a question.

'Stevie...' you say. 'Stevie if it was a girl. And if it was a boy, I'd have called him Miles.'

Aaron calls. 'Just a couple more weeks and I'll be home.'

'Are you okay?' you say.

One full week back in work, you return home on Friday evening and pour yourself a glass of wine. The apartment has been quiet for a few days. You lean over the cool evening balcony. The sea, glassy and still, merges with the horizon in the fading light.

Both at home and at work, you have been gentle in everything you have done. Every child you have dealt with, every meeting; you have slowed your body, measured your breaths, focussing just on the task ahead. Holding steady. You have fielded comments from staff and colleagues, 'You're well now? All okay?' You have smiled, nodded, reassured until you can almost believe it yourself. Almost.

You gaze out to sea and you make out on the very edge of the darkness a white hat with blue plastic flowers. The knitted costume clings as the Breton woman wades deeper with short measured strides until the seabed seems to disappear beneath her. She treads water a few hundred yards out to sea. She lowers her head and strikes out; the slow plash of her arms pulling on the water, the rhythmic kick of her legs. Her sturdy body tilts. Her proud head is turned towards the continent. You watch until all you see is the horizon.

The Helper of Cattle

Farah Ahamed

DR PATEL SPRAYED ON some eau de toilette, knotted his silk paisley cravat, slung his jungle hat by its string around his neck and ran a comb through his hair. After cramming the pockets of his polyester safari jacket with his notebook and pen, he smoothed down the flaps and checked his image in the mirror. The Maasai beaded belt, which the Lodge receptionist had presented to him on arrival, was stretched around his waist, buckled on the last notch. Patel gave his reflection a satisfied smile. It didn't matter where one was, one needed to keep one's standards.

Flies buzzed near his head. He batted them away and looked around his tent. The Lodge definitely presented great possibilities for Amber Investments. Yes, there were other lodges in the Mara, but none so luxurious in such a remote setting – on the side of a volcano no less! The army-green canvas walls of his room were decorated with African masks, batiks and beaded artefacts, and there was comfortable four-poster bed. The veranda looked out on to the vast expanse of savannah, which was covered in a layer of morning mist. In the distance, the rising sun had spread a pinkish hue over the sky. This five star Lodge would be the jewel in the crown of Amber's hospitality portfolio. And he, Dr Patel, would be the one to make it happen.

He strolled down to the front of the Lodge where a 6x6 Pinzgauer was waiting to take him on a game drive. Patel climbed into the back, and the vehicle jolted along the dirt road through the ravine. Cold air whipped his face as he sat in the back, wrapped in red and white Maasai blankets. His driver, oblivious to the chill, had only a red shuka draped around him. He throttled the engine as they bumped over a mound of dirt.

'We're on the edge of the Oloololo escarpment,' the driver said, 'about 6,500 feet above sea level. From here you can see all 120 kilometres of the Mara game reserve.'

'Splendid,' Patel said, 'and soon this whole place will belong to Amber Investments.'

The driver braked sharply and turned to face him. 'You mean you're here for business, sir?'

'Of course, it's why I've flown in from Nairobi.'

The driver fiddled with the radio equipment fixed in the dashboard until it crackled. He spoke in Maa, received a fuzzy static reply, then restarted the engine.

'Is everything alright?' Patel said.

'Yes, sir.'

'Very good. And I'm *Doctor* Patel, not *sir.*'

'So you're a medicine man, like my uncle?'

'Not exactly. People who know me well like to address me as *Doctor.*'

'Aha,' the driver said, 'now I understand; it's because you're a *wise* man?'

Beaming, Patel straightened in his seat. 'I believe so.'

'Maasai also give titles to people when they've got special qualities. So you're a man like that?'

'I wouldn't wish to brag,' he said, 'but my friends and colleagues in Nairobi rely greatly on my opinion and advice. What's *your* name?'

'I'm Olekorinko, but you can call me Ole, *Doctor* Patel.'

Ole stopped when they came to a clearing in the scrubland and a signpost, *MARA NORTH CONSERVANCY*. Beside it was a makeshift wooden stall. A Maasai woman in red and blue cloths and a heavy beaded collar was piling charcoal into sacks with her bare hands. A child knelt on the ground helping. Ole called out to them and the woman walked towards the car and peered in. Her ear lobes had long holes and when she grinned, Patel saw that two of her middle front teeth were missing. The girl had slanted eyes, a broad flat nose and lighter skin. The woman extended a hand to Patel.

'Jambo,' he said, without taking her blackened palm.

'She's my sister,' Ole said.

'Yes?'

'She was cursed.'

'By whom?'

'By the Chinese. And now no one will marry her.'

The woman turned away, pulling the child with her.

Ole started up the vehicle, swung it round and swerved to avoid a termite hill.

'But who on earth would buy charcoal out here,' Patel said, 'in the middle of nowhere?'

Ole shrugged. 'Our land was grabbed from us and now our cattle have nowhere to graze. But we have to eat, so what can we do? Just to make this makaa, I was forced to chop an acacia tree which was more than a 150 years old. It's not good, but we are desperate.'

Ole slowed down and handed Patel a pair of binoculars.

'You see those black shapes moving across the plains? They're a million wildebeest on their migration heading towards the Mara River, where they'll cross into the Serengeti looking for greener pastures.'

'Then they're not unlike us humans.'

'It's the rhythm of nature that drives them,' Ole said, 'not greed.'

From the undergrowth came a strange kuk-kuk-kuk call

and a loud flapping. A black and white bird rose up from a tree.

'That's the martial; Africa's largest eagle,' Ole said 'But in the Mara, birds are not the only predators.'

A sharp breeze rustled through the trees, and Patel pulled the blankets tighter around him. The car hurtled along the bumpy track. Ole decelerated and waited for a monkey to cross, with a baby hanging from its belly.

'Do you have children?' Patel asked.

'Meishooiyiook enkai inkishu o-nkera,' Ole said, 'is a Maasai prayer. It means may God grant us cattle and children. Both are a sign of wealth. Cattle are currency and give power.' The vehicle swayed through the long grass. 'What about you, Mzee?'

'No, I don't have children or cattle.'

Ole laughed. 'Then you are a poor man.'

'It's all relative,' he said, gazing out of the window.

They lurched forward and halted under a thorn tree. Ole pointed to the large birds circling a pile of carcasses.

'Those are white-backed vultures feeding on the remains of a kill.'

'They look viscious.'

'The bones you see aren't always of animals,' Ole said. 'Traditionally we don't bury our dead, but leave the corpses for scavengers.'

'Then I better pray nothing happens to me out here,' Patel joked.

Ole looked him in the eye. 'We don't hesitate when it comes to protecting our land and traditions.'

They rattled across the plains through the short grass and shrubs, and Patel stood in the back, looking out from the open roof through binoculars.

Ole drove up behind a herd of grazing wildebeest and nudged the car into its midst. Patel was close enough to see the saliva drip from their mouths as they chewed; he took a photo on his phone of the animals bucking and pawing the ground.

'What funny looking creatures,' Patel said. 'They look like a mixed breed assembled from spare parts: the forequarters of an ox, hindquarters of an antelope and the mane and tail of a horse.'

'Maybe,' Ole laughed, 'but like many of us they prefer to stick to their own.'

The animals grunted and snorted, making gnu-gnu sounds.

'We call the males the clowns of the savannah,' Ole said. 'During this season they make mating cries and perform antics to attract the female.'

'We all have our courtship styles, I suppose.'

'Don't be fooled by their comedy act,' Ole said. 'They're very territorial. The first signal a bull will give is to urinate or defecate to warn other bulls to keep off. After that he will get ready for a proper fight.'

The car edged forward through the long grass and the wildebeest galloped out of the way. The radio crackled with a voice and Ole adjusted the knobs.

He turned to Patel. 'My colleague says the wildebeest are about to cross the Mara river bank. We must hurry if we want to catch the killing.' Ole turned the vehicle around, his foot pressed hard on the accelerator. Patel was thrown from his seat and bumped up and down, until Ole slowed down and parked near a cluster of trees.

Patel sat up, shaken. 'I hope I haven't injured my back.'

'The Mara will be an experience you will never forget, Doctor.'

Another Pinzgauer was already parked by the bank. The driver leaned out and greeted Ole. A tall man in a business suit and dark glasses was standing in the back, looking through binoculars.

'That's one of the other guests from the Lodge,' Ole said. 'He's from Somalia.'

'Why's he wearing a suit and tie?' said Patel, waving to greet the stranger.

'He's not a tourist.' Ole wiped the dashboard with a rag.

For a while they could hear only the sound of the swollen river gushing. Then came a low rumbling and a mighty splash as a group of wildebeest plunged themselves into the river. Patel shrugged off the blankets and adjusted his binoculars with both hands. The crocodiles were already lying in wait for the wildebeest and one by one, as each creature entered the flowing water, they attacked it in pairs, thrashing and turning to pull it further out, into the faster currents. At the bank, a crocodile was holding a wildebeest firmly by the neck and dragging it into the deepest part of the river. The creature kicked and flailed as the great reptile wrapped itself around its body and began pulling it under. In the darkest waters of the river, a black hump could be seen advancing towards the fight.

'You see the hippo?' Ole asked. 'Now see the wildebeest being defeated.'

The crocodile was struggling to keep its grasp on its prey as the hippo sunk its teeth into the wildebeest's hump, turning the swirling water pink. They battled over the carcass until the hippo finally broke the crocodile's grip by going underneath the wildebeest's neck and lifting it out of the water. The crocodile slunk away.

Patel leaned forward, his elbows resting on the roof. 'Unbelievable. I've never witnessed anything so primitive. I thought hippos were herbivores?'

'Exactly, but they're very dangerous. During the migration they become opportunistic carnivores. The wildebeest don't stand a chance.'

'They'd be better off avoiding the river, wouldn't they?'

'Maybe, but the wildebeest can't resist.'

In the next car the man had turned his binoculars in Patel's direction.

'He seems to be marking you, Doctor,' Ole said, restarting the vehicle.

'Why me, Ole?'

'Maybe he wants to know where you bought your outfit.'

They returned to the Lodge where Dr Patel was met at the entrance by a waiter in a red and white Maasai shuka and beaded decorations around his ankles and wrists. The waiter offered Patel a damp towel to cool himself and a glass of fresh passion juice.

'Karibu, sir.'

'Very good, I can see you know how to treat your guests here.' Patel dabbed his forehead, then wandered down to the dining area on the balcony.

Flies hovered around sugar bowls set out on tables laid with crisp white cloths. He looked out across the vast dry plains with dusky shadows. The clouds were low, the sun was bright and not a leaf stirred. He loosened his cravat.

The waiter ushered him to a table, drew out a chair, and gestured for him to sit down. As the waiter left, a slim young man came striding across the balcony. Patel pulled his chair closer to the table and covered his protruding belly with a starched napkin.

'Hello,' the man said. 'I'm Tom, the Lodge manager for Smith Brown.'

They shook hands, Patel introduced himself and held out his business card. Tom sat down opposite him. The waiter appeared with a tray of pastries and took their order for tea and coffee.

'I hope you enjoyed the game drive,' Tom said.

'I sure did,' Patel began, taking a bite of a croissant slathered with strawberry jam. 'The croc fight was a sight to behold. I'm not a sentimental man, but I couldn't help feeling sorry for the wildebeest. Big as it was, it went down in minutes.'

'The Mara has its own food chain which never fails to surprise.'

Patel picked up the jam jar and slid a sticky thumb over the label: *MARA'S PRIDE*.

'Yup, local jam,' Tom said. 'You could almost call it home made. The Maasai initially resisted growing strawberries, but we flew in an expert in Change Management from London. It's for their own good. They have to accept they can't go on being nomadic pastoralists for ever.'

Patel wiped his mouth on the napkin. 'I'll get straight to the point, Tom. Your directors will no doubt have told you why I'm here?'

'I gather your company is looking to acquire the Lodge.'

The waiter returned with tea and coffee, and placed a fruit platter down in front of them. There was a rustling in the trees beyond the terrace and a Maasai woman appeared. She stood with a stick in her hand and Patel recognised her – Ole's sister. He turned his attention back to Tom.

'Yes, Amber Investments, where I'm the Safari Division Manager. The lawyers and auditors have submitted their due diligence reports for the directors, but before we make the official offer tomorrow, I'm here to assess the human resource potential.'

'Today it's lodges, lodges, lodges,' Tom said. 'Everyone wants one.'

'Absolutely, because there's money to be made.' Patel lifted a chunk of pineapple to his mouth, which slipped from his fork onto the floor.

'I should warn you,' Tom said, 'the Lodge is not without its baggage. As you know, the Maasai have suffered greatly over the past few decades. First they were displaced by the colonial British, and then had their land taken from them by the Kenyan Government. More recently Xinpin Gu invested in the region. For five years mini buses full of Chinese tourists descended on the plains each morning, more than thirty at a time, leaving so much litter from their lunch boxes, the monkeys started to depend on it for food.'

'If they were doing so well, why did Xinpin decide to sell up?' Patel said, before spearing a passion fruit with his knife. He sliced it in two, scooped out the slippery black seeds with a spoon and slid them into his mouth.

'The Lodge was set on fire one night,' Tom said, 'and Xinpin was spooked. They pulled out of the deal, saying it was bad feng shui. The company have since put their investments into mining.'

'Well we can't change the past, even the recent past. Our concern is for the future.' Patel looked out past the porch; multi-coloured hot air balloons floated peacefully in the sky across the plains. He glanced at the bushes. The Maasai woman had disappeared.

The waiter began clearing the table. Patel stopped him and asked for another basket of rolls and pastries. 'And more of that jam, please.'

'Smith Brown,' Tom continued, 'has tried to reverse some of the environmental damage. We've also built a school and dispensary.'

'Excellent.' He reached in his pocket. 'I'll take some notes Tom, if you don't mind.' He wrote a heading, *MARA LODGE*, and underlined it twice. 'Well, Amber has bigger and better plans.'

'Really?' Tom raised an eyebrow. 'Come now, we all know Amber's here for the exact same reason.'

Patel dusted the crumbs from his jacket. 'Maybe, but Amber's different. We're an indigenous multi-national, not a foreign investor, and have the Maasai's interests at heart.'

'Of course, as we did.' Tom adjusted his tie, and folded his arms across his chest.

'Well, I wish you luck. After the raid last month, I for one, will be glad to be out of here.'

'The Lodge was attacked?'

'My office was ransacked. They took my computer and phone, and that week's takings.'

'What did the police have to say?'

Tom shook his head. 'I didn't report it. To be honest, I handed in my notice the next day and then Smith Brown decided to sell. We can't do business in a lawless land.'

'That's precisely my point,' Patel said. 'No fire or raid can frighten Amber. We're used to the challenges of transacting in Kenya.'

Ole appeared and had a short exchange with the waiter standing a few feet away. Tom stood up.

'Ole, give our guest a walking tour of the Lodge and show him everything that was destroyed in the fire.'

'Thanks, Tom,' Patel said shaking his hand. 'I'm confident Amber has a great future here.'

Dr Patel followed Ole round the back of the Lodge and up the hill.

'You see that orange-coloured fruit up there?' Ole pointed to a tree. Patel went closer. The fruit was covered in worms gorging on its flesh. Ole shook the branch and some fruit fell and landed at Patel's feet. He stepped back and the worms scattered.

'Sometimes we have to shake the whole tree,' Ole said, 'to get rid of a few worms.'

Patel opened his jotter and wrote: *Maasai can be heavy handed over small things.*

Ole tore off a leaf from a nearby tree and rubbed it between his palms. 'Smell this,' he said. 'Depending how you use them, these leaves can cure skin infections or act as a venom and make your muscles swell up till you die.'

Patel sniffed the sprig and wrote: *Can make homeopathic remedies and poison. (Suggest at next director's meeting herbal medicine R&D centre for retail division?)*

Ole jumped from rock to rock, with Patel trailing behind,

struggling with the upward climb and holding on to branches that lined the path. The sun was directly overhead and pounding down on him. He stopped to catch his breath.

'How much further?'

'You're not fit, Mzee,' Ole called.

'I'm not used to this type of activity,' he said. 'Mine are of a more intellectual kind.'

'As we say, you can't force water uphill.' Ole laughed. 'You take your time.'

Patel stood in the shade and leaned against a tree. The jungle hat offered no protection, the belt strained at his waist and the double breasted safari suit clung to him. He took off the cravat and stuffed it in his pocket.

Ole climbed down to the ledge where Patel was standing.

'You should remove those,' he said, pointing at Patel's boots. 'They'll make you lose your balance.' His own sandals were made from leather strips and an old tyre.

'Not these.' Patel lifted his foot to display the ankle high shoe and ridged sole. 'They're specially designed for the bush.'

From the scrub came the shrill call of tiwi birds. He tucked away his notepad, and clipped the pen into his top pocket.

'We should head back.'

'The Maasai have a secret,' Ole said.

'Oh?' Patel propped himself against a large rock and observed the panorama of bush-cloaked hills and the cloud silhouettes drifting across the savannah.

'We know when it will rain, when a lion is near, and what kind of a heart a man has.'

Shouts of laughter came from up ahead. At the top of the knoll, Patel could make out the shapes of children playing with a ball.

'Are they yours, Ole?'

'Only those three,' Ole said. He pointed his club to the lighter skinned child holding a football. 'But that Chinku is my niece. In my clan many believe she's from the devil.'

'What do you mean?' Patel shaded his eyes.

'From China.' Ole turned away and bounded up the rocks, disappearing into the under-bush.

The children gestured towards Patel and the girl with the ball threw it at him. He caught it and was about to throw it back when the Maasai woman he'd seen earlier appeared from the bushes. She pointed her beaded club at Patel and yelled. She moved closer, hissing at him through the gaps in her teeth and snatched the ball off him.

Patel backed away, stumbled and caught his shoe on a protruding root. The next thing he was on the ground and the woman was looking down at him.

'Leo ni leo. Ata ona,' she said in Kiswahili, before spitting on him.

He understood: Today is today. You will see. He wiped his face. 'What about today? What will I see?'

Ole was back. 'What's going on here?'

Patel looked up, clutching his foot. 'I slipped.'

'Ha,' Ole said, 'the buttocks never mistake the ground.'

The woman shouted and jabbed her stick in the air.

'What's she saying, Ole?'

'I told you, my sister's a witch, a mchawi. She went mad when the Chinese possessed her.'

Patel tried to lift his leg and winced. 'Help me up, will you Ole? I think I've sprained my ankle.'

Ole held out his hand.

The woman spoke again, in a lower, more measured tone and raised her club over Patel's head.

'What's she saying now, Ole?' he said, brushing down his jacket.

'That your children and cattle will die and you'll lose your mind.'

'Why, Ole? What have I done?'

'She says the truth will be out soon.'

Ole took Patel's arm and put it round his shoulder.
'Twende, let's go, Mzee.'

Patel began to limp down the hill, leaning on Ole.

After the long, slow walk back to the Lodge, Dr Patel changed into long, khaki shorts and a yellow polo shirt and then relaxed in an armchair in the cool interior of the lounge. He rested his ankle on a footstool, ordered a fresh lime juice with plenty of ice and wrote in his notepad: *Maasai women are volatile. Recruiting female staff could be problematic.*

The waiter set a tray down on a stool and fixed his stare on Patel.

Patel looked up. 'Is something the matter?'

'I'm studying your face.'

'Well, would you mind doing it somewhere else?'

'Yes Mzee.' The waiter didn't move.

Patel put down his pen. 'Since you're standing there, I may as well ask you, do you know anything about the fire that broke out while Xinpin was in charge?

'Of course,' the waiter said. 'I'm Ktio, everyone who meets me knows they'll find me here and they'll leave me here.'

'What happened?'

'When our land was snatched by the Chinese, our elders travelled to Nairobi and explained to the Commissioner that our clan and livestock had become disorganised. They asked for compensation. The Commissioner told them it was impossible and to stop complaining, because all tourists and investors are the guests of the President.'

He nodded. 'I see.'

'This made Engai Nanyokie, our Red God, furious and he decided to take revenge by starting the fire.'

'The gods play an active role here, do they?'

'It's their duty to protect us.'

'Young man,' Patel said, 'these are historical complications which can't be resolved overnight by the gods. All one can do is try and erase bad memories and focus on good prospects in the present.'

'Ni kweli, Mzee, you're right,' Ktio said.

Patel jotted down: *Maasai-reputation for being suspicious and paranoid not without foundation.*

The Somali guest in the dark glasses appeared at the threshold holding a briefcase. Ktio left Patel and led the man to a nearby sofa and offered him a drink. The two men talked animatedly. Shortly after, they were joined by Ole and the three of them poured over a map. Without acknowledging Patel with even so much as a wave, they left, Ole carrying the briefcase under his arm.

A few hours later Dr Patel went to his tent for a lie down. By the evening, his temperature had risen and he was feeling week and feverish. The dim light from the lantern by his bed cast strange shapes around him. He could hear animals grunting outside the thin canvas of his tent. A night bird hooted. Patel gripped the edge of the blanket at the sound of scuffling. He fumbled for his phone and flashed the narrow beam from the torch around the bed. It died a moment later. He raised his head with an effort from the pillow and saw that Tom and Ole were standing at his bedside.

'Are you feeling alright?' Tom said.

'I think I've a fever.'

'I heard about your small accident on the hill,' Tom said, 'but I had no idea it was so bad. I was worried when you didn't show up for dinner.'

He was shivering. 'Could I leave for Nairobi right away?'

'I'm afraid not,' Tom said. 'The airstrip closed at five thirty and no-one's allowed to drive in the Reserve after six.'

'Is there a doctor around?'

'Unfortunately he was called away on a personal matter.'

Patel pulled back the covers. 'Look how my ankle's

swollen,' he said. 'It feels like lead.'

Ole stepped out of the shadows with a lantern casting a yellow gloom over the tent. 'I can bring my uncle. He's a laiboni, a medicine man.'

Patel groaned, 'Not now, please.'

'It's like an elephant's leg,' Ole said. 'See the way the skin is wrinkled and decaying.'

'Nonsense,' Patel said.

'The poison is spreading.'

'Don't be ridiculous,' Patel said, 'it's just a bruise from the sprain.'

'My uncle can do a ritual cleansing,' Ole said.

He lifted his head and looked from Ole to Tom. 'Not in a million years, Tom.'

'This sickness is caused by an internal imbalance,' Ole said. 'It is i–tikana loibor, the white disease.'

'What the hell's that?' Patel said.

'Your blood will turn white, your stomach and liver will swell, and Mzee will become weaker and weaker.'

'Oh for goodness sake,' Patel said.

'May I?' Tom pulled the skin under Patel's eyes, checked his pulse and reflexes. He turned to Ole. 'I'm no expert, but I can tell he's getting worse. I'll go and get the first aid box.'

'Someone has put a mganga, a spell on Mzee, which has overthrown him,' Ole said, shaking his head. 'I'll inform my uncle to prepare ntasim, a special medicine.'

'No,' Patel moaned. 'Please no.'

'Anand,' Tom said, 'I'm not keen on alternative medicine either, but under the circumstances we don't have many options.'

'Yes Mzee,' Ole said. 'If you don't co–operate you could be dead by morning.'

When Ole and Tom had gone, Patel struggled to sit up, but collapsed onto the pillows, drenched in sweat.

He fell in and out of sleep. When he woke, he could hear

footsteps and people talking outside. Then a rustling sound much closer, inside the tent and a movement in the corner.

'Who's there?' he shouted. 'Show yourself.'

A Maasai woman stood at the foot of his bed. Her silver jewellery flashed in the dark. She moved to the side of his bed and raised her arm; her bracelets jangled against the beaded club in her hand.

'Don't hurt me,' he said. 'My wallet's over there and you can take my phone.'

She flung his phone aside, struck a match and held the flame to his face. In the distance he could hear drums throbbing and incantations. Red and yellow lights flashed around the tent, then darkness enveloped him.

When he came to, his bed was surrounded by a dozen Maasai. They moved backwards and forwards, ululating and waving clubs and sticks over him. He turned his head on the pillow and found Ole leaning over him.

'Please, no more,' Patel mumbled.

'Drink.' Ole brought a gourd close to his mouth.

Patel clenched his lips. Then fingers clamped the back of his neck, his head was wrenched back and his mouth forced open. A salty, milky substance was poured down his throat and he began retching.

The following morning Dr Patel sat bundled in thick red and white checked Maasai shukas in the back of the Pinzgauer. On his face were yellow and white markings and his leg was wrapped in cow dung and leaves. Ole's uncle maintained that Patel had been afflicted by sorcery and if not treated promptly, an incremental swelling and madness would take over his body. The blood and milk mixture was to help eliminate the poison.

And now Ole was driving him to the airstrip for the flight back to Nairobi. From the airport he would go directly to a meeting with Amber's directors who were anxiously awaiting his evaluation. He'd made a final comment in his notebook that morning: '*Maasai: a superstitious and difficult lot. Will need focussed re-training.*'

'The air is muggy because it's going to rain, Mzee,' Ole said, pointing to the sky. 'It's a good omen.'

The sun was hiding behind dense clouds, and a thick gloom hung across the savannah.

They came to the signpost, *MARA NORTH CONSERVANCY,* where Ole's sister and niece were standing by the sacks of charcoal. Another Pinzgauer drove up and parked. Ole stopped and shouted from the window and the man wearing dark glasses sitting in the back exchanged greetings with him.

'That's our Somali friend, Mr Aideed,' Ole said. 'We're preparing for a special ceremony today. He's sponsored a goat.'

'A goat?'

'We'll slaughter it to purify the Lodge after yesterday's problem,' Ole said.

Patel was silent, slumped on the back seat.

'Also, now my sister won't have to sell makaa and I can afford to go to Little Mogadishu and buy a new phone.' Ole called out to his sister and she came over. She peered at Patel, waved a piece of paisley cloth at him and blew her nose on it.

He jerked his head back. 'Ole, please drive on,' he said, 'or I'll miss my flight.'

The sister spoke to Ole.

'What's she saying?' Patel asked.

'That you've been honoured with a Maasai title.'

'Oh yes?'

'You are now Oloishiru Ingishi, The Helper of Cattle.'

'I assure you,' Patel said, 'I shall endeavour to earn that title.'

'You will, Mzee,' Ole said, 'by never returning to the Mara. You wouldn't want to be ill again, would you? Thanks to my uncle, you were lucky this time.' Ole revved the engine. 'From the beginning, Mzee, I knew you were a *wise* man.'

Patel turned in his seat and looked over his shoulder. Through the billows of red dust he saw Mr Aideed placing a parcel in the woman's outstretched hands.

The Inn of the Two Witches – A Find

Zoe Gilbert

I WAS RECENTLY COMPELLED to visit a writers' group in rural Kent. Railways being what they are these days I ended up in the wrong village at the wrong time. Being stuck there, I spent a desultory couple of hours in the Coach and Horses, an ugly new-build pub where I told the ragged woman behind the bar of my woes. 'A writer?' she said, looking duly unimpressed, but once I'd bought her a half of Oscar Wilde Mild she softened. Perhaps it was my compliments on the incongruous horse brasses, but after her second drink she belched and told me she had something I might be able to use. After some scuffling out back she returned with a shoebox (Nike). 'Found this when we razed the old pub,' she said. 'Can't make much of it.' In the box were pages covered in small, crooked handwriting. At the top was the date 10th December 1930. I couldn't exactly turn down this peculiar gift, so I lugged it home to London with me, feeling travel-sick on the train from trying to read the tiny scrawl. It took me many weeks, what with my demanding writer's life, to type it all up. Some words I had to improvise, but here is a transcription of the contents of that Nike shoebox from Kent.

Should you have found this paper intact then you are to read an explanation of sorts a confession if you wish so help me God

Three years or maybe more Jessie Conrad has been coming to sit with Robert & me at our inn the Coach & Horses & during all her visits Jessie has talked of her Joseph it is six years now since he passed away God rest his soul & she has told over & over the fond memories the hard memories sometimes too so Robert & I have as good as got to know Joseph alongside Jessie – when she sat with us at the round table in the corner of the front saloon for cards or dominoes looking out at the grass & line of elm trees she sometimes smiled she sometimes grimaced though that was likely her bad knees they were a bother to her always even in stillness sitting cosy in our pub – then her head would make its little wobble that was her familiar trait it would get more familiar as the evening went on with the taking of brandy always brandy even as times got harder for us we would fill Jessie's glass the poor woman & she would tell us stories – when she did this I recall she would always begin with remembering where she & her Joseph were living at that time the big old farmhouse at Pent with all its cats & rats & the ghost of a robin always visiting she said or at Oswalds over in Bishopsbourne where her Joseph died God rest his soul – I grew fond of hearing about these houses I got a sense of them the whitewash hall the back kitchen each room where Joseph sat or Jessie pottered & so to me Oswalds was like a house in a book I could see it in my mind

Poor Jessie I never met a woman heavier in the flesh she has such trouble to walk even with her crutches & tires so quickly I daren't imagine how she looked after her Joseph & two boys all those years & he such a worrywort he worried himself to death is how it seems to me – I've suffered with my back myself so very bent I've got as I've aged but I've little flesh on my bones & Robert's miserly ways have caused me little strife in our better years not like that Joseph with his nerves also his temper God rest him – but poor Jessie she may be weighed down with her pain & sorrows & with her own limbs & bosom the very girth of her yet when she smiled to remember him & began to tell a tale her puffy face lit with love & the fondness that forgetfulness of harder times can bring she was despite it all a pretty thing – perhaps it was this that made my soft spot for her grow so I felt tenderly towards the woman almost motherly dare I say though I never raised my own it was this made me generous with the brandy even when Robert glared & began to make low comments about our empty coffers & the brewery asking for accounts he was right but I couldn't help it I would always try to help the woman

Robert had tried too in the beginning he saw the sorry state of her still mourning her Joseph after years gone by & taking comfort in the brandy & in a little round of cards when we both saw how she liked to bet how her round face lit up when there were coins on the table stakes I should say we thought this our own blessing for we believed we could cheat the cards so Jessie would win – with her happiness at heart both Robert & I tried to play badly to make sure she would win some shillings some pounds even we were doing better then with the earl coming in regular with his cronies drinking fit to sink a ship but it was difficult to give her coins even this way for while she loved to gamble she was so careless at it & anything we lost to her we won back again without wanting or trying–after the earl stopped coming by the inn such a fall in our fortune & our takings Robert put a stop to these attempts though seeing as they rarely worked I didn't see why he took so hard against it so we played cards still but for lesser coins & still I poured brandy for poor Jessie for Robert & me too though lately he's took to hiding the bottles & marking down the tots she's drank – last week he showed me I kept a ledger he said this is what she's had off us in liquor & she should pay it all back we'll be homeless before she is at this rate I scolded him for heartlessness but I saw the figure on the ledger not small now & it will grow & Robert may be mean but he may also be right

So it was on 21st October of this year Jessie visited again nothing strange in that it being a Wednesday & she being expected Robert had hid all but one brandy bottle which he held back give her ale first he hissed so I did & Jessie so hot & bothered from her journey & carrying with her a case this time she supped it down in one long gulp – I've a dilemma she said when she caught her breath her head giving its little waggle & she held the case on her lap this is the very last story I have by my J.C. she said (that is how she called her Joseph) & though I need the money so very badly I am very loathe to sell – Robert came out from behind the bar then he was pretending to polish glasses but we had served nobody but ourselves the last two days you would sell it? he asked & he stared at the case & Jessie sighed indeed I have sold them all to keep a roof over my head & bread on the table she said I have lived like a mouse to eke out the money but I am down to nothing now & I owe rent on the house she hugged the bag closer with her big broad arms.

Robert came & sat down by her they are worth a lot then? he asked & Jessie nodded they are original manuscripts she said I typed every one for him myself it breaks my heart a little to sell them & to part with this last one I fear will break it entirely but what am I to do? the last three months I've paid no rent on Oswalds &I am hungry she said her head wobbled & there were tears in her eyes – Jessie you sit quiet I will fetch you a meal I said don't worry you will feel better & though Robert glared at me he did not follow me into the kitchen but stayed by her & her case – while I cut her some bread & cheese & a quarter pie I pictured the cottage Oswalds that Jessie had described so many times & it nearly broke my own heart to think of her put out of the home she'd shared with her Joseph God rest his soul I had tears in my eyes by the time I carried the plate back out – then I saw Robert had already got her to open up her case & the manuscript as she called it lay on the table – it's worth quite a lot is it? Robert was repeating & Jessie nodded oh yes I sold every set of originals at a fine price & this last one I have I thought one of his best though J.C. didn't agree she smoothed down the top page of typed letters & I peered down THE INN OF THE TWO WITCHES it said it makes me shudder to write it now but at the time it meant nothing much – Robert said may I read it I'll be most careful you can be sure & I thought that was a strange tone for him awfully polite but it made Jessie smile & she handed him the manuscript before her eyes swivelled towards the bar so I fetched her more ale – when I gave it to her she took my hand & before she opened her mouth I knew what she would say she had been asking me more & more often would I get out my Ouija board for her & I had protested but it had got harder & harder to say no each time to find an excuse for she knew I had used it in years past I had told her the story myself but it had been meant only to amuse not to put ideas in her sweet puffy head – I only ask she said for I wish to consult my J.C. before I sell this last story of his & your Ouija board is the only means she was pleading with me I said no Jessie I can't I've not the knack any more this is what I always say the real reason being one I shan't repeat but that has haunted me since that terrible night with the earl when I swore I'd never use it again – before I could go on Robert interrupted have you read this story yourself Jessie? he asked oh she said of course I typed it with my own fingers but I've not read it for many years now though I am sure it was a good one – Robert had a certain look in his eyes a kind of meaning meant for me to catch while he said to her indeed it is a good one & you would surely make a fine profit from it let me fetch you a brandy while you eat up that bread & cheese & he scooted off behind the bar ah! he called I will have to get fresh from the cellar Helen will you help me with the hatch? & he glared at me to follow him out down the passage.

When we were out of her hearing Robert hissed I can get her to sell that story easy enough & if she will then pay us back for all the brandy she's had poured down her neck while she's been here we'll be good for another order & keep the brewery off our backs he looked triumphant that gleam in his eye & I was suspicious I said how on earth will you be doing that? you can't consult her Joseph for her that's what she wants – Robert grinned he beckoned me close & spoke in my ear that story he said it's not kindly & when she sees it she'll be glad to part with it she must have forgot its nature over the years so I will show her & bob's your proverbial it'll be sold in a jiffy he sounded quite sure so I asked what do you mean it's not kindly you don't sound so kindly yourself – well Robert said one of the witches in that story is awfully familiar if you know what I mean & you'd have to be silly not to see it when Jessie reads it she'll change her mind about her *dear* J.C. how much he loved her & she him she'll see he thought her a dreadful creature really & she'll want shot of that manuscript sure as eggs are eggs & Robert laughed then stopped himself – I was furious you'll do no such thing I said you'll not tamper with that poor woman's happy memories it's all she has but Robert said exactly that's the problem here she has memories & no money & I for one would rather it were the other way about he started down the cellar steps & I followed him you're cruel I said I won't let you ruin what small joy she has left in fact I'm going up right this moment to take that manuscript out of her reach – Robert took me by the wrist if we don't pay for an order the brewery man will smell a rat it will only be a matter of time before they shut us down is that what you want? he knows I love our inn the Coach & Horses it is our home even if it is our struggle too & never have we been so close to losing our grip of it Robert spoke again we have to get her to sell that story & if you don't have a better idea than mine then after her third brandy I will make her read it

Standing there on the cellar steps of our dear inn that was where the idea came to me to save Jessie from believing anything bad of her J.C. but to get her the blessing she needed to sell the story it turned me cold to think of it but there was nothing else to do – I peeled Robert's fingers from my wrist I said to him I will get the Ouija board & you will leave that woman in peace you'll not let her near that manuscript tonight – Robert looked at me hard he smiled then he went down the steps & came back with a full brandy bottle he said take this let her drink freely if you think you can make her sell it he put the bottle in my hand but did not let go he went on & you are wise I will indeed keep that manuscript hid from her & if she hasn't agreed to sell it by the end of this evening I will sell it myself – I did not like the sound of this but a plan was forming in my mind a good one though I didn't like it so I said very well but you keep it safe for I know this will work my way will be much kinder & as I ran back upstairs with that bottle I felt quite superior to my mean husband & I believed I could do it – I went straight to the loose skirting where the Ouija board has been hid all these years I saw it were stained several letters blacked out by spilt ink how that happened I knew not but even after I swore off it the earl still had a liking for taking the board out in the back bar private with his cronies there was nothing I could do now since I had but one of the dreadful things so help me God

Robert had the manuscript back in his hand in the window seat of the saloon he was saying to Jessie he would very much like to finish reading it such a fine story & being worth so much it was a privilege he was weasling anyone could see it but Jessie when she saw the board in my hand heaved herself up with a smile broad as anything her head waggled Robert gave me that meaning look from behind her back I said Jessie let us go up to the back bedroom for some privacy & we will talk to your Joseph will you manage the stairs with your crutches alright? – of course she nodded & exclaimed I could climb a mountain to speak to my J.C. though I knew that weren't true with those knees of hers like crumbled buns but she followed me panting

& we stopped twice on the way up Jessie leaning against the wall – the chair in the back bedroom being that dainty one with the fine turned legs I sat Jessie down upon the four-poster & made her comfy against the pillow it is our only four-poster I am quite proud of it & she looked a grand sight sitting there while I lit some candles we still hadn't electric in that room – we were just getting settled the Ouija board across her lap when there was a knock & Robert entered he paused a moment in the doorway as if he'd had a fright then he said you two look a pair of witches there bent over your dark doings & he laughed quite loud & you forgot the bottle he said & he put the brandy & two glasses on the side table & looked at me meaningful again let the liquor flow he said I'll be downstairs reading & he left

It was a kind trick I planned to play a trick with the best of wishes for I've only ever wanted to help my dear Jessie so I pulled the chair up close by her & placed the pointer on the board that lay on her lap – I did not tell her the proper method that everyone present should have two fingers on the pointer instead I kept that job for myself it would make the trick easier to pull off so I only told her she must ask questions herself at this she gasped & said I must speak to him directly? her eyes blinked back tears her head waggled & she whispered J.C. I do miss you & when she said that I felt sure I did the right thing to keep her from reading the story – Jessie went on can you hear me J.C.? she asked I pushed the pointer to 'YES' there was no sense in causing her any doubt & she gave a little sob I felt the board wobble but poor Jessie smiled at me bright as a girl & said I talk to you often J.C. while at home but it is a place you never lived I don't suppose you hear me then do you? – God forgive me I did not know how best to answer this I pushed the pointer to spell out her name. This was when I saw the difficulty the ink stain covered both 'E' & 'S' as well as 'F'& 'T' so after the 'J' I thought fast I added a 'C' to make

J C

It was enough Jessie began to babble wiping happy tears her head joggled like a puppet's & she began telling of her trouble with her knees & the struggle she had with a publishing man over a book she had written about her Joseph & all the friends of his she had not seen these last years lonely in Kent but glad to be in the county he loved – she did not mention the story it was as if she had forgotten so when she faltered I said go on ask him she looked askance so I took up the brandy & poured us each a large glass for courage honestly I needed it to steady my own nerves sitting before my friend & fooling her I took a sip Jessie glugged hers & set the empty glass back down then she nodded & took a deep breath that tipped the board forward – J.C. she said I confess I have been selling original copies of your works the very pages I typed out for you only out of necessity I promise so that I can pay my rent & eat she looked up at me as if for the reassurance she sought from him that gave me a pang of guilt in my gut I took another sip of brandy then I pushed the pointer so it spelled

YOU DO RIGH

Alas the 'T' was beneath the ink – Jessie frowned I whispered he must mean 'right' & she nodded thank you she said though that is an odd turn of phrase not like him at all this was a worry I could not in a month of Sundays speak or write like Joseph Conrad himself author of books & famous ones at that but before I could take another sip of brandy Jessie spoke again J.C. she said it is the greatest comfort in the world to hear you say that but I must ask for your blessing now to sell a copy of a particular story it was a favourite of mine when you wrote it but I believe you thought it bad – she cringed a little not wanting to go on so I spelled out

WHICH 1

I was glad the numbers at least were not stained by ink – Jessie leaned over to pour herself another glass & I had to stop the board from tipping onto the floor then she emptied the glass & said quickly The Inn of the Two Witches that is the story I wish to sell – she beckoned for me to lean close then she whispered he hated that story so much he would not read it after it was published I fear he will say no! – This put me in a bind I thought for a moment I had better be like the real J. C. lest Jessie get suspicious but I would make it come right in the end even Joseph Conrad could change his mind so I spelled out

NO

Then since I could not use the 'R' obscured by ink to say the word sorry I spelled out

APOLOGY

No apology does that mean I mustn't be sorry? Jessie asked she had mistook my meaning but really it was for the best she seemed to believe he might give his blessing after all – in relief I reached for my glass & sipped again & when I turned back to the board Jessie had her fingers on the pointer – I had not planned for this but I saw the hope in her face & saw that it would not matter so long as I could move it where I needed to the trick would still work – so I may sell it The Inn of the Two Witches? she asked her voice rising higher her head waggling it was excitement at speaking to him once more she really believed he heard so I began to edge the pointer towards 'YES' at the bottom of the board but it would not go instead it slid fast under our fingers across the letters across the black ink stain & it spelled out

NVR

What does he mean? Jessie whispered but I had not chosen those letters & did not like to say that it looked very much like never – how I longed for a nip of brandy then I tried not to think of times past with this board with the fear it put in me but already Jessie was asking J. C. what do you say? I know you weren't fond of it but in my opinion having read everything you wrote that story is one of your finest – again the pointer moved where my fingers did not agree it spelled

BURN I

My stomach filled with dread & first I wondered if Jessie played a trick on me but I looked into her puffy face it was a picture of confusion pale & as sweaty as my own in the candle light she spoke low to me again saying does he mean he lives in hell? but that cannot be my J.C. was a good man he suffered for his temper & she stared down at the board – so did I noticing again that the 'T' was obscured by the ink stain & it was clear to me what those words meant that 'I' should be 'IT' then I felt a little light in the head I wished to stop a moment but Jessie was asking again what's that you say J.C.? just as if they spoke on a bad telephone line & there were crackles in the message – the pointer scooted once again though I felt no shove from Jessie's fingers & it spelled

I AM AHAMD OF I

This was meant to be a little game one I could win but now I did not feel I was playing – Jessie too looked grave at me perhaps she saw fear in my face I said to her he means ASHAMED I could not lie my trick no longer mattered in that moment – oh J.C. Jessie cried you should not be ashamed of a single word you wrote they were all brilliant I wish you would not worry any more you ought to be at peace now & she began to weep the board shook with it under our hands & the pointer spelled out

BURN I NOW

Jessie's tears stopped her face was flushed & she said but it is precious not just to me to many people in this world your sons too

YOU DON RMMBR

The pointer moved fast it jerked about the board as if it was angry & I was quite wet with sweat under my arms on my brow God help me I wished so much to stop but Jessie sighed & said perhaps you are right J.C. you usually are & if burning it will make you happy it will make me happy too – her words were coming slurred but her glassy eyes were calm & she gave me a weak sort of smile

We sat in silence then Jessie closed her eyes she looked exhausted there against the pillow & a long time passed while I heard the little rustles of her breathing & I felt how hot her fingers were on the pointer beside mine – after some minutes I had gathered myself together I began to move the pointer to where 'GOODBYE' is written on the board this being the traditional way to end & send the spirits away Jessie's eyes stayed shut but her fingers stayed tight by mine I began to push but to no avail the pointer began to make a slow track across the board spelling

I LOV YOU J

It was then to my horror Jessie's fingers drifted from the board before I could point to 'Goodbye' her hands lodged in her lap breathing slowed & deepened she was sound asleep & though I shook her she would not wake & there was nothing I could do

I could not sit beside that cursed board I left Jessie to rest there in the back bedroom a great queen on her four-poster I needed cold water to splash my face & wash my dry mouth I needed most of all to think – my hands now they were not on the board shook like the elm leaves outside in the wind as I went along the passage hoping Robert would not be waiting to question me but in the saloon there was only the manuscript lying on the table by the window so I sat down beside it & rubbed my aching head – there were only two stories I could tell myself now & neither of them did I wish to believe the first was that Joseph Conrad really had spoken through the Ouija board & the second was that Jessie had pushed that pointer about so swift & so surprising seemingly to both of us – I searched for a reason why she might do such a thing & it struck me she wished to keep that manuscript so badly her last memento that she made the board refuse to give its blessing this theory fell apart though since the board had told her to burn it & told her twice – this left the other story which was worse that Joseph Conrad really was ashamed of what he wrote & really told us but if this was true we had not completed the session we had broken the rule we had not said 'GOODBYE' – I felt sick it was too dreadful to think of that Ouija board any more so I picked up the manuscript & decided to read it myself

It was a peculiar story indeed & one meant to frighten when I'd had fright enough for one night but what turned my blood cold first was not the odd men at their odd games with each other but the part where the traveller entered the inn& saw the two witches as he called them – they were not really witches just unfortunate women it seemed to me yet witch was not the worst thing he called them he used all kinds of insults such as weird harridans unspeakable frights feeble creatures horrible grotesque appalling decrepit objects of disgust & dread – one of the women had a puffy face the story said it repeated this detail of puffiness several times as it did that this woman's head trembled & all the more so when she was excited & the poor old thing walked with the help of a crutch the story said – I read this part again to be sure my tired eyes did not add their own fancies to the words written there but they did not & I saw Robert was right it was not kindly – but even worse upon my second reading I saw that the other old woman is thin with a terribly bent back & for a moment then I saw Jessie & me together in the back bedroom just as if I looked in through the small window Jessie's head wobbling as our fingers moved on the Ouija board & her puffy cheeks growing red & I saw myself bent over the board the hump in my back showing worse than ever & there beside us Jessie's crutch leaning at the bedpost

Something in the whole night seemed to turn askew then as if fate looked down & toyed with me first the Ouija board now this there was nothing to do but read on & hope sense would come to me so that is what I did while the wind rushed through the elm leaves in the black outside the window – such a strange story I never read before & such a devilish device as was described in its pages I never heard tell of or would have imagined for myself so cunning & cruel was it this bed at The Inn of the Two Witches that could kill a man the contraption was a kind of four-poster the canopy of which might descend & suffocate the sleeper – what imagination can dream up such things I shuddered to think & upon dropping the pages on the table once more I shuddered all the more for where had I left Jessie sleeping but on our only four-poster bed?

I scrambled up the stairs Jessie I called Jessie but there she lay a great lump on the bed the same as I had left her the Ouija board had fallen to the floor the brandy bottle stood where I'd left it only a third of the liquor remaining such grand measures she had poured herself & then slurred her words & fallen asleep so quick – I thought of Robert then his sudden change of tune going to fetch the bottles he'd hidden in the cellar telling us to let the liquor flow with that look in his eyes I had hoped he meant to help & that seeing what trick I meant to play he believed it would go easier if Jessie were a little worse for wear – but the night had put me on edge the story most of all & I wondered what he really meant & had he a trick of his own to play – it would not be the first time he meddled with the spirits he'd put sleeping draughts in the earl's whisky once when he & his cronies had got frisky & wished to play at William Tell in the saloon with a shotgun

& a lemon from the bar – there was not a sound from Jessie my own heart thumped so loud I did not even hear her breathing & that was when it crossed my mind I'd read in the story of a body lying dead on the devilish bed & here she was so help me God I could not stop the thought & my legs gave way & I toppled

That was where Robert found me I don't know how much time had passed but he was kneeling beside me & propped me up on a cushion there there he said did you have a fright? he went to pour me a brandy from the bottle on the side table – oh no you don't I said I'll not touch it get me water then I remembered what had made me fall & before I could help it I looked up at the bed & when I saw that Jessie was gone that was all it took to get me on my feet & edging towards the door – what have you done with her? I asked my heart thumping again but Robert smiled & said the lady is downstairs taking a cup of coffee we've been having a nice little chat

I suspected him still I said you made her read it then you weasel but Robert shook his head oh no he said the manuscript made very nice kindling to get the fire back up we thought it for the best it was cold enough down there to freeze the proverbials off a brass monkey & he smiled again jollier than I'd seen him in months – if you don't believe me just ask Jessie he said I never saw such a grin as when she crumpled that paper down into the grate she is watching the flames now still grinning no doubt – I was speechless all I'd gone through & he had let the story burn as if it were yesterday's newspaper it was too much to take God forgive me I felt the anger rising up in me as Robert stood there smiling his hands in his pockets & I remembered then Jessie telling how her Joseph would pace his brow furrowed his hands shoved in his pockets too –as if everything was normal he went on saying but you read the story too when you came down earlier you must agree it's an ingenious invention & he stepped closer to me the cheek of it I thought so I said no it's an insulting one if you ask me but Robert said not the story you silly thing the bed – we both glanced at the four poster then the eiderdown rumpled from Jessie's weight Robert said it made me think we might refurbish this back room & advertise for a higher class of guest we could really make the most of this fine bed it's a shame not to use it – his eyes gleamed as he patted one of the wooden posts he went on the kind of guest that has a bit more cash to spend & we'd only need have them to stay once to be back in the black in a jiffy

I stared at him as he went to inspect the four-poster I saw a morbid meaning in his words & believed he surely did not mean a fresh polish a new eiderdown but something far more sinister something only the fiendish inventor of that story could dream up – I could not speak but Robert still smiled now he said I thought that Jessie might stay here a while to save herself the rent she might entertain our new high-class customers with tales of her famous writer husband she might become an attraction – he shoved his hands deeper in his pockets that was it I bolted & even though I slammed the door before I ran down the stairs I heard that man laughing & laughing in the back bedroom

It was only much later that I could be persuaded to sit down & listen to their plan & though Jessie was as sweet as ever & Robert's eyes no longer gleamed God forgive me I still saw something nasty in it – the genius idea as Jessie called it for Robert's sake was indeed to convert our four-poster bed into the deathly contraption written in the story but with the purpose of falsely advertising it as the original that had inspired the author – I objected that the story was now burned but Jessie assured me it was printed in books it had been read by many and being such a good one was surely very famous by now & admirers of her Joseph's work would come flocking from all over the world to Kent to visit the Coach & Horses we would all three be rich – Robert added we would say this was the real Inn of the Two Witches & his laugh seemed a little cruel to me remembering those two poor women so harshly depicted but Jessie was delighted – I still suspected he was not exactly himself but I bit my lip I decided I would bide my time

So I have done & the truth is that hardly a soul has called on account of the bed & the advertisements & while Jessie finds out the brandy wherever Robert has hid it & I sit down to play dominoes with her in the afternoon with the bare elms creaking outside the window Robert does not join us – I hear him creeping about upstairs improving the contraption making that canopy slide down & back up as silent as he can this he tried to reassure me is simply to impress to tourists when they finally come

If one day my beloved Coach & Horses should fall down or be destroyed be it by fate or the hand of man then perhaps this my account will be found where I will leave it in the crack of our cellar wall & it will stand as a confession of sorts or at least an explanation for what may come next – I both dread & hope for my own preservation for Jessie's for a comfortable life here where I have made my home & if a traveller should go missing one day a higher class of gentleman perhaps with cash to spend then you will know that Robert made the most of his refurbishment & that Jessie Conrad lived happy til the end knowing she fulfilled her Joseph's wishes to burn his manuscript & what's more if you ever read that dreadful story of his you will know that it was a kind of wicked prophesy so help me God

Mamas

Grażyna Plebanek

Translated by Scotia Gilroy

'It's queer how out of touch with truth women are.
They live in a world of their own, and there has never
been anything like it, and never can be. It is too
beautiful altogether, and if they were to set it up it
would go to pieces before the first sunset. Some
confounded fact we men have been living contentedly
with ever since the day of creation would start up and
knock the whole thing over.'

        – Joseph Conrad, *Heart of Darkness*

MAMA FATOUMATA FELT A warm trickle of sweat drip from
under her wig. She wiped it away with an impatient
movement of her hand and smacked her lips. This didn't
change the look of disapproval on her face. Mama Fatoumata
didn't like to smile. She didn't think it was appropriate for a
working woman, a mother of six, a politician whose career
was now hanging by a thread. Why? For a reason so stupid that
she tut-tutted again: because of a lack of men!

Everything always starts with a scuffle. Who's taller, who's
better, who's richer, whose cock is bigger. As if one couldn't
return to the ancient practice of sharing. In the old days, when
a man went out into the fields, his father, brother or uncle
might pay his wife a visit while he was gone. The man would

drive his spear into the ground in front of the threshold as a signal – 'Don't enter!' And the husband would wait outside until his relative had finished having intercourse with his wife.

What was wrong with that? It's how marriages were within the clans so that property wouldn't be divided. A cock is a cock, no matter what nationality or ethnicity is written in a man's ID document.

Eth-nic-ity. What a word! As if people were born different. Mama Fatoumata had given birth to six children and had raised over a dozen more. She knew – without a doubt – that any apparent differences between people were insignificant. Unless, of course, there's an albino involved.

Everything turned ugly because of all the divisions; separate boxes, labels, and all that hair-splitting. And how! People raged and stormed, clashed and lashed each other, drank each other's blood and bit off each other's cocks. But all these damn cocks were exactly the same!

Mama Fatoumata scratched her forehead, but it didn't bring her any relief. Beads of sweat had formed furrows in her face powder, and were now washing away the remaining layers of makeup coating her skin, threatening her carefully drawn-on eyebrows.

The idea of legalising polygamy was as risky nowadays as it was revolutionary. It's not as if it were something new; people had lived that way for ages. But at a certain point the continuity had been broken. A new master and a new god had entered, breaking the continuity like a drop of sweat smudging the black arch of an eyebrow.

Monogamy was introduced. One woman, one man. Because that's what the foreign god wanted. And because it supposedly prevented AIDS. But how could it really prevent it, since there's never been a single man since the world began who's been able to have sex with only one woman for his whole life, and no woman could promise herself to just one man. Well, she could, but keeping her word is a different matter.

After they slaughtered each other, there weren't many people left. More women had survived. The male population was really slim, numerically speaking. Now there were three women for every man, or actually four. The statistics included old men and young boys, even though they weren't capable.

'This is a real problem!' thought Mama Fatoumata. She'd had this thought countless times that day, and most days recently. It was a gloomy month – the rainy season outside and in the soul too. They mourned the dead at this time every year. Sadness was rampant, like weeds. But weeds have to spread so there'll be something to pull up. Mama Fatoumata was looking forward to that.

She was born a woman of action, like all the women in her family. They worked like dogs all day long, which is why they got so mad when they saw the men getting all wound up, and then grabbing those stupid machetes and cutting off each other's even stupider heads. Heads that the women had fed, cradled, caressed and scolded for years, beaded with sweat, just like the sweat now dripping from under Mama Fatoumata's wig. Humans needed heads and other body parts. Mama Fatoumata couldn't stand wastefulness.

They'd slaughtered the women, too. No one was spared their fury. The machetes never dried, a red line had sliced through the country like a rapidly-spreading disease. In the end, very few people were left alive. So how was life to go on? Who would father the children? They hadn't thought of that.

Mama Fatoumata looked around. There was nobody in the corridor, so she pushed her wig all the way back. What a relief! she thought. The debate was still going on behind the closed door. She'd left the chamber as if to go to the toilet. Really she just wanted some space to set things straight in her mind. She needed time to think about how to win over Mama Scholastica. If her faction supported Mama Fatoumata's idea, they'd be on the home straight. In homes full of children.

The problem was that all the young women in the

parliament unanimously opposed the legalisation of polygamy. They shouted that their fight for equal rights hadn't been for this – to be assigned a number such as 'first wife,' 'second wife,' 'third wife.' As usual, short-haired Rokhaya shouted the loudest, proudly sporting a milk-stained blouse. And the other young women all rallied behind her.

Of course Mama Fatoumata had easily convinced all the male members of parliament to legalise polygamy. The problem was that there were only seventeen of them, whereas there were eighty-two women, most of whom were young. She fanned herself with a leaflet on which were printed in bold letters: 'One for all, all for one,' 'Sisters unite!' and 'Women support women.' An expression of restrained approval spread across Mama Fatoumata's face. It was clear those young women who sided with Rokhaya could afford higher-quality paper.

Well, who wouldn't give them money! Their breasts were bursting the buttons on their blouses and their heads were filled with nothing but strange mumbo-jumbo, as if someone had ploughed them and planted foreign seeds. There was one thing Mama Fatoumata couldn't get her head around: why couldn't the young women see what would inevitably happen? She shut her eyes and imagined them sticking their claws into each other's wigs. And over what? Over a man! Yes, there was another storm brewing, and it had nothing to do with *eth-nic-ity*.

She felt a hand touch her arm. Mama Scholastica was standing over her.

'They'll kill each other if we leave them one-to-one!' she blurted out the tail end of the thought pounding in her head.

Mama Scholastica immediately understood what Mama Fatoumata was talking about. She sat down next to her.

'There's one man to every three women,' she muttered, 'but in fact there's really one to every four, not counting the ones that aren't capable.'

They sat for a while without speaking, savouring the silence in the corridor. The debate was taking place behind a door that was so tightly shut that not a single sound seeped through. All that could be heard was a calming murmur of water from the nearby toilet. The cistern had broken two days before.

'We have to think of something,' said Mama Scholastica hoarsely.

Sitting beside Mama Fatoumata she looked like a grizzled heron next to an over-fed pigeon.

'After you went out,' she said, waving towards the door, 'they put forward a ridiculous idea....'

'What now?'

'Not only do they keep waffling on about how *demeaning* polygamy is but...' Mama Scholastica shielded her eyes with her hand, as if the light were dazzling her, '...they want to start importing.'

Mama Fatoumata felt the floodgate of her drawn-on eyebrows bursting. Drops of sweat were now pouring into her eyes and her mascara was mixing with her face powder, creating a brown sludge.

'Import what?' she asked, for the sake of form.

'Men.'

Mama Scholastica, who never wore makeup, lifted her slender fingers from her eyes with the annoying gesture of a person born with good manners.

'Young Rokhaya has just proposed to resolve the lack of local men by importing them from neighbouring countries. And maybe even from other continents.'

Everything went dark before Mama Fatoumata's eyes. She wiped off her smeared mascara with the edge of her hand.

'In bulk?' she wheezed. 'Or individually wrapped in vacuum-sealed plastic?!'

'They want to build new factories that would attract male workers. They're also thinking of scholarships for students. They would pay them well. You know they're good at collecting money.'

Mama Scholastica cast her sad gaze down at her flat chest, or maybe it just seemed that way to Mama Fatoumata. Her vision, blurred by her makeup, may have been playing tricks on her.

The murmur of water suddenly began to upset her.

'They ought to import a plumber,' she hissed.

'Apparently the best ones are from Poland,' Mama Scholastica muttered, thinking of something else. 'In any case, in Europe they're afraid of them.'

'And what did you do when they started talking about this import?'

'I tried to talk some sense into them.'

'I would've given them an earful!' Mama Fatoumata waved her fist at the closed door.

'They shouted me down. They don't understand that if they bring young foreigners here, another war is on the cards.'

'And that's why I keep saying it's better to stick with the few that are still here and share them,' Mama Fatoumata huffed.

'I even read them a quote from a book by Ken Bugul about how love means sharing,' Mama Scholastica whispered pensively.

'You did well,' said Mama Scholastica, without conviction.

Before the war Mama Fatoumata had worked as a cleaner at the school where Mama Scholastica had been the headmistress. When the massacre began, Mama Fatoumata had saved Mama Scholastica and her family, risking her own life and the lives of her loved ones. To this day she still had doubts about whether reading books was a safe path in life.

'But they started quoting another book, by another writer named Mariama Bâ.'

'What does she say in that book?'

'That polygamy leads to pain and suffering, humiliation and AIDS. They say they want monogamy because it means respect. And it's romantic.'

'It's what?'

'*Ro-man-tic.*'

Mama Fatoumata wanted to tut disapprovingly, but instead she snapped her fingers.

'Think of something!' she said to Mama Scholastica, outraged. 'You're wise.'

'Me?! All I know about is books.'

'Alright, so let's fight with what we've got. Books!'

'What do you mean?' Mama Scholastica looked as if she had woken up from a deep sleep.

'What are they reading now?'

'Something about vaginas. And sisterhood.'

'But what do they read under the bedclothes? I ask because I've done my fair share of cleaning in my life, and I'll tell you this: you have no idea how many smutty books I've swept out from under the beds in girls' dormitories.'

Mama Scholastica looked as if she were fighting the urge to scold Mama Fatoumata; instead, she took her iPhone out of her handbag. One of the consequences of the great massacre was that the country had been able to shift to a simple economy after the war, thanks to which it had become one of the most highly computerised countries on the continent. The members of parliament were all given modern telephones, which were indispensable when the parliamentary debates dragged on. They could order groceries from a nearby shop straight from the chamber and have them sent to their houses. They could pay through their phone, too, leaving the other hand free for voting.

Mama Scholastica punched something into her phone and handed it to Mama Fatoumata.

'Frederic Beigbeder… Is it a book about war?'

Mama Scholastica shook her head, and then nodded.

'The content doesn't matter, only the interpretation. Shall we defeat them with their own weapon?' she said, rubbing her hands together. 'They want to be free, liberated, don't they?'

'Yeah, and… *pro-gress-ive*.'

They stood up as if on cue.

All heads turned towards them as they walked in the chamber. Mama Fatoumata's entrance always caused a stir because she sailed into rooms like a battleship.

'…and that's why we propose creating programs that encourage young men to spend time in our country. Temporarily, with an option of extending,' Rokhaya said, concluding her speech from the podium.

'… the species,' someone added under their breath.

Applause filled the room.

'Are we all in agreement?' asked Rokhaya.

'Almost, sweetie,' said Mama Fatoumata, energetically brandishing the phone and barging her way towards the podium. 'I just have one thing to add, and the idea came to me from my, uhhhh, favourite writer. I'm sure he's your favourite writer, too.'

They looked at her, intrigued. They were aware, just as she was, that this was the first time in Mama Foutamata's life that she'd ever talked about books in any context other than dusting them.

'The writer's name is…' Mama Fatoumata brought the iPhone screen close to her face. 'Frederic Beigbeder. Oh! On the cover of his book there's a bullet.' She turned the phone towards the room. 'A bullet with a red trail behind it. And do you know what the title is? *Love Lasts Three Years*. Yes, three years, and not a day more. That's what's written here. Clear as day!'

She stopped talking and looked around the room. Rokhaya was staring at her with a mocking smile. A screen lit up behind Mama Fatoumata and someone gave her a thumbs-up from the back of the room – it was Mama Scholastica, making use of the room's technological capabilities to have the cover of Beigbeder's novel projected on the huge screen. Now the bullet glowed red behind Mama Fatoumata in all its glory.

'Three years,' she boomed from the podium. 'Some guy

will come here, he'll take our money and three years later he'll be gone! Is that what you want? Three years and that's it? Is that your *ro-mance*...?'

Rokhaya raised her hand to say something, but Mama Fatoumata pretended not to see it.

'A different woman every three years! Hopping from flower to flower. And what about AIDS?!' she thundered. 'A husband who has several wives at least knows he has to provide for his kids and his wives. And if he can't afford it, he doesn't get married. But what about these ones? They'll screw you, give you a kid, wash their hands of you and then bugger off home! Who'll raise the kids for you then? All of you work, and your mothers do too. Who'll look after the kids, I ask you?'

'What about romance?' called a voice from the audience.

'It lasts three years!' Mama Fatoumata raised three plump fingers above her head. 'Ro-mance lasts three years, that's what it says here. And not a day more.'

'How many?' someone asked from the back of the room. Mama Fatoumata recognised Mama Scholastica's voice, which was quavering with barely hidden amusement.

'Three!' Mama Fatoumata roared, and she raised three fingers in the air again. 'Three years. Three years!'

'Three years, three years!' the male members of parliament joined in.

'How many?!' Mama Fatoumata cupped a hand to her ear.

'Three years! Three years!' Others joined the chorus, and raised three fingers in the air.

'Three years!' Continuing to chant, Mama Fatoumata glanced at the circle of women surrounding Rokhaya. Behind them the shouts were growing louder, someone began to clap in rhythm, and steady drumming could be heard from somewhere.

Mama Fatoumata stood at the podium, conducting the chanting crowd, and when the shouts reached their climax she raised her arms above her head and called for silence.

'All those in favour of the reinstatement of polygamy, say "Aye".' The crowd roared their approval, plunging their three-fingered salutes back into the air. 'The Ayes have it', she shrugged, catching Rokhaya's eye. And as fresh chants of 'Three years' resounded in the chamber, she headed towards the door triumphantly, with all the others trailing after her. The crowd spilled into the corridor and the door closed behind them.

Only Rokhaya and Mama Scholastica were left in the chamber. They looked at each other in the silence that had suddenly fallen.

'And what now? Will it be like in the old days?' asked Rokhaya.

'You still have a lot to learn.' Mama Scholastica was trying really hard for her voice not to sound like the voice of a former headmistress.

Rokhaya ran a hand through her short hair. She didn't look angry, just stunned. Mama Scholastica could barely restrain herself from giving her a reassuring pat on the arm. She had daughters and daughters-in-law her age, and she knew how exhausting it was to work while trying to raise small children.

'To learn?' asked the young woman. 'But how?'

Mama Scholastica tried to make her voice sound as convincing as possible.

'From books. From books, my child,' she said.

Fractional Distillation

SJ Bradley

ARRIVED SAFELY, I WRITE, although the signal bar's empty. *Hope the kids aren't giving you too much grief x*

I gulp the humid air, and lean against the hire car. When I find a signal, perhaps in the next city I pass through, I'll send the text.

It's a long drive to the middle of nowhere, and I seem to spend half my life in a car on my way to it. I drive through a canopied darkness, the road hacked from the undergrowth like a tunnel, headlights on, neck streaming. Leaves flutter and jerk with the movement of release from animals jumping; I grip the wheel, keep my eyes on this road, what of it there is.

340 degrees. Residue, ship fuel, bitumen.

The lower reaches of the tower hold a less volatile liquid. It's one step below diesel, thicker, emerging at a much higher boiling point.

Suddenly the jungle stops, and I come out into the open, the sun blazing like hot oil. I get out, flash the security guard my ID, and he shows me to the site office: a fabric-sided gazebo, with tables resting on temporary flooring.

'Thomas?' It's the site foreman, overalled and red-faced. When he shakes my hand the dirt moves between our palms like an industrial floor sander. 'Powerful hot out there,' Davey says. His West Country drawl brings to mind white cottages and cream teas.

'It's a world away from Albuquerque, alright,' I say.

'Sooner we get started, the better; we need the rig-up started today,' he says. 'There's been a lot of rumblings about this extraction.'

'We expecting anybody?' I say.

'Hopefully not, but you never know. Come.'

Outside, the trucks are already at the business of clearing. They crawl around the site, digging holes for the mud tanks, a place for the tower. Once the roughnecks have put the kit together, the extraction will start; the lower wheel forcing crude oil from the field underground, overflow pouring into the mud tanks.

As I watch one of the caterpillar trucks trundle between tree stumps in the dirt, I hear Davey mutter, 'Shit.'

I turn. It's there, small and colourful, so distant you almost might not notice it, but there, all the same. Scraps of red and blue and yellow, tucked in behind trees to the west. Canvas flapping, and the unmistakeable insect scratch of human activity.

'For fuck's sake,' he says.

'What do you think they'll do?'

'Probably nothing,' he says. 'Chant slogans and wave banners. They look like they think it's 1974. Still – better try and get the job done before they can do anything.'

260 degrees. Diesel.

The second lowest point up the distillation tower gives us a fuel with slightly longer molecule strings, one that doesn't release so many quantities as petrol when combusted. Yields per barrel of crude are lower. Its boiling point is higher because the strings, being longer and more enmeshed, wrap around one another like noodles in a dish. As with other fossil fuels, it contains a small amount of sulphur, and a non-metal oxide which is soluble in water.

On any usual extraction, the site would have been running by now. Mud tanks installed, the tower flaring, the plunge and whoosh of the oil and burn-off roaring. But no. The site's just a murmur of voices: Davey, sweaty, twitching, moisture pouring into a darkening shirt collar.

'Bloody tree huggers,' he says. 'Didn't I tell you?'

At that point, I almost envied them for having the cover of the forest. 'What can they do?' I say. 'Hippy twats.' The site's in a university campus sized clearing, and up there, on the horizon, stands jungle dense as an encyclopedia. Between the trees canvas moves, and a flag flutters, broad yellow band up top, a horizon of red and blue.

'Already done it,' he burrs. 'Sabotage. They've done something to the fuel tanks, I don't know what. Taken bolts out of the fucking pipeline...' he gestures at the machinery standing in the humid air. 'Everything we've got, they've done something to it. The more they damage, the more it costs. They've taken bolt cutters to the tower chain, fuck's sake.'

A bus window glints on the hill. I watch, feeling a dry itch in my throat like insect wings. 'What about the security guards?'

'Useless,' he says. 'Must have been asleep.'

'What's their bus run on,' one of the roughnecks calls. 'Unicorn farts and fairy dust?'

'It'll be one of those hippy chip-van ones.' Davey doesn't take his eyes off the camp for a second. 'Biofuels.'

'Not getting anything done today, are we?'

Davey rubs his face. His forehead wrinkles like pastry flaking in a bag. 'I'll ring Head Office as well, give them an update.'

'Poker, anyone?' Joe, one of the roughnecks, hard-handed and at a loose end, boiling in his overalls. 'Not much else to do today, is there? You want in, boss?'

I write another text in my drafts folder: *We could be here a little bit longer than we thought x*

Davey shakes his head slightly, his eyes sweeping the flutter of canvas. 'Don't get too comfortable, boys,' he says, directing his comments to the roughnecks. 'We'll be back on the job before you know it. I want an inventory. Look at everything, I want to know what's working and what's not, what's been damaged and what, if anything, is salvageable. Check *all* the moving parts. If there's obstruction in the tower shell, I want to know. I'm not having us rigging it all up, only to have an explosion the minute we start extracting.' The men start to move off, and Davey clicks his fingers at Joe. 'You. Look at the breakables. Sort through the leftover bolts for the tower, count how many are still good enough to use. Look at them *properly*, to check they haven't been sanded off. And look at the mud tanks. I want to know they're alright to hold the overflow once we start.'

The truth was, none of us wanted to be out here any longer than we had to. Not with the wandering spiders and the infernal, never-ending heat. 'I'll help,' I said. 'What else am I going to do today?'

Alkalenes (by-product). Methane, ethane, propane, butane, pentane, octane.

These compounds – highly volatile and flammable – are a by-product of the cracking process. They remain afterwards, when there are not enough hydrocarbons to saturate the bonding positions.

Joe shrugs, and shakes his flask. There's a tinny sound, like the noise of an old washer draining its last gurgle. 'Now, with Tar Sands,' he says, gesturing over at a flap of green on the horizon. The light's failing quickly, stars coming out over the canopy. 'They didn't like that at all.'

'That's right.' A boy with thick eyebrows and a pair of aces. 'They were there before we even arrived. Hundreds of them, blocking the site off. They'd built a whole village out of sheds and tree-houses, all over the shop. Couldn't even get the trucks down.' He turns away, and with a clip pushes a token over the table. Yellow, edge-dotted, circular things that look like they've come from the game Connect Four.

I look back up towards the camp. It's a struggle to make anything out. Night has fallen fast, and there's no shapes or light, only a star line above what must be the tree tops. 'Better not be any more trouble,' I say.

Joe tips his flask. 'If you want to worry about anything, worry about getting finished on time.'

'The security guard reckons that every hour behind schedule,' the other lad says, 'costs the company a hundred thousand dollars. At Tar Sands, they sent in bulldozers.' He pushes a hand over the table, to demonstrate. 'Razed the whole lot to the ground in under an hour.'

I look to the tower, the spot where they've dug the hole for the tanks. The wheel over the tank arm will turn slowly, clinking, the chain rattling up and through the arm. This is always how it is. Things move slowly, emptily, in their rhythms and at their speeds, until the tower is lit. When the top compounds flare and burn, whooshing and thumping, that's the sound of the site running. Blooms of oil will strike a rainbow along the earth, ground sparkling with a full spectrum of colour.

The way this blackness is falling, though, sharp as a door closing, in a minute we won't be able to see anything at all. Up on the hill there's a sudden shout, human voices, hundreds of them.

'Christ,' the roughneck says. 'Ask Davey for his torch. I can't see a thing here.'

'I need it.' Davey's voice is clipped, a talking telegram. 'Keep playing if you want, but do me a favour, will you? Take cover. Health and safety.'

'What?'

A hand grabs at my back, and pulls me behind one of the trucks. Then I hear it. A roar up on the hill. Loud engines, jeeps. The quick lamplight of Davey's torch moves over the ground, first one way, then another, catching fallen branches, leaves, something that looks like dead legs. It's disorienting. I think the sound comes from the west, but it's hard to tell when you don't know which way you're facing.

'Get down,' Davey says, and pushes me to my knees.

My nose hits rubber. Tyres, that's what we're hiding behind, the jeep.

Something cracks. The ground's soft, warmer than I expected, and my knee crushes something. It's the same feeling as smashing a snail shell. 'Christ, Davey,' I say. 'I think I just killed something.'

'Could be a spider,' Joe says. 'Better hope it's dead.'

Then there's another crack, and another. Louder than the crack of shell. Airguns, firecrackers. Real guns. A distance away but the sound travels. There's not much between us and it. I'm too scared to look.

'Stay down,' Davey says.

'What for?'

Men shout. The voices are far away but they reach us. Screaming and shouting, protestors. It's the sound of people frightened and trying not to give it away. The sound of people trying to hold their ground. *Krak-krak*, I hear, and the voices descend into muttering silence.

'Are they shooting?' Joe breathes, by my elbow. Davey shushes him. 'What's going on over there?'

Davey's eyes are wet, and whiter than bone. A crack. I peek out. Flares of orange spike the night.

'Yes,' he says. 'Should be the army.'

'Whose?' I say, but he doesn't answer.

I look again, narrowing my eyes, an attempt to keep the whites hidden. I'm holding onto the wheel arch. Through slits I see movement. A flag on a pole, a crowd of people making their way out of the forest, downhill and towards the site. Two of them might be chained together, although it's hard to tell at first.

There are more of them than I'd thought. Behind the first two, others march, double file, then suddenly, behind them there are fifty, a hundred more, streaming out like bedbugs from a dirty mattress.

'Jesus,' I say. 'Davey, look.'

They run around half-dug holes, avoiding the edges. I would have thought at least some of them would fall in, but they seem to know exactly where they are. 'Son of a bitch,' Davey says. 'Come on, come on.'

Then there's another sound. A voice, megaphone-distorted. A thump of syllables, mangled by static. A language I wouldn't be able to understand even if I could hear it properly. It's coming from where the protestors were, up behind the trees.

'What's happening?' Joe asks.

Sharp flares of fire. All around the site, protestors run towards the jeeps, the trucks, and fall down against them, as though pulled by a powerful magnet. 'I don't know,' I say. The person on the megaphone is still shouting, but nobody seems to be paying any attention.

There's a pair of the protestors still up, marathon-sprinting idiots, running towards our jeep. Flapping in khaki and tie dye, faces half-covered. Both wearing woollen hats. They run awkwardly, each with one arm swinging free, the other inserted into one of these barrels. The metal tube hangs heavily between them, their arms locked in as if, inside, they're holding hands.

'Fuck off,' Davey shouts. 'Get away, or we'll shoot.'

Joe hoots. He knows as well as I do that Davey hasn't got a gun. 'Motherfuckers! This is even better than Tar Sands. Shit!'

Shots fly. Davey ducks, then me. Sharp-rattle sound of many barrels firing. Over on the hill and from our left. Where I came in through the newly-cut road.

'Keep down,' Davey grunts.

The company handbook says never put yourself in danger. Site gear must be worn at all times. Hard hats, steel boots. Fall arrest equipment. There's no page in the handbook for a situation like this though. I don't know what to do, and I can tell Davey hasn't much clue either.

A thin veil of singing rises. It's all around the site, ghostly and well-meaning. 'Christ preserve us,' Joe says. 'If I'd known they were going to sing, I'd have brought my ear protectors.'

'Shut up, Joe,' I manage.

Voices come from the other side of the truck. Two thin melodies, a man and a woman, singing unfamiliar syllables. They raise their voices, as if calling to the other protestors across the site.

I hear shouting, and see another set of people crossing the site, slowly, with slivers of metal flashing across their chests. One of them stops in front of a set of protestors by the digger. He puts out a foot, and leans down to shout in their faces. Somewhere over by the tower, a megaphone squeals and crackles.

Headlights sweep the earth: a truck coming in from the side road. The engine's loud, rattling, but we can still hear the *pop* of guns, and screaming from over by the mud trucks' dig site. I can't tell whether the protestors have stopped singing, or whether I just can't hear them over the engine. I duck back behind the jeep, just in time to see boots hitting the ground on the far side. 'Get in,' commands a voice, rough and heavily accented.

Davey motions us to be quiet. 'Soldiers,' he mouths. Joe's flask flashes; he nudges me, and offers it across.

'I said, get in!' the soldier repeats. 'It's better to come now, or do you want things to be worse for you, eh?'

The protestors on the other side of our truck raise their voices in defiance. They're still singing. Joe wipes his mouth, giggling.

'Get in the truck,' the soldier says, 'This is your last chance.'

The woman's voice rises. 'Oh,' she's saying, or maybe, 'No'. It comes to us in the same rhythm as a barking dog trapped in an alleyway.

Metal clicks against metal. Somebody bangs on the side of the jeep, and she keeps shouting 'No.'

'I warned you,' the soldier says.

'Fuck!'

A gun explodes. Ringing in my ears. I feel the aftershock in my fingers, the ripple of the bullet all along the bodywork. Along the wheel arch, where my head's resting. Something pisses from the truck, spraying into the dirt. Petrol. I stare down, and notice something dark pooling by the front tyre.

Davey pushes me further down. The tyre rubber scrapes my right ear. He's muttering something, I know that because I can feel his breath, smell the whisky, but I'm still half-deaf, and don't know what he's saying. I open my drafts folder. Fingers shaking, I type, *You were right. I never should have come here.*

Davey's hand forms a pincer. He's saying something, the same words over again I think, but my ears are still squealing and I don't know what they are. I shush him, and keep texting. If these are the last words I type, I want to be sure I don't miss anything. *Love you, love the kids. Make sure they know xxx*

'Thomas,' Davey says. 'Tom.'

At last, gradually, I can hear him, an echo bouncing down along the side of the truck and into my ear. 'What?' I say.

'They're not firing at *us*,' he says.

40 degrees: Petrol.

Reaching the top of the distillation tower, the compounds become less viscous, and more volatile. Of all the products gained from fractional distillation, petrol is the one most highly prized, and most in demand. Each barrel of crude oil yields only perhaps 30-40% gasoline through condensation. The demands of economy call for something closer to 50%. This volume can be produced by 'cracking' the larger molecules in a thermal decomposition reaction, where large molecules are vaporised and passed over a hot catalyst, breaking the chemical bonds.

A digger passes, momentarily blocking the sun. Roughnecks scramble up the rig like monkeys. There's one tightening bolts near the foot of the tower, another towards the head. Everything, every bolt and plate, has to be screwed in before the distillation can start. Once it gets going, the metal will be hot enough to melt skin; the tower's over two hundred feet tall, you don't want any of it sliding loose.

It looks like scaffolding, with lines and chains running off it everywhere. I've never seen them work so fast. Tightening bolts around the pipes, running lengths of chain hand-to-hand from the tower top, looking for weak links. Three men stand by the foot of the tower, signaling to a driver dangling the mud tank from the front of his truck. They're all over the site, these lads, and I don't know their names. Oil-faced and grimy, sweating like soldiers in a war.

'Clear.' Joe's on the tower top. He's been checking the chains and cables are in the right place. Six lines for power and diesel. Once he's down, the last job will be to check their strength; to check the top line can hold the rig by itself, in case something goes wrong, and the tower ends up being lifted out of the ground by the pressure of the oil.

If they keep going at this rate, we'll be ready to start extracting this afternoon. They're a quick team, this lot – perhaps the speediest I've ever worked with.

There's been a steady flow of vehicles away from the rig-up, now that everything's almost in place. 'You've done a lot of these jobs,' I call to the driver.

He leaves it by the site fence, alongside two other parked trucks. 'Thirty years, man and boy. You?'

Down in the field, a digger sinks the mud tank into the cut hole like a coffin. 'Can't even remember,' I say, shaking my head, and for a moment I can't.

Another truck approaches, and he waves it into a space alongside. 'Just here,' he shouts. 'Don't block the gate.' There's a mark like a chainsaw bite in his forearm, healed white and lumpy, like blancmange. 'Keep going until it's done.'

'Do you want to spot check, Davey, or shall I?'

Davey's hammy face condenses with sweat. I glance at him, his tumbling belly, his fat arms.

'Second thoughts, I'll go,' I say; I don't much fancy his chances up the tower.

I climb the square ladder, holding tight, only looking at the bolts and plates directly in my eyeline. These lads have done a good job. The bolts, burnished and bald-headed, look as though they were moulded into the metal. Struts criss-cross the tower, a farmer's gate laid sideways. I reach across for one of the other struts, and snap my spirit level against it to check the angles. The degrees are right; everything's perfect. I can see the forest through the scaffolding, although I try not to.

Every foot I climb, I see more of the same. Tight bolts, perfect crossings. I reach the treeline, then climb further, and leave them behind. From the apex I see it all. The power lines running from the tower, and the new fence around the site. The canopy. A solitary green flag leans sadly out of the trees, toothpick-small. It's not good to look down from this height.

'All clear?' Davey shouts.

It takes twice as long to climb down. I grab the ladder so tight it leaves marks in my hands.

'Yes,' I say, once I'm back down. 'Start her up.'

Davey begins the process of clearing, waving the roughnecks back beyond the safety line. The lines at the top of the rig tighten, stretching until there's no more give, and lift the tower clear of its pedestal. I count on my watch, ten seconds, twenty. Davey watches too, by my elbow, but keeps turning away, back to the road.

'They come back?' I ask.

'No,' he says. 'But I can't help thinking they might.'

I signal 'ok', and the tower drops. The lines at the top start to buzz. 'That one who was in front of our truck won't be coming back any time soon.'

Davey grunts. 'Their Government's done a deal for the oil. It's not for the likes of them to stop the extraction.' He listens to the power lines, and nods. 'Terrorists, Thomas, that's what they are, and if their Government have any sense, they'll be charged for it.'

A clank. The chains start to move. The pumps start to nod slowly, and the mud tank is washed with a swirl of crude oil.

The road seems to go nowhere. Long, and twisting, with the burning blue sky spreading out high above. I feel like I've spent hours behind this wheel already. Even in shades my eyes stream with the blaze from it.

The protestors left leaflets. There's one jammed under my wiper, rattling against the windscreen. Each time it settles against the glass I try to decipher the header. It looks like it's been photocopied a thousand times. The word *unsustainable* flaps against the screen.

I glance at the mileometer, and see that I have travelled twenty miles already. Still another hundred to go.

The company advises against visiting local markets. In some countries, the town centres can be even more dangerous than the site. They definitely don't like you going before the site's running. But this is the end of the job, and I'm all packed. Clothes, laptop, tablet, timesheet, passport. Dirt clings to everything. It'll be gathered in the bottom of my bag when I unpack, weeks from now.

Over the hill, I see a distant huddle of buildings, the village which is the next town along. It disappears, and I keep driving towards it.

Sometimes you get unlucky. Most towns don't have a market every day, or else you find yourself there on a day when the market sells only cheese, or milk, animal hides or farming equipment. *Here, darling, I brought you a scythe.* But today there is a market, quite a large one, busy. A dozen stalls in a street with wooden fronts, and flapping green tops. I open the car door to the smell of something delicious and meaty.

The first stall holder says something, telling me not to touch perhaps, or asking whether I want a full set of everything. He gestures around the stall, fingers briefly lighting on this cup, that bowl, making a broad sweeping gesture across the whole cloth.

Shaking my head, I say, 'English.'

He grimaces and makes a series of hand gestures. Four fingers, pointing at a mug, ten fingers. An index finger, two fingers. I watch them move, the length and grace of them, mesmerized, wondering whether they are the same hands that made these cups. There's no way of asking. The two of us could be here all day trying to understand one another. 'I'll take it,' I say, handing him a note.

He waves it away, and picks up one of the cups. Lifts it to his lips, mimes drinking. Says something else, voice slightly raised this time.

The water. That's what he wants to know, about the running water that's supposed to run along with the extraction site. Sanitation is not my concern. I've had to tell locals this on almost every job. There's a phone number for somebody at the company – that's the person they have to call, a woman who sits behind a desk somewhere in Abu Dhabi, somebody called Sharon who has the power to get things done, somebody I have never met. I mime using a pen to write the number down, and he waves me away, as I knew he would. I move away, quick as I can, trying to make my hurry look casual.

At the next stall, a cascade of scarves drapes down one side of the display, undulating gently in the breeze. A turquoise scarf catches my eye. Brighter than the sky, and with broad silver lines down each edge. 'This one,' I say. I also spot a small wooden box perfect for my daughter, and a beetle carved out of wood, for my son. He'll touch its spiny legs against his palm, make it jump along the carpet. Frighten his sister with it, perhaps. If he still likes doing that sort of thing.

The stallholder holds up some fingers, and I hand him a few dollars.

And then I'm in the car, driving away. In the rearview mirror I watch children playing soccer in the dust. How much can you miss? I turn my attention back to the road. Once I went away on a job like this, and came back to a walking girl, and a boy who could hop on one leg and hula. 'Are you sure you're my boy?' I said to him. 'Because this big boy is so much bigger than my little boy.' He'd laughed, showing me a full row of front teeth. 'Silly Daddy,' he'd said.

180 degrees. Kerosene: jet fuel.

Common air pollutants: Carbon monoxide from incomplete combustion; the formation of oxides of nitrogen, from heat and pressure in the jet engine; sulphur dioxides, from impurities in the fuel burn.

It's so bright on the concourse. A plane stands parked up against an embarkation tube, and a luggage buggy rolls around on the tarmac beneath its wing. Sudden cold rushes over my arms like frost, the air conditioning blasting viciously into every corner.

'Did you pack this bag yourself?'

The woman unzips my carry-all. She looks at the scarf, the beetle, the box. 'Gifts for my family,' I explain.

'Alright.' She waves me on.

I repack my bag by a row of blue mesh seats. This place could be anywhere. There's the Costa, the Pret-A-Manger, duty free. The smell of coffee rises. It's a familiar scent taking me back to the high street at home. I go towards it, squinting against the runway glare.

The girl behind the counter looks bored. 'Can I take your order?' she says.

'Americano, please, and this,' and I show her a bottle of water from the fridge.

'Coffees are served from the end.'

I wait, and watch a family at one of the tables. Two sweet kids in stripes, and a mum. The children, a boy and a girl, aren't quite old enough to know how to colour: they scribble all over, bubbles and lines, on the paper, on the table, creasing the paper with their enthusiasm. The mum kicks at a tombstone-sized Samsonite, and scrolls through her phone.

At these moments, the airport at the end of the trip seems like the start of a holiday. All four of us could be on our way to some unfamiliar place, some new city where we walk between strange walls in a hired apartment, touching light switches that work the wrong way, sockets with two prongs or three prongs or no apparent switch. It was easier when they were younger, like those two. When we invariably forgot to bring adaptors, so that there'd be nothing to do but sit together, all four of us crunched together on one sofa, playing cards and talking, our eyes straining to make out suits and numbers, giggling and making stupid jokes, while exchanging cards across a table in the dark.

Legoland

Agnieszka Dale

THE MAN'S SKIN IS white. An interior design catalogue might call it 'Victorian white'. His shirt is white too, with a few red stains on the sleeve. He is standing on this empty train, his nose almost touching hers. He looks like he must have been a hard Lego to construct. Thousands of tiny white cubes, tiered, like fluid-filled lumps, one on top of the other. And that's just his face. Hands, too, she notices. So white, for all their intricately locked tiles, their latticework of overhanging shadows, brick on brick. He must have taken months to complete. A fortnight at least just to achieve his delicate blue eyes, framed by perfect Lego eyelashes. Or more than that. Maybe even a year, in total, to make him, here in Great Britain.

He brings a Lego knife up against Inga's throat. She can see his fingers better now. She counts all the little Lego blocks. Eleven pieces per finger, with each finger ending in a pink, one centimetre-cubed brick with a thin plastic nail on the side.

'Don't,' she whispers. Can the Lego man hear her? Can he hear at all? Can he talk? Can he feel anything? Or is he just Lego?

The plastic feels odd against her throat; not cold particularly, but smooth.

'You're hurting me,' Inga gasps. She tries to unhook his arm but he is leaning into her, wedging her against the window, his blocks so unmoveable against her; his grip so tight around her wrist.

He presses the knife harder against her skin. The pain increases. It shouldn't hurt as much as it does, just as when you step on a piece of Lego barefoot. Inga had done that many times. Once, in the middle of the night, when getting a glass of water from the kitchen for her youngest. She keeps a jar of filtered water on the kitchen counter. She never lets them drink straight from the tap, doesn't trust the Victorian pipework. Today, she's left them with her older sister. She doesn't always trust her older sister. It's not easy being the younger one.

With the knife still hard against her throat, she looks to the window. Berkshire landscape rolls out like a carpet, the grass so green – fluorescent almost – that it hurts her eyes. How many fluorescent Lego blocks would it take to rebuild the countryside? she thinks. Her eyes begin to water. The plastic pushes deeper, as she gulps at nothing. She would drink anything right now, from any tap.

'I don't want to die,' she tells him, desperately. Her head is spinning from the pain, the thirst. She doesn't want to die. She hasn't even lived yet; always living for her older sister, rather than herself. Brought into this world for her, so that she wouldn't be alone.

Lego Man shakes his head. Can he hear her?

'I'm not originally from Legoland, like you,' she tells him. 'I wasn't born in Great Britain, as you can probably tell from my accent. I'm from near the Baltic Sea. The Baltic area. It's nice.' This is a safer option maybe than telling him exactly where she's from. And don't we all come from water really? From the sea? Ah, the thirst. Who knew a knife against the throat could make you so thirsty?

'I'm a good person. I have a job. I write short stories. I've got a publisher and everything, and am becoming established in the field,' she pleads.

He shrugs, like he doesn't care about her life. Or maybe he doesn't believe her. A Polish woman, a mother, in her forties, can't be *that* well established. Established in what exactly? For being a second-born, seven years after her sister? Second children hardly ever become 'established'.

Maybe he has been programmed, like a robot, or a soldier with tunnel vision. Recruited from Legoland to quietly sort out the 'overpopulation problem' and, to him, it doesn't matter where she's from, or that she came second to her sister. But maybe he can tell, anyway: always a foreigner in a foreign country, conceived in Chile, born in Poland, nursed as a baby in Colombia. When she returned to Poland at the age of three, she feared Polish children. She spoke better Spanish than Polish but stopped using it when other children laughed at her bilingualism. Her sister didn't. She was old enough to retain it, and often conversed with their parents, in fast, idiomatic Spanish with a Bogotá accent that Inga couldn't follow. Inga tried to re-learn Spanish at university but couldn't block out the sound of children laughing; her sister's fluent speech. Later, Inga spent some time in the States, before moving to Britain at the age of 26. But now she is just a Polish woman. To the white Lego man, this is all she is, and all others think of her too, no doubt. It probably doesn't matter. Not much anyway.

Only now she notices his smell. He smells like plastic; like her daughter's Barbie. The knife chokes her as if it were a rope. She coughs twice. Maybe he just hates women? All women, Lego or not. Or maybe he just hates real people. Non-Lego people. She can smell bubblegum on his breath as well as something else: a rotten tooth. One rotten Lego piece in a mouth of perfect white.

'There's a letter,' she rambles, 'I always wanted to write, and send, before I died. To Windsor.'

His blue Lego eyes blink. 'Windsor,' he says. Or maybe she says it to herself, in her mind, full of fast thoughts, all chasing one another, playing 'It.' All she feels is fear. At its best. At least she feels something.

He gives her a piece of paper. It's made of a very thin sheet of Lego, so thin it looks like real paper. And a Lego pen all the colours of the rainbow.

'You want me to write it now?' she asks. 'Can I?' She should have asked for a phone call, but maybe this is better. She wouldn't be able to talk now, anyway. And who would she call? Her sister?

So she'll write, because she is a writer. She starts with a full stop. No other thoughts come. But there's so much she wants to say before dying. In some ways, it would have been easier to turn to Polish now. The language she speaks to her parents. They still use Spanish words from time to time, especially when cooking: *leche*, or *queso*. They use Spanish fruit names, too, as so many of these exotic fruits weren't sold in 1970s Poland, so they didn't know the Polish names. Now it's different of course: *everything* is available, especially fruit and veg. Warsaw must have more vegan cafés than London. Warsaw, London's younger sister.

'Take me somewhere quiet,' she tells him. 'Better still, take me to your leader.' She is 41 after all, and she doesn't want to waste time talking to a middleman. She looks around the carriage. It's empty, and clean, evidently a new train, with the green seats, each sporting little yellow ears. There's just Lego Man and her. Which company runs this one? she thinks. There are 28 different rail operators in Great Britain: Southern, Virgin, Southeastern, East Midlands, First Great Western, and South West, to name a few. The patchwork of different companies involved in running trains is still confusing, even after thirteen years of living here. The voice announcing the stations is the same, or similar. It's a man's voice. A tired man, too polite to yawn, not mid-sentence at least, but whose voice has an undeniable trace of yawn behind it. She imagines he looks like your average trainspotter, a man who liked trains so much as a boy he got a job running one.

Lego Man nods, as if he has taken an order from her. He pulls her towards him and lowers the knife to the small of her back, so others might not see what he's doing. He walks closely behind her as they move towards the door. It's new, this situation, and yet, she has been here all her life, being pushed around. The knife is new, and Lego Man himself, but he's just an older sibling really, bullying her along. She's used to being bullied. Even her children bully her. They shout at her, they bite her, they hit her when they're angry.

It's King's Cross station. They are taking the stairs down. So it's going to be a Tube ride, she thinks. Somewhere central.

'Who is your leader?' she asks. 'Is it royalty?' There must be royals among Lego, residing in some ivory Lego tower. First born, of course.

They get off at Oxford Circus, a good spot for shopping but not for dying. She always imagined she would be alone when it happened. Her sister is older, so she would die first.

Ah, the buzz of Oxford Street. When she first arrived, in 2004, this street was so exciting, heaving with people from every corner of the Earth, so many different faces, colours, accents. Now, as Inga surveys the shoppers, the point of the knife still pinching the skin of her back, they all seem the same. Even if they look different, they have changed – unified somehow – against her. And yet, she still feels a flicker of that old excitement, always eager to catch a glimpse through great glass facades of Topshop, Mango, or whichever. Who doesn't like shopping! Even second children deserve a treat sometimes.

Now Lego Man is shunting her across the road. A taxi screeches to a halt, almost hitting them. He doesn't seem to notice. The smell of his rotten tooth wafts over her, from behind. But it's not the breath that bothers her the most, it's his heart. His rotten Lego heart. They head down Regent Street until he pushes her sideways, into Hamleys, the toy shop.

It's the worst kind of building to take kids into – dark, tight, Victorian. But since Star Wars took over the basement, her kids love it. She takes her kids with her everywhere. Even if they are not with her, she imagines them there. The consumer version of Pavlov's dog dribbles again. Shop! Shop! Inga remembers she needs to buy a present for one of their neighbours, Katie, who turns five on Tuesday, and if she survives until then, she promises herself that she will. She'll go and visit Katie, with her children. But Lego Man doesn't want her to go to the basement. He points to the escalator. Up a floor. And another. It's easier to think about Tuesday. What would Katie like? Lego? All kids love Lego. Katie is a first born, lucky Katie. And this is where they are now; the top floor. The Lego floor, shelves and shelves of brightly coloured boxes, all arranged around a central, show-stopping construction: a Lego Queen.

Lego Man stops pushing Inga and falls quiet out of respect. As he kneels, the little Lego hinges in his knees make an arpeggio of cracking sounds. He gestures to Inga, as if introducing her to the queen. Inga wonders if he is a second child after all. She recognises something in his servitude. But then he takes out the Lego knife again, and prods it into Inga's side. First for sure, a bully.

'Ouch,' says Inga, then bobs a curtsy.

Lego Queen nods, as if ready to listen but not for long. She has no time for people born second.

Can Inga speak now, before the queen? Among all these people shopping, taking pictures with Her Majesty? Will anyone hear? Will Inga hear herself? Again, she feels the knife, more painfully this time.

Sometimes, at the end of the day, she feels like she could sleep forever. Just sleep. She wouldn't have to be there for her sister in that other world, when she woke. But there are things to say before her death. Just things she's been thinking about. Thoughts. Not feelings. Thoughts.

'Talk,' says Lego Man. A threat, not an invitation: if Inga didn't talk, he would kill her. She wasn't a subject of the queen after all; she was just a foreigner, a second child.

'The shop will be closing in five minutes,' says a shop assistant, dressed as a giant Lego bunny. Or maybe it's not a costume; maybe he *is* Lego. He is saying this to everyone, politely. Another second-born maybe.

Lego Queen stands up from her throne, as if about to leave, and her corgi jumps to the side, barking. She stares down at Inga expectantly, and her knees begin to tremble. The queen may be made of Lego but she's still the queen!

Slowly and distinctly, so that her accent might be understood, Inga says: 'Your Royal Highness. Please, have mercy, and forgive me for being born outside Great Britain. Even though I am not first but second. Whatever I do, I'm always second.'

Lego Corgi starts growling at Inga. This can't be the friendly pooch that she loves so much from *Hello* magazine, always sitting so imperiously on plush velvet cushions. She buys it every week. She wants to be in *Hello* too.

'Forgive me, Your Majesty, for my foreignness. My foreign dog who barks too much. My foreign cat who I don't really like. For the birds in my foreign cage, which keeps on breaking. My foreign car, with its foreign tyres, all of which always get bloody punctures! The food, *pierogi*. So delicious when hot. All the foreign contents of my house, and my body too. I sometimes get foreign objects in my eye, usually my left one for some reason. I have foreign thoughts. Often. Forgive me. Please. For the birthmark on my right breast, in the shape of Madagascar, a foreign place, which men seem to like and compliment me on. Please forgive me, for staying while all my foreign friends have returned.'

Lego Man clips her across the cheek with the side of his hand. She wants to slap him back but lacks the confidence, or perhaps the willingness to fight – that second child thing again. Even at 41, she still feels like she doesn't have the right to fight back. Her cheek burns, but she's been hit before. What interests her more is why? Why is he hitting her? Is it because she mentioned her breast to the queen? Or because she talks too much, or has an accent? This is progress: she wants to know. In the past, she would have accepted it, no questions, and just stood there, face stinging.

'Please make your way to the entrance. The shop will close in four minutes,' says Lego Bunny, leaning into a microphone behind the counter. Lego Queen takes a step towards the escalator, then another; her corgi, Lego Man, Inga and others all trailing behind her. The escalator squeaks as they all slowly descend.

'I don't want to be foreign! To be listed! To be slapped!' Inga shouts, grabbing Lego Queen by the hand. 'The term *foreign* has become a disease in the last year or two, a kind of criminal status. Am I offending Your Majesty and all Your Lego subjects with my foreign, non-Lego ways?'

Until recently I hadn't given my foreignness too much attention. I was just a Polish person living in London, someone who arrived when Great Britain opened its borders in 2004. I thought I was allowed to come here, work here, contribute. I thought I was welcome. But now I feel I was breaking some law that had yet to be written. I was always second-grade. You just never told me.' The escalator is moving so slowly. She wants to go faster.

The queen pulls her hand away.

'Three minutes left,' says Lego Bunny.

Lego Man picks up Lego Corgi just as the escalator reaches the bottom. Inga follows them.

'Your Majesty, please hear me out.'

A new floor. Baby toys. Three more barks. Maybe Lego Corgi doesn't like baby stuff.

'Please. Your Majesty. I want to help, and I can. I have so much potential. Because where is the law that states that I am useless and need to go home? Show me the act of Parliament? Point to the clause. Maybe it is an unwritten law, whispered in stately homes and terraced houses, passed between neighbours, or from generation to generation, through thick walls and thin. A law that says: Second children are no good. Not as important, somehow, as first. Maybe *I am* breaking a law, a law that has not yet been written, and I'm a criminal now, in this country, in the eyes of your subjects. Do you know that my own children, born in this country, make fun of me because of the way I talk? My children. I'm scared of them sometimes. Of their accents. The purity of their speech. Believe me; I am not a bad person. I do not want to be a hooligan of any sort. I do not want to be breaking any law. Is it a common law perhaps? Long-standing, unwritten but taken as read? Never publicly declared. Or maybe it's still being drafted? The law of an imperious dog sitting on a velvet cushion, barking at an underdog?'

'In two minutes this shop will close,' says Lego Bunny. The queen glides further down the escalator to another floor. Lego Man is standing on the step behind her holding her handbag, like a butler. Does he expect to get knighted for holding her handbag so well? Is there a special category in the New Year Honours list for this?

'I must say, Your Majesty, I never felt any resentment before the referendum. Confused occasionally – like which box to tick in the ethnicity section of my local gym's membership form. In Poland, I was white. Just white. Boring white. Here, I am 'White Other' – white confused, more like. Secondary white. I checked in Photoshop, with a colour picker, to be sure how much other I am. On the form, opposite 'white other' I just wrote what Photoshop told me I was – my personal white, Hex number: FBF3F3.'

They reach the next floor: hi-tech toys. Gadgets. Flying. Remote-controlled. Robotic. Soulless. There are hardly any customers left. Lego Queen stops, looks around, picks up a

Mini UFO Saucer-Drone from one of the nearby tables and drops it into the handbag Lego Man is still holding for her, as he looks the other way.

Inga can't see Lego Bunny anymore. Maybe he doesn't belong on these lower floors. He seemed nicer than Lego Man, who is now glowering at her, as if to say: *Hurry up, this is the queen you're talking to.*

'Your Majesty, I was wondering if I am indeed that much other or foreign. I have taken the liberty of checking Your Majesty's British family tree against mine, the foreign one. I noticed – I'm sorry, I'm so sorry for noticing this – some Polish names. Foreign branches to your royal, British, family tree. How nice, I thought. A few German too. I have German friends and relatives, you know.'

Lego Queen zips shut her handbag, still held by Lego Man. She smiles for the first time. The corgi's tail is wagging. She got herself a freebie. Even the queen likes freebies. Lego Man is smiling too, and his grin says it all: 'Oh, to be knighted by the queen, made rich and famous, like the very first child. The only child.'

'I am a second child, Your Majesty,' Inga says. 'But I don't like it very much. It doesn't help me in life.' She is standing by the front door now, she can feel the draft.

'The shop will close in one minute,' says Lego Queen.

'Your Majesty, I'm requesting a royal pardon, so that I might lead a good life in the country where I invested my future and made my home, with my children, born in this country. Born first. And second. And third. They don't understand the whole foreignness thing. Or what impact it will have on them to be born second, or third, if returned to a land that's foreign to them. They don't get this at all.'

Lego Queen looks at Inga. 'I have a party to go to,' she says, 'and things to do.' Her voice is gentle, but with a soft Lego accent. 'What do you need, my dear? Speak now, we are closing the shop.'

Inga suddenly wants more rather than less. Make me loved, she will say. Or, you know, at least make me first. The first child. Touch both my shoulders with your mighty sword, will you? I want to be a descendant to your Lego throne, please. The next queen. She'll say this in a minute. When she gets her courage back. When she forgets that she is second, and less loved. Unable to speak up when the time is right.

'A box of Lego, for Katie, please,' she asks.

The Double Man: An Hotelier's Tale

Giles Foden

IT WAS ALREADY LATE in the evening – one of those noiseless summer evenings during which the London traffic is unaccountably dampened down – when Mr Kelodia arrived back at the hotel. At least fifteen years older than me, he had been on the staff longer than any of us, and we all looked up to him. It was always to him we went, when there was a problem at work, rather than the general manager. Holders of that position came and went. Twain's, the large corporation that was our employer, liked to move general managers between countries on a two-year cycle.

Despite his patent abilities, Mr Kelodia had remained as concierge at Twain's Bloomsbury for two decades. It is an impressive building on one of those little streets which, running between Tottenham Court Road and Gower Street, suddenly deliver you from urban confusion onto a quieter pavement – out of which rises, via a lamplit stairway with an ornate, cast-iron balustrade, the double-fronted Edwardian façade of Twain's.

It was here that Arjunbhai – Mr Kelodia, as I always used to call him – presided, keeping down the disorder that, like lava from a volcano, always threatens to rise up in a hotel. For with each new guest comes a new story and new possibilities, good or bad. One has to try to see into the heart of these tales, as if looking through frosted glass or the halo that forms round the moon on a cloudy night. It is a process which demands vigilance about how one's first impression can change, and how what is obvious may not be true. Sometimes, though, the first impression is right. The moon is nothing more than the ring around it; the snap judgment made in the lobby, spot on.

It often used to strike me, in those days, how little I knew about Mr Kelodia's own history. I made meaning of little pinches of knowledge, hardly as much as would fit in a woodpecker's beak – such as the light-flecked photograph of a savannah landscape, with a flat-topped tree and a patch of maize, which he insisted be hung behind us at reception. When I asked him why he called crisps 'chips', he said it was 'how we said it at home'. At first I thought that was India, but in the staff room he had a little silver-plated teapot marked E.A.R. He later revealed that this stood for East African Railways and that he was a Ugandan Asian.

The photograph, which on closer inspection revealed the opening of a path in the clump of maize – a winding track going off into the distance – he would one day explain as being near the site of his grandfather's first shop in Uganda. 'It was in a village called Rubirizi,' he confided, adding that there were often elephants nearby. 'They would come out of the marsh and proceed to trample the maize.' His English, like mine, was slightly old-fashioned, and mangled with the forms of another tongue.

No, Arjunbhai did not give much away. One could gaze for years into his eyes, which are the colour of green Chartreuse and have a glint of the fox, without being able to tell what is going on behind them. It was thought at the time, as he wore a ring, that he was married, but no one knew then whether this was true or not.

To a fellow member of staff, his debonair reserve could be frustrating. Over the years, my irritation with his secretiveness would grow. But as he approached the front desk, on that noiseless summer evening which began the unfolding of my story, I felt a rush of relief. For there was a problem that evening and Mr Kelodia, who knew how to act quickly, was the only man to deal with it.

Tall and elegant, wearing his usual light grey suit, he placed his palms on the veneer. 'I am sorry I had to go out, Marisa. I see that you telephoned my mobile phone. What is the difficulty please?'

'Something has happened in one of the rooms, a cleaner says. A broken door. The guests have left.'

'So, you have called Pickering?'

Dave Pickering was the hotel handyman. 'Yes, he's up there now, but I think you should see. It is an interior door and –'

An expression of panic passed across Mr Kelodia's brow. It was as if his self-possession had crumbled, and he was reduced to a state of immobility. Watching his lips fix on his thin mouth and a frown develop on his brow, I was confused. I felt a pang, I must confess, though of what I didn't quite know.

Now I understand. It is not just to the identity of others that we must beat a path along the tangled *levada* of life; to see ourselves, too, we must lift away the straggling foliage that enfolds human secrets, that greenery of ongoing life which is always threatening to encase us completely.

'What number?' he said, his mouth moving at last.

'204,' I replied. It was a room infrequently used.

He nodded pensively, as if he already suspected that this was the number of the room in which the event had occurred. As he nodded, all signs of the previous, disconcerting moment of collapse vanished. His forehead became smooth again. He was once more the silver-haired majordomo whose cool, if very occasionally impatient temper infused the whole establishment.

'What was the name of the guest?'

'Well, there were two men. A Mr Brown and a Mr Jones.'

I had a memory from the previous night of them checking in, both in white mackintoshes and dark blue suits. 'Not gentlemen – I thought it odd that they took a room together.'

'What address did they give?'

'Let me see.' I punched a few keys on the computer. '*Little Birds, Chobham, Surrey GU24*. I am guessing "Little Birds" is the name of a house.'

'Possibly.' As his lips formed round the word, Mr Kelodia's green eyes gave another flicker of anxiety. 'I will go up there now.'

'Shall I come with you?' I asked, in my innocence.

'No,' he said, sharply, and turned towards the lift across the lobby.

As I watched him walk, I realised that I had never seen Mr Kelodia move so fast. He tended to *glide*, but not this evening. Something was clearly amiss, every bone in my body agreed about that. And you know what, my own limbs wanted to follow his as he strode across the lobby. But I kept to my post, which is what he would have wanted.

I had the story from Dave Pickering the next afternoon, when I came back on shift. He was a football-loving young man from Kent or Essex or one of those other counties on the edge of the great swamp of London, into which immigrants, dislocated folk such as myself and Mr Kelodia, are being continuously absorbed. Welcome to the swamp, the levels of which are as hard to ascend as the slimy sides of a fish-tank that no one has bothered to clean; welcome to the swamp, where we salve our loneliness with labour, trying to forget the triggers that brought us here; welcome to the swamp, where against the odds we might preserve certain rituals of that world beyond, the past.

These were the voices I heard, coming here as a younger woman, from an island in the Atlantic.

Yet Dave also came from a world beyond the city, he too

was a kind of settler. He might have been driving a white van if he had not enrolled on Twain's apprentice scheme for works and estates. Now, instead, he wandered happily about the hotel corridors with his ladders and tools (he had a sort of leather belt from which the latter hung), repairing broken ceiling tiles or going down into the basement to see to the boiler.

The Twain's apprentice scheme had recently been singled out by the government as a matter of national pride. 'An excellent scheme,' the Minister for Tourism had said in an article in the appointments section of one of the British newspapers (it was the first thing I had ever seen about Twain's in any of the papers). 'Exactly the sort of thing we need across the whole hospitality sector, if we are to keep the fixtures and fittings of Hotel UK up to the required standard.'

Dave was quite good looking, in a brutal sort of a way, and I knew he'd had relationships with one or two of the maids. I used to be a maid myself, when I first came from Madeira (I was a maid there, too), so I recognised how that kind of thing could happen. That was at Twain's Hyde Park, before I came here and got promoted to receptionist. It's a good company like that. We move you through the ranks if you stay.

'I thought it was just one of the interconnecting doors,' Dave told me. 'From room to room like, that we open up for families. It had been busted, anyway, splintered near the lock. So I goes in and pushes it open and there's a room all right but it's not *there*, it's not the room I expect.'

'What do you mean?' I asked.

We were in the staff room, drinking coffee. It was surprisingly light for a basement room, with a large window through which you could see the tops of the trees in the square on the other side of the street. On the near side – looking askance and upwards through the black-painted iron railings – I liked to watch people's feet moving along. If it was summer and the sash was up, I would listen out for fragments of their conversation... utterances from the flow of life like that pitiless narrative, laden with the pollen of suffering and poverty, which had brought me from Funchal to London.

All humankind has a secret song of pain and hope that taps away inside us with the same rhythm as our heartbeats. It's not unnatural that we should seek that these tales should be told; what is surprising is how so often the telling involves some narrative not just of love or family, but of work. In my case, and Mr Kelodia's, the story is bound up with all three.

As he picked up his thread, Dave's shaven head was bobbing about in perplexity. 'It didn't open into the next door room as per the corridor. There's a little tunnel instead.'

'And? Did you go down it?'

'Course I did, Marisa. Was only bare brick, mind, with a bit of strip lighting. Didn't even know we had a power conduit down there.' He sipped his coffee and knitted his brows, as if considering the mysteries of mains distribution units and current loads per outlet.

'Well?'

'There was another door at the end. Another internal hotel room door, like, but older than the norm. And that one had been broken into, too. I look inside, natural, and it's like someone's living in there. There's clothes and stuff and er – this is the strangest thing, loads of files and a computer. And all them files had been pulled off the shelves and opened up...'

At that moment, the door to the staff room itself opened. Mr Kelodia's noble head appeared, and in he walked. He stood for a moment looking at us, as if lost in surprise. 'I see,' he said, eventually. 'I suppose you are talking about the repair that Pickering undertook yesterday.'

Dave coloured, and so did I. There was no reason that we should have done so, except perhaps a sense that we had broken some imagined prohibition of Mr Kelodia's – a forbiddance which, in his languid fashion, he then made fact.

'May I ask you?' he said, his fox-like eyes flashing with more than usual intensity, 'may I ask you *not* to discuss that with any other staff? Not Mr Haverstock, especially.' Haverstock, a greedy man with a scarlet face and double chin, was the general manager of our Twain's. 'I'll explain to you why. That room which you discovered, Pickering, that room which a pair of drunk guests saw fit to break into last night, has been closed off for many years.'

'Why?' I asked.

'It is a long story, Marisa, and perhaps I shall tell it to you in full one day. The gist of it is this. A long time ago, someone died in that room – someone dear to the founder of the Twain's chain. He asked that the room be shut up exactly as it was and we at Twain's Bloomsbury have respected his wishes.'

'You mean, with a *body*?' Dave was aghast.

'Don't be facetious, Pickering. The body...' His voice tailed off. What on earth was he going to say next? 'Is in its proper place. No harm done. And so we'll say no more about it, my friends, yes?'

'But we can't not tell Mr Haverstock.'

As I spoke, Mr Kelodia came across the room to the window, where a light breeze was moving the tops of the horse chestnut trees in the square next to the pavement. There was as yet only a hint of darkness in the summer evening but the blossoms of those trees shone like white candles.

Arjunbhai was silent for a while, gazing at the moving blossoms until a sparrow, landing on the railings, interposed itself in his field of vision. It began pecking at the flaking paint of the bars. 'I will deal with any difficulty, you need not worry at all about that. Successive managers here have been unaware of the existence of that room. It would only cause Haverstock trouble in his career.'

Coming round behind us like a wraith, he touched me gently on the shoulders, then left the room with his customary glide. In the window, embarrassed by the lack of nutrition in the ironmongery, the sparrow gave up the battle and flew off.

'Bloody odd, if you ask me.' Dave's thick fingers fiddled

with the top of a milk carton. 'Reckon we should tell Haverstock after all.'

'We mustn't,' I said. 'Not if Mr Kelodia doesn't want it.' I suddenly felt protective towards him.

'If you say so. But it's not nothing, what happened.' The carton jerked and a blob of milk flicked onto his jeans. 'Bloody hell.'

'Let me do that.' I took the carton from him and pulled it open, then went for a cloth to the sink, where Mr Kelodia's teapot was waiting to be polished. It was ancient, that teapot, the colour of old lamps.

Once Dave had drunk his coffee and left, I sat alone, with my empty mug in my lap. A spell of time must have passed, for I became aware of the last of the evening light, hanging on the verge of the room like a nervous bride. Already it was criss-crossed with the shadows of the iron railings outside the window.

Looking at these again, I suddenly thought of another hotel, the Apollo, in Madeira, where palm trees cast shadow lines across the forecourt. It was a place at once parochial and cosmopolitan, full of evidence of change, yet somehow itself resisting that change. Guests described it as delightfully Victorian in the visitors' book but I found it oppressive.

This was in fact where, in a frilly white pinny and black skirt, I first worked in a hotel, as a teenager. It was certainly a grand place, almost a palace, which made much of its history as a stop-off for imperial travellers as they made sea voyages between Britain and Africa – the long, straight wakes of their steamers standing out in the photographs whose alignment along walls it was my job to adjust after dusting. Walking past, the general manager there, a hirsute man who boasted of having served Churchill tea at the Apollo in his youth, fairly often used to grope me as I was aligning the pictures.

That man was the reason why I got the job at the Apollo, and why I left for England: he was my uncle. For so many years he, or his memory, held me back from everything – from marriage, children, the whole works. Freezing me up, he was the reason the nearest that I used to come to passion was watching Brazilian telenovelas on the Twains' cable menu, my favourites being *Sangue do Meu Sangue*, *Caminho das Índias* and *Cúmplices de um Resgate*.

Now I only watch them to keep up my Portuguese, all the pent-up desire that I once felt, watching those passionate melodramas, having been dashed away by a peck of vermillion powder on my head and all that followed. 'Do you agree?' he would ask me, in the end, after asking me another question beforehand – I who was immobile, who was unable to speak, who was waiting for love to sing in her heart at last. 'You know that in business you have to make decisions very quickly?'

It would be some months before the secret of the other room was revealed. I suppose that, as we got on with our jobs day to day, Dave and I more or less forgot about it. Mr Kelodia seemed on the surface to have returned to his usual imperturbable self. He dealt with guests with his customary aplomb, moving across the lobby in his trim grey suit, a Mont Blanc fountain pen in his top pocket, ready to be whipped out to write what he called a 'notelet' to one or other of us members of staff.

Now and then, though, watching him (not out of any personal interest, or so I allowed myself to think), I became aware of a residual worry nibbling at Mr Kelodia's temperament. At the same time, my irritation with his unknowability, no doubt irrational, bubbled away inside me. It took the shape of a desire to strip away his façade, to dig under his urbanity, to shake the knowledge out of him. I'd receive my own notelets, always addressed 'Dear Marisa', with a mixture of frustration at being told what to do and a need to please him.

During this period, the anonymity under which Twain's had previously existed, except for the acclaimed apprentice scheme of which Dave Pickering was a beneficiary, was suddenly exploded. Split open, like the green casings of the horse chestnuts on the street outside, when people stepped upon them.

It seemed that the company, which was a public one, was subject to an aggressive takeover bid (I am not, and despite all that followed remain not, an expert in these terminologies, so please forgive me if I tell them wrong). The newspapers were reporting things like SECRETIVE HOTEL GROUP RESISTS BID and ACTIVIST SEEKS MORE TRANSPARENCY AT GUARDED TWAIN'S and CHANGING TWAIN'S PROVES TRICKY. These articles seemed to suggest that the problem was that the majority owner of Twain's was somehow not out in the open and should be.

Before the days of intimate involvement, I never gave a moment's thought as to who owned the company. And I wouldn't have given these reports much attention, were it not for the fact that, as I read the crumpled paper in the staff room one evening, the so-called 'activist investor' (which, I have come to understand, means a shareholder who wants to change how a company is run) was revealed to bear the name of Karnabhai Kelodia.

One evening, not much later in the summer, I was sipping my coffee in the staff room, inspecting a cobweb that had begun to form above the window. The pattern of my thoughts was taking the same line they had taken ever since I saw that name in the papers. Was this Kelodia some relative of our own Mr Kelodia, Arjunbhai?

I felt I was within my particular rights to ask him, despite the general distance he kept from us, that sense one might as well try to jump a twenty-foot wall as get to the heart of him. In full awareness of such imaginary obstacles (and now I know they were mainly imaginary), I was that very evening about to go and confront him when I heard footsteps on the pavement above.

I looked up and in the dying light saw two pairs of black

lace-up shoes and the hems of two white mackintoshes. I knew at once it was them.

'Tonight it is, then?' asked the voice of one.

'Yes. We've had the signal from the main man. Let's check in now.'

I saw a cigarette ground under the heel of one of the shoes, and then they moved away down the pavement towards the balustrade and main door.

I sat for a second or two trying to make some sense of the statements I had just heard, valiantly fixing my attention on interpretations that decoyed me away from the malign ones my mind was leading me towards. But it was all in vain. Putting down my coffee mug, I rushed back up to my post in the lobby, sprinting up the stairs.

'You're not due back on for twenty minutes!' said Jenny, my co-receptionist, as if correcting me for feckless behaviour.

'Never mind that. Those two men who just came in, what room did they book into?'

'Um...' Her lacquered nails (all these young women have false ones now) skittered over the keyboard. '204. Brown and Jones.'

The same two names, of fictional heritage no doubt.

'Have you seen Mr Kelodia?'

'No, not for an hour or two. He's off duty, too.'

'Do me a key for 204.'

'I can't do that.'

'Just do it.'

She did as I asked, then sulkily handed me the slip of plastic. My heart thumping with immense rapidity, I ran across the lobby and pressed the button on the lift. On reaching the second floor, I ran down the carpeted corridor to 204. I put my ear to the door and listened. I could hear a low muttering within the room, which I took to be the conspirators talking. Then there was the sound of an impact and splintering wood, followed by steps and finally silence.

I could feel the plastic key, slick in my palm, but suddenly didn't dare to use it. What were these men after? Summoning up my courage, I passed the key into the slot. The door opened with a quiet click and I peeped in. No one was to be seen. The room was untroubled except for flakes of wood from the broken internal door. I crept noiselessly across the carpet, moving like an automaton.

For reasons I could not have explained at the time, I allowed myself to be drawn to a fate unknown, down the secret corridor which I had heard described. The lights in it flickered, making strange shapes on the bare walls. I could see another light too – a thin vertical line at the end of the tunnel. With cautious steps, trying to stop my feet scraping on the concrete, I advanced towards it.

Reaching the slit of the door to the other room, which was where the light came from, I stood still as death. I put my eye to the crack. To my horror, I saw Mr Kelodia kneeling on the floor. His arms were bound. Above him stood the two men. One – let's say he was Brown – had his arms folded; a lighted cigarette hung from his saturnine lips. The other, Jones, was introducing a long spike, like a knitting needle or kitchen skewer, into Mr Kelodia's ear. He was keeping him still by grasping a handful of his silver hair.

'This is a message from your brother. Unless you sign the paper, it's gonna go farver an' farver into your ear. Now, I don't want this to get messy, so – do us a favour.' He moved his hand a little and Mr Kelodia gave a cry of pain. I watched a pip of blood roll down his jaw.

'Hurt?' said the other man. 'Have a fag.' He took the cigarette from his mouth and jammed it into Mr Kelodia's forehead.

'Aaaah!' Mr Kelodia fell sideways, and Brown kicked him in the ribs.

Terror, which should have made me flee, instead impelled me forward into the room. I flung myself against the bodies of those two men with the force of the ocean storms that batter my native island. They fell to the floor. I suppose my hope was that Mr Kelodia would take the opportunity to get to his feet and run. But he remained lying on his side. What might have been a hoarse 'no!' issued from his mouth.

The mackintoshed men stood up; with imbecile wonder, they looked at me, sprawled on the floor next to Mr Kelodia.

'What's this then, the girlfriend?' said Jones. He grabbed me by the arm and hauled me up. 'Who sent you here?'

Limp in his grip, I felt his other hand shove around my dress in a vile mockery of loving. 'What's your game then?' He came to my identity badge and pulled it roughly off, throwing it to the floor.

'Hotel skiv.' Then he shook me impotently. 'Speak to us!'

Suddenly there was a movement below. Jones doubled over. Mr Kelodia had kicked him in what I have learned, in this country, to call the crown jewels. In response, Jones visited savage violence back on Mr Kelodia with his own feet, stamping on him and kicking him with those same black Oxford shoes which, shortly earlier, I had watched through the basement bars.

Eventually Brown restrained him. 'Christ, Paul. This is no good. Let's get out of here.'

'We can't do that,' said Jones, breathing heavily. 'Don't get paid less we get the signature.'

'Who are you?' I said, getting onto my stockinged knees, next to the moaning heap that Mr Kelodia had become, to which I stretched out a comforting hand. 'What do you want?'

'Oh, she talks does she?' Keeping his eyes on me, Jones gave poor Mr Kelodia another kick. 'Pete! Girly here wants to know who we are. We's little birds, ain't we? Fly away Peter, fly away Paul, all of that. Come to get a little something. You gonna let us take it back, in our little beaks like?'

Addressing himself to Mr Kelodia, Brown produced a long, devilish knife from the pocket of his mackintosh. 'Or do we have to cut her? It's your choice.'

Seeing that he was in deadly earnest, I began to tremble. Then I saw Mr Kelodia give a tired nod. And to my shame, I didn't know whether he meant that they were to injure me or that he would sign.

Brown bent down and cut Mr Kelodia's bonds. He pulled him up and placed him at a chair at a desk in the room. It was only then that I became fully aware of my surroundings in that other room. Somebody *had* been living here, it was true – there was a little bed – and not only that, they had been using it as an office, too. There was a computer, and a telephone, and a fax, all the usual office things – including a Mont Blanc fountain pen, which Jones picked up off the desk and thrust in Mr Kelodia's hand, before moving to one side of the desk, leaning on it as he waited for the signature.

Brown, meanwhile, was still standing over me with his knife, in a pose which suggested that he was about to plunge it into my right shoulder. His hand, I remember, was very hairy.

It was another hand that moved, in the end. Arjunbhai had just signed when a dark object spun through the air above me and struck Brown – in the forehead I'd discover. Straightaway he fell backwards. A lump hammer tumbled to the floor beside me. Jarred by shock, I watched Dave spring into the room, his eyes blazing. He leaped towards Jones, simultaneously drawing a screwdriver from the leather carrier round his waist. With exaggerated movement, but slowly enough for me to realise it was not in fact a screwdriver but a chisel, he plunged it into Jones's thigh.

A look of surprise, followed by a grimace – one as twisted as the horns of the Minotaur, I shouldn't doubt – passed across Jones's face. Then he staggered and fell backwards. I gave a scream of horror and then there was silence for a second. Blood began to pump out of Jones's leg in rhythmic spurts – slowly at first, then faster, soaking his white raincoat and spraying the floor.

Dave turned to me and said, 'All right love?' As he spoke, I saw with wordless dread that the abominable Brown had sat up, the impression of the hammer clearly visible in the middle of his forehead and, in his hand, the blueish grey of a pistol. He lifted it, pointing it at Dave's back. At that moment yet another hand – the hand of a South Asian man, Mr Kelodia, Arjunbhai – appeared at the side of Brown's neck and jabbed him, very hard, with the fountain pen. Brown's hand descended limply, losing its grip on the gun. Then he too fell down, convulsing amid the reddening wings of his coat.

And I was glad because that fellow deserved the very worst.

Mr Kelodia, battered and breathing heavily, stood up over Brown. The burn on his forehead glowed like a Hindu sign – one that I would myself grow to recognise. 'I may have signed,' he said, still holding the pen, 'but I did not agree.'

A few days later, after the invading thugs had been taken away under police guard in ambulances, after the secret room had been gone over by the forensic specialists employing powders and solvents, after everything except Twains' reputation had been more or less cleaned up, we went back down the corridor. It was then that Mr Kelodia told me that the words which he had spoken over Brown were a proverb from Uganda. He was part of an Indian business family there, he explained, one that had been established by his grandfather in the 1930s, and had prospered until a dictator threw them out nearly half a century later.

'We came here to England in 1971, my brother Karna and I, and we built up our business in hotels and other areas. But I did not like the way he practised. He was ruthless – he cared little for his guests and nothing for his staff. All he wanted was profit. So, there was a schism in the family and we agreed to separate our interests. We signed the agreement in this very room. And it was from here too that I resolved to work clandestinely, running all the Twain's hotels at the same time as working in one. I would come back in here by that secret tunnel so none of you would know.'

'You worked in here? Why? When?'

'At night mainly. I believe that to really run a hotel well, you have to be with the staff on the ground. And I suppose I did not want to live the playboy lifestyle anymore. I was through with all that, Marisa. When I was a young man I was all for helping the poor. Somehow I forgot it all in the intervening years, until we had to leave Africa. And then everything had to be rethought. I lost my wife about that time too. Cancer. I suppose I was depressed.'

'You said someone had died here – I mean before.'

'In a way that was true. It was me who died here, my old self, and the family unity that we had in Uganda. But really I was a double man, living in two times and places in the same moment, one running a corporation, the other still totting up accounts with a slide rule in a dimly-lit *duka* back in Rubirizi.'

He sighed, as if craving the childhood dream of that remote African place. He'd later tell me a *duka* was like those corner shops they have in England, but more basic, selling Omo soap, tinned fish, razor blades.

'So I withdrew,' he said, sighing again. 'I shut myself up in this room and ran my businesses from here. Not just Twain's. All kinds of businesses right across the world, with nominee shareholders. I got a kind of perverse delight out of it.'

He paused, looking round the room. Dave had removed the carpet tiles onto which spots of blood had sprayed, but there was still a sense that this light dusting of horror, which we had seen settle on the ordinary blossoms of life, would not easily be wiped away.

'But not anymore,' said Mr Kelodia resolutely, still speaking of the hidden path he had taken all these years. It was as if he too like me had seen again, flickering in his mind, the spasms of the wounded men. 'Come on, *twende.*'

'What?'

'It's Swahili. It means let's go.'

We went down to the staff room to make ourselves a drink. Coffee for me, tea for him from the pot marked E.A.R. Jenny was there. She scuttled out when she saw us.

'Why did they come, really, those men?' I asked, flicking the switch on the kettle.

'My brother's own businesses had started to go wrong. He was still very wealthy, but not enough to buy Twain's at the market price. He sent those thugs to harass me into agreeing his takeover at a discount. Haverstock was in on it. I suppose he saw a chance to make his fortune.' Mr Kelodia gave a little chuckle and I saw his green eyes glint in the half-light. 'I shall like to see how he can do that in Pentonville prison.'

'What will happen now?' The whole thing had been in the newspapers, of course, and Dave had been making the most of his new status as an action hero.

'Well, my brother lives in Dubai. I suppose the British police may try to extradite him from there, but I expect he will get out of it. I don't really care. I am more concerned, Marisa, with what will happen here. I am an old man now. I do not have many years left...'

His voice tailed off. I looked at him. By now a scab had formed on his forehead from the cigarette wound. In time it would become a scar.

The kettle came to the boil.

In the silence that followed I found myself looking away from him, up through the bars at the street above. There were two pairs of shoes there. I thought I recognised one of the pairs as Dave's boots, which had translucent soles filled with air. The other shoes were a woman's patent heels. Could they have been Jenny's? Once she had told me, apropos of nothing, that Dave smelt of machine oil. The window was open and I listened, but the couple above were silent too. I wondered if they were kissing... and I wanted to jump up and kiss

Arjunbhai, very much.

But something held me back at that moment. Contradictory feelings rumbled like lava flows within me. Immobile, unable to speak, I felt like a character in one of my Brazilian melodramas, but in this case the actress had forgotten her lines.

Glancing at Arjun standing above me, I could see the wrinkles in his brow, the flecks of black in his grey hair. Still unable to move, my brow knotted, I sat looking up at the light which flooded in from the world beyond the sash, silently willing a little bird to land on the ironmongery and tell me which song to sing.

Guided by Conrad

Jan Krasnowolski

SOMETIMES I THINK OF my grandfather, Jan Józef Szczepański, and what he must have been like during the war. He would have been in his twenties at the time, much younger than I am now. A lieutenant in charge of a partisan squad in the forests of Southern Poland. I can almost picture him: slim, a field cap brandished with a crowned eagle logo on his head, sporting a battered leather jacket and green breeches, always with a Luger hanging from his belt. And the look in his eye – sharp as a razor.

He must have been so different from the person I knew, decades later, and yet somewhere in that old man I remember so fondly there must have been a trace of this young, brave soldier.

My grandfather's squad was part of the *Armia Krajowa*, the Home Army: a massive resistance movement of over 400,000 volunteers, founded in February 1942 out of the *Związek Walki Zbrojnej* ('Armed Resistance'), and absorbing most other Polish underground forces. Following the German's invasion of Poland in September 1939, my grandfather had joined the resistance movement immediately: a former officer of the Polish Army that had been defeated in the 'September War', as the invasion became known, he was eager to fight.

They answered to the Polish Government–in–Exile, which by 1940 was based in London. So while my grandfather, and thousands of partisan soldiers like him, lived, slept and fought all year round out in the forests, the wider campaign was being discussed and devised in London. Both orders and supplies came from Britain. The RAF planes used to fly in from the West, parachuting down weapons, ammunition and medical aid for those camped out in the woods: only knowing where to drop them thanks to carefully timed fires, specially lit to guide them to the drop points. The Command had their particular signals as well: they would communicate with the partisans in Poland by playing a specific tune on the BBC European Service – for example, Chopin's Funeral March – a certain number of times at a certain hour. This signal would tell the partisans that the drop was confirmed, and that the fires should be lit. Fires in forest glades were easily visible for the brave RAF pilots flying at night over occupied territories, as they flew so low.

The weapons contained in those parachuted capsules made a big impact: the STEN sub-machine gun quickly developed a reputation for its simplicity, as well as its tendency to jam when overheated. Even the Brits who occasionally parachuted down with those supplies developed not just nicknames – they called them 'The Dark, Silent Ones' – but also mythic status. These were commandos trained for special tasks by the British Army, and sent to assist the partisans – 'The Forest People', as they were known – in their missions. They would operate just outside of Kielce, a town in the South of Poland. There were vast forests down there, perfect for disappearing into after each mission. But they could never stay in one place for long. The Nazis scoured the forests for them relentlessly, forcing each squadron to constantly relocate; and once on foot, even under cover of darkness, the Luftwaffe reconnaissance teams could spot them. For the Forest People, the war effort mainly consisted of acts of sabotage, blowing up trains loaded with military cargo, attacking the Germans' outposts and gun turrets; the aim was simply to make the occupiers feel unsafe, under threat, endangered. Occasionally the partisans would also undertake assassinations (high-ranking Nazi officers), or executions (snitches working for the enemy).

It is difficult to imagine life as a partisan. The reality must have been harsh, brutish, gloomy, being forced to make cruel choices on a daily basis. Living in the woods, in improvised dugout shelters, would eat away at your health as well as your morale. Even with the RAF drops, there was always a deficit of medical supplies, and never enough food. If injured, partisans would not let themselves be treated in Polish hospitals, as it would mean instant capture and, with Nazi propaganda branding all partisans 'bandits', they were treated accordingly when captured. Partisans were not considered soldiers fighting for their country, but as criminals who had to be wiped out. As a result, the Nazis did not recognise a captured Home Army soldier as a 'prisoner of war' protected by certain basic protocols, and would instead perform barbaric acts of torture on them. And simply because violence begets violence, partisans would treat a captured Nazi similarly. An ordinary German foot soldier – the Wehrmacht, as they were known – might have been given a chance: let go, and sent barefoot and without a weapon to find their own way out of the forest, but anyone found wearing a black uniform with two SS bolts could expect no mercy.

War makes people grow up fast. It forces them to face situations, which we, the lucky ones, who live in a peaceful time and part of the world, can't imagine. War deprives; it undermines your humanity and brings out your basest instincts as you struggle to survive. It takes an extremely strong individual to resist this process – this blurring of values – and remain righteous.

To beat this dehumanisation, and all the other traumas and still be able to carry on with life... that was the greatest challenge.

How do I know all those things?

I learned them from my grandfather. As soon as the war

was over, Szczepański started to write. By the time I was born
– 1972 – he was a well-established author.

As he set out in this pursuit, he decided he also wanted to
see the world. Shortly after World War II, the Cold War began
– and it became extremely difficult for a person living in a
country behind the Iron Curtain to travel. But Szczepański
found his way. He joined a 'Globetrotter Club' which made it
possible for him to travel as a passenger on cargo ships all
around the world. In the early sixties he even travelled to
Spitsbergen, working as a cook as part of a scientific
expedition. He climbed some of the highest mountains,
travelled across Europe, Asia and both of the Americas. He did
his best to win back all the years that had been taken from him
by the War and to simply enjoy life. And he kept on writing,
to great acclaim in Poland – short stories, novels, essays,
screenplays, even translations – mostly focussing on the stories
of human beings navigating extreme situations.

I have read almost everything he wrote, but if I had to
pick my favourite, I would say the collection of short stories
titled *Boots*, published in 1956. One of the stories acquired a
high profile in Poland, but not entirely for the right reasons.

In the title story, Szczepański depicted a situation where 26
Russian soldiers from the anti-partisan R.O.N.A. squad
surrendered to a group of Polish partisans. They were Russian
renegades, who had joined the Germans as the Nazi's Eastern
front ground slowly towards Russia. R.O.N.A. squads were
organised and led by SS Brigadeführer Bronisław Kamiński – a
Russian officer, who'd defected, taking all those under his
command with him. In 1942 he had established his own little
breakaway army that welcomed Russian deserters, POWs, and
criminals recruited from the prisons. R.O.N.A. soldiers served
the Nazis zealously and proved to be outright savages when the
Germans deployed them to suppress the Warsaw Uprising in
August 1944. They massacred civilians, raping and stealing as
they went, leaving thousands of dead behind. At the end of

1944, when they realised that the Third Reich's days were numbered, they decided to abandon ship and changed sides again, fleeing their barracks for the woods in search of partisans to befriend. They brought with them guns and ammunition as a token of their surrender but, even with this bounty, the partisans were reluctant to embrace them. These Russians could not be trusted, they felt; they had changed sides twice already, betraying first their own country, then the Nazis. The Poles were not in need of such allies, and, what's more, many of partisans had lost relatives and friends in the Uprising. They were craving vengeance. And it soon emerged that the Russians had relics from the Uprising on them: jewellery and watches they had robbed from civilians in Warsaw. Their role in these recent atrocities was beyond any doubt.

The decision was made to eliminate the Russians.

Most of the partisans were happy with this verdict. But there was more to it than just revenge: the R.O.N.A soldiers were well-equipped, with sturdy weapons, warm uniforms, and comfortable marching boots, all of which had caught the partisans' eyes from the very beginning. The lack of proper uniforms and boots was one of the greatest challenges faced by the partisans out in the forests; they marched in shoes that would fall apart, their uniforms were makeshift and arbitrary. So, after all 26 of the Russians were executed – near a small village called Krzepin – the partisans removed all the boots from the dead bodies and shared them out. The main character in Szczepański's story, a young lieutenant nicknamed 'Gray', was the only person who looked on the whole episode with disgust; but there was nothing he could do. He had no power to stop the execution and, despite his internal protestations, he could not justify stopping his comrades from robbing the dead Russians. He knew that many of them were practically barefoot by this stage, and that winter was coming.

This incident made Gray realise that the cruelty of war did not lie solely in one's enemy's actions, but also in one's own

– the way it forces you to change yourself, and the ease with which it blurs the difference between right and wrong. Like a disease, it contaminates all who touch it; regardless of which side they are on.

Szczepański had this short story published in a magazine and shortly after he received some feedback he did not expect. He was accused of disparaging the war heroes who'd fought for freedom, with some critics claiming that he must have made up the whole incident so as to build his own literary career on a controversy. Very few people at the time really understood what he was trying to say with the story.

From the very beginning Szczepański was considered a difficult writer – honesty is quite often a difficult thing to swallow. But the tensions which arose around this honesty empowered him and his writing, and over the course of his career, became his trademark.

Now, almost fifteen years after my grandfather passed away, his *Diary* has just been published and I read it with curiosity and delight. He wrote in his diary on almost a daily basis, his entire life, since the day the war was over. Times after the war were unimaginably hard, but he was persistent, and never gave up. As I read the *Diary*, I get to know my grandfather much better, and I develop a better understanding of who he was. Over the years, he occasionally refers back to those 26 executed Russian soldiers, as if he never came to terms with the narrative of that story.

Because it really happened, and he had to live with it.

I know. So much about my grandfather and not a word so far about Józef Konrad Korzeniowski, an immigrant from a country that did not formally exist at this time, who became one of Britain's greatest writers.

But there is a connection that links these two writers forever.

Joseph Conrad's books influenced a whole generation of

Polish writers, known as the 'Generation of Columbuses'. Writers born around 1920, who were just about entering their adulthood when the war broke out. The very name 'Generation of Columbuses' came from Roman Bratny's book *Columbuses. Generation 20*. Szczepański was one of them.

Imagine maturing in those times: newspapers soaked with Nazi propaganda; no TV, no internet, not even a radio (for, under the Nazi, rule you could be shot just for owning a radio). But with this censorship came resistance: people had an urge to read, to gather their own information about the world, and to find a space in which debate could take place freely. Conrad's books provided that space. Firstly, they described the exotic, far away worlds - places that for young Poles were completely out of reach. On top of this, his books depicted people, like them, who faced great moral dilemmas, where one wrong move could lead to terrible consequences. So, for my grandfather and the others of his generation, Joseph Conrad meant much more than just a favourite writer – he became a moral compass.

To fully understand how massive an influence Conrad's writing had on this generation one should read Szczepański's essay 'In a Great Ship Owner's Service' (from his essay collection *Before an Unknown Tribunal*). Szczepański talks about how the eponymous character from the novel *Lord Jim* became a role model for him and his friends: 'We suddenly realised that Jim was one of us – in our own world. And thanks to him, Joseph Conrad also became one of us too.'

'I always wonder,' he writes, 'if Conrad [...] had any idea that he brought to life other Jims – naive lads, idolatrously looking up to the face of a wise sailor.'

In the same essay, Szczepański tells another story from his younger days.

Again, it was during the War. He still lived in Kraków (this was before he joined the partisans), and one day he got an unexpected visitor: Jerzy. A friend from the old times, a lad he had gone to school with. Now, this young man was in trouble. As part of a resistance group in Warsaw, he had become a fugitive, after one of his comrades had been arrested by the Gestapo. Being aware of the secret police's brutal interrogation methods, it was clearly only a matter of time before they would start tracking him down. So Jerzy came to Kraków: to hide; to wait it out until things cooled down. Confined to my grandfather's flat, unable to leave for fear of capture, he started reading a book he found there to pass the time. An edition of *Lord Jim*, no less! Jerzy read it with increasing excitement. This book 'got him'; he started comparing Jim's situation to his own. And so, to *not* act like a sailor who had abandoned a sinking ship, Jerzy resolved to go back to Warsaw at once. He remembered he had left a photo of his girlfriend in a drawer of his desk, in his flat, and he felt sick at the thought of the secret police finding it. Perhaps the Gestapo had not got there yet; maybe he still had a chance to remove the photo before it fell into the wrong hands.

My grandfather tried to talk some sense into him, but to no effect. Jerzy returned to Warsaw. He did it because he believed he was doing the right thing, but also, because he did not want to be a coward, like Lord Jim. Obviously the Gestapo already knew his address, and they ambushed him the moment he arrived. Jerzy was arrested and, a few weeks of brutal interrogation later, publicly executed.

'What mask has Conrad used, to hide his God?' writes Szczepański. 'Because He is there, between the pages of Conrad's books. He is there, as a law, not named as such, but just as strict; not to be loosely interpreted.'

'We too were aware of this law hanging over us, perennially. And many of us have died because of it. Jerzy was only one of them. It was our metaphysics.'

Conrad, Capital and Globalisation

Dr Richard Niland

BORN INTO A NINETEENTH-CENTURY Polish culture that had experienced political dismemberment through the designs of the Prussian, Russian and Austro-Hungarian empires, Joseph Conrad's subsequent life and career saw him carry an awareness of this formative encounter with empire beyond the horizons of Europe to the world at large. Despite the major cultural and geographical shifts of Conrad's life and work, in his posthumously published *Last Essays* he explained that his writing 'had a consistent unity of outlook.'[1] This Conradian unity has frequently been found in his treatment of the power and limits of empire, but his engagement in life and art with the interrelated peoples, places and forces of modernity in a global context also sees Conrad's writing acquire a further unity through its scrutiny of both newly-emerging and embattled residual tendencies in a globalising world. If the idea of empire is famously elusive for Marlow in *Heart of Darkness*, what, then, is the nature of the global in Conrad's writing and how does it shape his estimation of history and modernity?

Fredric Jameson has identified four major positions on globalisation: that there's no such thing; that globalisation has always been with us in some form or another; that globalisation marks a significant modern intensification of underlying economic structures and networks on a global scale; or that globalisation marks a particular phase of multi-national capitalism bound up with postmodern society.[2] Conrad's work incorporates options two and three, while gesturing towards number four, highlighting both the origins and the economic, cultural and political interconnectivity of a period now regarded as a prelude to the globalisation of the twenty-first century. *The Mirror of the Sea* Conrad's autobiographical evocation of his years in the merchant service, offers a vision of the world characterised by intensified global trading and commerce, with contemporary seamen the inheritors of those who worked 'the famous copper–ore trade of old days between Swansea and the Chilian coast, coal out and ore in, deeploaded both ways, as if in wanton defiance of the great Cape Horn seas'.[3] In the same work, Conrad's allusion to 'great Indian famine of the seventies' and 'dashes across the Gulf of Bengal with cargoes of rice from Rangoon to Madras'[4] draws attention to the myriad global crises and responses of peoples, markets and commodities. Conrad's language reflects the networks and technology that facilitates the flow of capital in a globalising world whereby 'A modern fleet of ships does not so much make use of the sea as exploit a highway.'[5]

An essential element of Conrad's global consciousness is his awareness of long waves of economic, political and historical development. Conrad's fiction itself, of course, appears in the middle of what historians often see as one of the major Kondratieff waves of modernity,[6] cycles of economic rise and fall that appear to characterise global economic development. Conrad's work can also be placed within what is known as the emergence of the world–system, deriving from the work of historian Immanuel Wallerstein and focusing on *longue durée* approaches to historical trends that have shaped contemporary globalisation.[7] In his essay 'Geography and Some Explorers,' which addressed the 'balance of continents'[8] in world development, Conrad offered a survey of history, placing his perspective in a post-Columbian context and dwelling on Iberian imperialism as well as the later exploration of the southern hemisphere. Elaborating on the expansion of European, African and Asian horizons, Conrad sees Columbus and his contemporaries as comperes to a history that can be characterised as global, adding 'suddenly thousands of miles to the circumference of the globe' and opening 'an immense theatre for the human drama of adventure and exploration'.[9] This approach later informed Werner Herzog's *Aguirre: The Wrath of God*, in which Iberian adventurers are determined to 'stage history as others stage plays.' Given the typical denouement of Renaissance historical drama, this staging invariably involves cruelty, death and destruction. For Conrad, the founding stages of Iberian imperialism also saw the 'greatest outburst of reckless cruelty and greed known to history'.[10] In addition to the global exchange of minerals, culture and commodities between Europe and the Americas, there is equally the shadow of disease and the legacy of death and decimation. Turning to his own times, Conrad delineates imperialism in Africa as 'the vilest scramble for loot that ever disfigured the history of human conscience'.[11] Conrad's work, with its isolated characters living in 'Godforsaken villages up dark creeks and obscure bays',[12] exists interstitially between a totalising capitalism and the residual efforts of its now superfluous pioneers, who paradoxically embody its most dominant traits. Jon Beasley-Murray has noted that 'the European state depended on a diffuse group of adventurers and n'er do wells to expand its sphere of influence until it covered the entire known world; but it had simultaneously to reign in this renegade subjectivity'.[13] In *Heart of Darkness*, Marlow journeys to Africa aware that 'the Company was run for profit',[14] yet the full brutality of Kurtz's actions is unnervingly brought home through its contrast with unscrupulous capitalist principles. Viewing the decapitated heads of Kurtz's compound, the result of unspeakable rites, Marlow notes that 'there was nothing exactly profitable in these heads being there'.[15] The darkness lies in the suggestion that a rapacious capitalist ideology might prove less morally iniquitous than an unbridled monstrous will, capturing the text's view that in this world we are offered a 'choice of nightmares'.[16]

Conrad's cartographical focus on the division of the world into the colours of competing empires in 'Geography and Some Explorers,' *A Personal Record* and *Heart of Darkness* points not only to the divisions of empire frequently associated with the scramble for Africa, but also increasing global contiguity though travel and flows of capital. If, for Conrad, the conquistadors discovered that there 'wasn't enough gold to go round',[17] his work returns repeatedly to the circulation of capital. In conjunction with his focus on failed traders and doomed voyages, such as those of *Almayer's Folly* and 'Youth,' Conrad's fiction centres on the cessation or interference with flows of capital and commodities, from the ivory of *Heart of Darkness* and the silver of the mine in *Nostromo,* to the voyages of *Typhoon* and *The Nigger of the 'Narcissus'*. Expanding on the subject of Conrad's fiction, *The Mirror of the Sea* draws attention to capitalism's demand for new markets, and the ways in which speed and efficient networks render the art of the craft redundant. Isolating the historical continuity of 'the seaman of the last generation, brought into sympathy with the caravels of ancient time by his sailing-ship, their lineal descendant',[18] Conrad's understanding of progress is frequently expressed in terms redolent of the writing of figures from Karl Marx to R.B. Cunninghame Graham in which 'machinery, the steel, the fire, the steam have stepped in between the man and the sea'.[19] 'The End of the Tether' recalls 'the halcyon days of steam coasting trade, before some of the home shipping firms had thought of establishing local fleets to feed their main lines. These, when once organised, took the biggest slices out of that cake.' The devouring nature of expansive capitalism, which 'prowled on the cheap to and fro along the coast and between the islands, like a lot of sharks in the water ready to snap up anything you let drop',[20] drives out the earlier trader: 'In a world that pared down the profits to an irreducible minimum [...] there were no chances of fortune for an individual wandering haphazard with a little barque – hardly indeed any room to exist'.[21] As such, Conrad echoes a constituent feature of Joseph Schumpeter's influential view of capitalism as 'creative destruction,' whereby 'The romance of earlier commercial adventure is rapidly wearing away, because so many more things can be strictly calculated that had of old to be visualised in a flash of genius'.[22] In 'The End of the Tether,' remnants of the flash of genius and its diminishing force in a rationalised capitalist world emerge in Captain Whalley's declining independence and fading vision.

In 'The Secret Sharer', the crisis of command experienced by the captain begins with a striking, hallucinatory image of displaced communities swept aside by the modernising world, rendering a landscape 'crazy of aspect as if abandoned for ever by some nomad tribe of fishermen now gone to the other end of the ocean; for there was no sign of human habitation as far as they eye could see'.[23] Despite this particular instance of absence, in Conrad's work the dilemma of the individual is frequently played out in the important context of the larger movement of peoples, with the subject of crisis and honour operating not only in the context of capital, but also that of labour and migration. In *Lord Jim*, the global connections of capital are initially made manifest through those with a vested interest in the Patna: 'The Patna was a local steamer [...] owned by a Chinaman, chartered by an Arab, and commanded by a sort of renegade New South Wales German.' In addition, the ship transports 'eight hundred pilgrim [...] coming from north and south and from the outskirts of the east',[24] and the novel places Jim within a complex network of globalised forces. In *Typhoon*, Captain MacWhirr's battle with the elements occurs in the presence of transient Chinese labourers, while the short story 'Amy Foster' recalls the experience of European emigration. In *Lord Jim* and *Typhoon*, both Arab pilgrims and Chinese migrants contribute to the texture of the connectivity of the world of the fiction but also to the political and social delineation of mobility, labour and markets. Additionally, these texts demonstrate one of the structuring principles of capital's dominance, namely its ability to keep class below decks. As one of the cosmopolitan sites of labour relations and a 'typical workplace of the nineteenth century',[25] the ship operates in Conrad's work as a nexus of the global and a site of the clash of forces over capital. Conrad's sharp focus on the individual trial reveals an uncertain response to the idea of a 'sovereign power enthroned in a fixed standard of conduct'[26] within this capitalist system. Indeed, the spectral elements of 'The Secret Sharer' and *The Shadow-Line* and their tests of command can be connected to sociologist Max Weber's view that, in such an economic system, 'the idea of duty in one's calling prowls about in our lives like the ghost of dead religious beliefs'.[27] Indeed, despite Conrad's fidelity to the memory of the crew in *The Nigger of the 'Narcissus'* and the solidarity of the shared hardship of the sea elsewhere in his work, the politics of his treatment of captains and crews has long been the subject of sceptical scrutiny. In his novel *The Death Ship*, which recalled texts such as *Lord Jim* and *The Nigger of the 'Narcissus,'* the anti-capitalist writer B. Traven observed how 'that greatest sea-story writer of all time knew how to write well only about brave skippers, dishonoured lords, unearthly gentlemen of the sea, and of the ports, the islands, and the sea-coasts; but the crew is always cowardly, always near mutiny, lazy, rotten, stinking, without any higher ideals or fine ambitions'.[28]

Throughout his career, Conrad's rather artisanal memory of the age of sail exists alongside the acknowledgement that we are 'bound to the chariot of progress',[29] even if this chariot is not unlike the ships of empire in John Masefield's contemporary poem 'Cargoes',[30] which elegiacally offers a vision of the declining romanticism of unfolding periods of empire from the ancient to the modern world. Nevertheless, Conrad echoes in certain respects Marx's analysis of production and mechanisation in *Das Kapital* whereby capital always seeks to break down barriers, to annihilate time and space, and to transform the primacy of human contact with nature. As a product of an era of rapid technological transformations, Conrad's work is attuned to the consequences of an 'earth girt round with cables',[31] aware of the age of the telegraph and developing communications, and conveying the sentiment of Kipling's 'Deep-Sea Cables', which spoke of the 'Tie-ribs of the earth' which have 'killed their father Time'.[32] In 'Travel,' from *Last Essays*, Conrad evaluated the forces that now 'encompass the globe [...] after the piercing of the Isthmus of Suez',[33] indicating their role in the shaping of a uniform, if not necessarily homogenous sense of place and culture. The spectre of capital, of course, informs much of this thinking, and it especially haunts *Nostromo*, notably through the US financier Holroyd, who expounds a view of globalisation derived from capital investment, followed by political intervention, as a 'theory of the world's future'.[34] Through the recurring image of time-pieces and railroads, *Nostromo* engages with the major time-space shifts of the nineteenth century which enabled the increased flow of goods and capital. These developments tend towards a uniformity of appearance in *Nostromo's* estimation of the aesthetics of modernity, whereby the 'material apparatus of perfected civilisation [...] obliterates the individuality of old towns under the stereotyped conveniences of modern life'.[35] In Frederick Treves' *The Other Side of the Lantern*, a round-the-world travel account of the type that Conrad claimed to despise and published in the same year as *Nostromo*, the traveller found himself on arrival in Delhi in a 'new and bumptious railway station, which might have been at Bournemouth for any characteristics it displayed'.[36] This structural synchronicity, which incorporates both anachronism and incongruity, troublingly transforms Bournemouth into a version of Melville's white whale, ubiquitous in time and space, with an object formerly particular and English becoming increasingly universal and global. This temporal and spatial confusion of modernity is also captured more generally in the narrative strategies in Conrad's fiction. From the chronological vortex of history in *Nostromo* to the simultaneity of the central events of *The Secret Agent*, with its attack on the first meridian, Conrad juxtaposes time in flux with moments of stasis, illustrating the view in the Preface to *The Nigger of the 'Narcissus'* where to rescue 'a passing phase of life' from 'the remorseless rush of time'[37] is one of the endeavours of Conrad's literary art.

While historical attitudes to empire inform Conrad's understanding of global history, the contemporary rhetoric of empire speaks directly to the globalising tendencies of Conrad's era. The years of Conrad's most celebrated works, *Heart of Darkness*, *Lord Jim*, and *Nostromo* brought together the high-point in British imperial awareness, the definitive end of lingering Spanish imperial ambitions, and the beginnings of US global prominence following the Spanish–American War of 1898. Conrad's settings and characters offer something of a composite portrait of the fate of historically dominant imperial and capitalist energies, with the fading legacy of Dutch trading captured in the figures of Almayer and Willems in the Lingard trilogy of *Almayer's Folly*, *An Outcast of the Islands* and *The Rescue*, to the evocation of distant Spanish imperialism that informs *Nostromo*. Conrad, of course, came to creative maturity in a literary and political culture that ruminated incessantly on the shape that empire and globalisation should take. In his influential study *The Expansion of England*, John Robert Seeley wrote of a global political and cultural empire that in effect constituted a 'world Venice, with the sea for its streets'.[38] Similarly, in 'The True Conception of Empire', Joseph Chamberlain condemned the idea of a little England and celebrated the universalising potential of the British Empire. *Heart of Darkness* interrogates many of these notions, initially placing Britain at the margins of the historical Roman experience of conquest, and also pondering the exchanges that occur between London and the ends of the earth, scrutinising centre and periphery in light of economic and political globalisation. In *Victory*, the vision of interconnected places and peoples is juxtaposed with the reality of failed enterprise, marking the distance between the cartographical and economic ideal and earth-bound reality. *Victory* wryly observes the 'unnatural mysteries of the financial world',[39] ironising the language of speculation by which all that is solid melts into air. Instead, all that is ideologically insubstantialised by way of the language of capital and markets clashes, in this instance, with concrete substance and circumstance. The initial plans for the Tropical Belt Coal Company foresee a tentacularly global capitalist outcome, but their realisation remains unfulfilled: 'We greatly admired the map which accompanied them for the edification of the shareholders. On it Samburan was represented as the central spot of the Eastern Hemisphere with its name engraved in enormous capitals. Heavy lines radiated from it in all directions through the tropics, figuring a mysterious and effective star – lines of influence or lines of distance, or something of that sort. Company promoters have an imagination of their own. There's no more romantic temperament on earth than the temperament of a company promoter'.[40] However, despite the economic failure of *Victory* and, similarly, in spite of the complexities of the Gould Concession in *Nostromo*, both novels evoke the protean 'temperament' of capitalist ventures and their contribution to the course of globalisation.

In a letter to R. B. Cunninghame Graham, on 20 December 1897, Conrad compared the universe to a vast machine that contained its own momentum, rhythm and design: 'It is a tragic accident – and it has happened. You can't interfere with it. The last drop of bitterness is in the suspicion that you can't even smash it [...] I'll admit however that to look at the remorseless process is sometimes amusing'.[41] Such scepticism mirrors the portrayal of globalisation as a tendency – remorseless for many, amusing for others – interwoven with the material development, nation, empire, character and culture in Conrad's work. Ultimately, the ships and journeys of Conrad's fiction at the turn of the twentieth century contain cargoes comprised of 'the seed of commonwealths, [and] the germs of empires',[42] promulgating a long-standing historical globalisation whose transformations through power and capital continue to shape the world in the early twenty-first century.

Notes

1.   Conrad, Joseph. *Last Essays*. London: Dent, 1926. p208.

2.   Jameson, Fredric 'Notes on Globalization as a Philosophical Issue.' *The Cultures of Globalization*, edited by Fredric Jameson and Masao Miyoshi. London: Duke University Press, 1998.

3.   Conrad, Joseph. *The Mirror of the Sea*. New York: Harper & Brothers, 1906. p15.

4.   *Ibid*. p68.

5.   *Ibid*. p119.

6.   Proposed by the Soviet economist Nikolai Kondratiev in his book *The Major Economic Cycles* (1925), and also known as supercycles or long waves, these are hypothesised cycle-like phenomena in the modern world economy. The proposed periods of these waves range from forty to sixty years, with each cycle consisting of alternating intervals of relatively high and low sectoral growth.

7.   Wallerstein, Immanuel. *World-Systems Analysis: An Introduction.* London: Duke University Press, 2004.

8.   Conrad, Joseph. *Last Essays.* p9.

9.   *Ibid.* p7.

10. *Ibid.* p4.

11. *Ibid.* p25.

12. *Ibid.* p9.

13. Beasley-Murray, Jon. *Posthegemony: Political Theory and Latin American.* London: University of Minnesota Press, 2010. p6.

14. Conrad, Joseph. *Youth: A Narrative and Two Other Stories.* London: Blackwood, 1902. p67.

15. *Ibid.* p147.

16. *Ibid.* p156.

17. Conrad, Joseph. *Last Essays.* p5.

18. *The Mirror of the Sea.* New York: Harper & Brothers, 1906. p120.

19. *Ibid.* p119.

20. Conrad, Joseph. *Youth.* pp228-29.

21. *Ibid.* p198.

22. Schumpeter, J. A. *Capitalism, Socialism and Democracy.* London: Unwin, 1970. p132.

23. Conrad, Joseph. *'Twixt Land and Sea.* London: Dent, 1912. p101.

24. Conrad, Joseph. *Lord Jim.* London: Blackwood, 1900. p13.

25. Osterhammel, Jürgen. *The Transformation of the World: A Global History of the Nineteenth Century.* Translated by Patrick Camiller. Oxford: Princeton University Press, 2014. p694.

26. Conrad, Joseph. *Lord Jim.* p53.

27. Weber, Max. *The Protestant Ethic and the Spirit of Capitalism.* Translated by Talcott Parsons. London: Routledge, 2001. p124.

28. Traven, B. *The Death Ship.* London: Picador, 1988. pp112-13.

29. Conrad, Joseph. The *Mirror of the Sea.* p252.

30. Masefield, John. *Collected Poems.* London: Heinemann, 1926.

31. Conrad, Joseph. *Last Essays.* p128.

32. Kipling, Rudyard. *Rudyard Kipling's Verse, 1885-1932.* London: Hodder and Stoughton, 1934. p173.

33. Conrad, Joseph. *Last Essays.* p123.

34. Conrad, Joseph. *Nostromo*. London: Dent, 1947. p77.

35. *Ibid*. pp96-97.

36. Treves, Frederick. *The Other Side of the Lantern: An Account of a Commonplace Tour Round the World*. London: Cassell and Company, 1904. p90.

37. Conrad, Joseph. *The Nigger of the 'Narcissus'*, edited by Cedric Watts. London: Penguin, 1987. pxlix.

38. Quoted in Bell, Duncan. *The Idea of Greater Britain: Empire and the Future of World Order, 1860-1900*. Princeton: Princeton University Press, 2007. p110.

39. Conrad, Joseph. *Victory*. New York: Random House, 1921. p5.

40. *Ibid*. p22.

41. Conrad, Joseph. *The Collected Letters of Joseph Conrad*, Volume 1. Cambridge: Cambridge University Press, 1983. pp424-25.

42. Conrad, Joseph. *Youth*. p54.

Live Me

Jacek Dukaj

Translated by Sean Gasper Bye

I. Virtual reality A.D. 1899

'It had become so pitch dark that we listeners could
hardly see one another. For a long time already he,
sitting apart, had been no more to us than a voice.
There was not a word from anybody. The others
might have been asleep, but I was awake. I listened, I
listened on the watch for the sentence, for the word,
that would give me the clue to the faint uneasiness
inspired by this narrative that seemed to shape itself
without human lips in the heavy night-air of the
river.'[1]

You are taking leave of your senses.

Your senses are taking leave of you, starting with sight.
Thick night has settled on the Thames. The sky is darkening,
the lights of the great city are going out. The lamps on the
ships and boats – these too are surrendering to the gloom.

Hearing goes next. Even the water has grown calm, the
sloshing of waves subsides, a sail once flapping has also fallen
silent; and no-one speaks a word, you have tried to make
conversation but it has not overcome the quiet.

Touch – for you have hands, you have the whole
receptorium of the skin – but you are all fixed to the spot,

there is nothing to do here in this narrow little boat, so this sense too withdraws. You retreat to the bare focal point of perception, immaterial and devoid of external stimulus.

Now it is words that nourish you. Now the imagination grows fevered.

Starved of external sensory input, you begin to feed on these substitutes; you begin to *live* Marlow's story.

In controlled, medical conditions of sensory deprivation, water tanks, or larger tank-like containers, are used. These are filled with highly saline water so that one floats freely on the surface of the liquid, effortlessly, finally unaware there is any liquid at all, that there is up or down, wet or dry, air or water, for one is free of the force these sensations exert; unaware of the presence of the body, for the water matches its temperature; unaware even of one's own existence.

Here we see how the dissolution of the subject progresses: the fading away of proprioception – our sense of orientation within the body – followed by the fading away of our internal orientation as to the sources of feelings, thoughts and biological forces. Is this happening to me? Am I causing it myself? This feeling – is it memory, fantasy? '[B]asically something that actually is initiated within us gets misidentified as from the outside'.[2]

Under sensory deprivation, a person's brain activity drifts towards phases that are physiologically characteristic of sleep. Brainwaves enter the theta rhythm, while the alpha rhythm dies away. Fifteen minutes of thorough sensory deprivation is sufficient to induce hallucinations in a significant share of test subjects.[3] 'When confronted by lack of sensory patterns in our environment, we have a natural tendency to superimpose our own patterns'.[4]

The motif of sensory deprivation forcing the mind to feed on its internal reserves recurs numerous times in *Heart of Darkness*, not least in our own inner experience of Marlow's story.

First, as you are sailing on a steamship sleepwalking its way down the western coast of Africa. A procession of days with the same void of blue, red, and white, the same rhythms of sound, the unchanging geometry of infinity. You've been suspended between life and life in a quasi-hypnotic inertia. And the first factor to break this monotony – a boatful of locals happening along – is a hammer-blow of hyperrealism: cold iron striking a fevered forehead...

And then, when rocked gently between wakefulness and sleep, lying on the deck of the wrecked riverboat, you semi-inadvertently overhear a conversation between the general manager and his uncle. And once again, their voices fill in for a whole universe of impressions: you build up a world from the content of their words and what those words arouse within you. This is when you first create an inner projection, an image of Kurtz. This is when you truly meet Kurtz the man – in your mind – in projection – in the void...

It occurs again as you steam upriver, where once more it is day after day after day of the same – until silence, calm, motionlessness and the monotony of nature force the mind to sate its hunger with stimulus from somewhere – from where? – from the past, from the imagination – was this your past? Did another world exist?

And later, when your senses are clouded with fog so thick and heavy that some of the ship's pilgrims are driven to the verge of a mental breakdown – for they are filling the vacuum in their perception with fears from their own subconscious...

And finally, it appears at the climax of Marlow's story, when you become sucked into the inner experience of Kurtz in the nocturnal darkness, in a clearing of nothingness – you and Kurtz – 'he was alone, and I before him did not know whether I stood on the ground or floated in the air' – there is only a voice – and you are even unsure whether you yourself exist or whether you have now dissolved in this experience, leaving nothing remaining.

And for that matter, every time the story presents you with an adjectival wall – 'immense wilderness', 'impenetrable darkness' – to what is this reality 'impenetrable'? To the senses.

This technique occurs too often to dismiss as an accident. Conrad trusted in it, even though he had no objective insight into the physiology of the brain via MRIs and EEGs. He had his own theory of art, humanity and inner experience.

'He was just a word for me. I did not see the man in the name any more than you do. Do you see him? Do you see the story? Do you see anything? It seems to me I am trying to tell you a dream – making a vain attempt, because no relation of a dream can convey the dream-sensation, that commingling of absurdity, surprise, and bewilderment in a tremor of struggling revolt, that notion of being captured by the incredible which is of the very essence of dreams...'

He was silent for a while.

'...No, it is impossible; it is impossible to convey the life–sensation of any given epoch of one's existence – that which makes its truth, its meaning – its subtle and penetrating essence. It is impossible. We live, as we dream – alone...'

He paused again as if reflecting, then added:

'Of course in this you fellows see more than I could then. You see me, whom you know...'

We can distinguish four categories of methods for experiential transference:

(i) Words.

Here, we are not conveying sensations. We must rely upon the active cooperation of the recipient. We convey only codes, *symbols of sensations* – trusting in the power of the other's imagination.

You read: 'the sun is blinding you'. And the sun is not blinding you – but if you concentrate, if other streams of stimulus do not distract you, and if you have a sufficiently rich database of associations – then the thought of being blinded by the sun evokes memory, imagination, an aura of emotions and impressions of being blinded by the sun, and your pupils will even contract.

(ii) Figurative art.

You look at a photograph or painting. You go to the cinema or the theatre. You listen to recordings. This isn't a beach, it is a picture of a beach – but it is now directly comprehensible to the very sense you are engaging. It is, of course, incomplete, flattened, agonizingly artificial – but it requires no independent decoding of symbols; it is also interpretable for anyone who has never been to a beach, never heard of a beach, has no notion of a beach.

Is this not how the majority of associations and impressions are first amassed in our imaginaria today? We read about an evening in the Sahara – and while we have never been to the Sahara, we have seen it on television, in the cinema, in pictures, on the internet, and thanks to this, words blossom into images for us, with no need to absorb page after page of detailed description.

(iii) Augmented Reality and its particular variant: Virtual Reality.

AR superimposes onto reality, as our senses perceive it, any number of layers of additional, artificial realities. Some of these layers only add new elements; others transform elements of the original reality; still others delete it, replace it.

VR is a kind of AR that deletes and replaces 100% of our sensations of the physical world.

To that end, we use equipment engaging our eyes, ears, the sense of touch in our hands, etc.; therefore, each sensory experience imprinted on your brain still passes first through the unique filter of the body.

(iv) Mind–machine interface. (Mind–machine–mind interface.)

Here, neither external equipment nor the sensory organs are required – stimuli are altered and induced within the cerebral cortex. The entirety of your most profound subjective experience of the world, of other people and even your own 'self' – existing in the body, existing in time – becomes the product of an author writing directly onto your neurons.

We are struggling up this ladder of artistic mimesis. (A technological digression.) Now, in the second decade of the 21st century, we are witnessing the final stages of the civilisation of writing; we are among the last generations to live experiences personally and biologically – *Homo sapiens* is attempting to leap from the second rung to the third, while already reaching for the fourth with the tips of our fingers.

The rise of MRI brain scans has caused an enormous shift in issues heretofore addressed by psychology, philosophy, religion and art – taking them from the realm of subjective cognition into the domain of objective knowledge, or at least the methodology of the hard sciences.

Thanks to fMRI – which captures neural activity continually as it happens – we now know that information about others' affective states enters into the nervous system in a similar way to information about our own affective states – it is only that we then process this information differently. We also know that as a result of listening to and telling stories, we grow more similar to one another at the level of brain activity itself, of our very neural patterns.[5] Empathy consists of emulating what others have undergone with the help of circuits designed to read the conditions in one's own body. Yet when information about another person is too scarce, the mind fills in the gaps using contextual knowledge and produces empathetic reactions by imagining or anticipating the other person's affective states.

The very feeling of *living an experience* – being an experiential subject, i.e. of actively causing events to happen and sensations to be felt – is also transferrable. We need only consider the illusion of possessing another body in VR: you perceive it in a first-person perspective, in its natural size and definition. This body speaks with a different, individual voice – but VR imposes the inescapable illusion that you are the one speaking. Then afterwards, back out of VR, your voice, i.e. the voice of your biological body, turns out to have shifted towards the frequency of your virtual body's voice.[6] You have already in some measure become the person you were living.

Writers have only words.

II. THE PATH OF LITERATURE

'[T]he artist appeals to that part of our being which is not dependent on wisdom; [...] to the subtle but invincible conviction of solidarity that knits together the loneliness of innumerable hearts, to the solidarity in dreams, in joy, in sorrow, in aspirations, in illusions, in hope, in fear, which binds men to each other, which binds together all humanity - the dead to the living and the living to the unborn. [...]

'Fiction - if it at all aspires to be art - appeals to temperament. [...] Such an appeal to be effective must be an impression conveyed through the senses [...]. All art, therefore, appeals primarily to the senses, and the artistic aim when expressing itself in written words must also make its appeal through the senses [...]. My task which I am trying to achieve is, by the power of the written word to make you hear, to make you feel - it is, before all, to make you see. That - and no more, and it is everything.'[7]

Before the 20th century accustomed us to reading literature with the ironic detachment of an old man, through kaleidoscopes of metatexts and the barbed wire of inverted commas, the natural, simply physiological, path of taking in literary fiction was to *live* it.

In the Preface to *The Nigger of the 'Narcissus'*, Conrad refines this observation to the clarity of a writer's manifesto. For what is the goal of an author of fiction? To cause their reader to live these fictional events. To feel what they have not truly felt – what has been put down on paper for them to feel. Subjective experience is always fed into us via sensory content - not on the plane of intellectual arguments and logical statements, but in just the same way as everyday real life speaks, meaning using image, sound, smell, touch, repertoires of sensations.

This is how Conrad argues for literature's exceptional position in the hierarchy of art. And this is not in the least a privileged position: literature alone has no direct access to its audience's senses. Music is heard, paintings seen, sculpture we may even touch – but text must first use words, i.e. a purely intellectual construction of meaning, to lead us into a state of autoillusion such that, in reading a description of a landscape, we seem to *see* it, in reading a description of drums echoing in the night, we seem to *hear* them, and so on and so on, eventually building to an illusion of *lived experience* set up for us directly in prose.[8]

Of course, this is not the only rationale or path for literature. In the art of creating a text – a text meaning a sequence of sentences written for the purpose of being individually interpreted by readers - two additional functions and traditions have secured comparatively solid positions:

The second: the function of text as a tool for discussing phenomena which do not exist in a form apprehensible to the human senses.

These are above all ideas and emotions. It is impossible to see, touch, or smell democracy, relativism, thermodynamics, a logarithm, or for that matter envy, fear, or melancholy. Only text allows us to perform direct, complex rational operations on these. They are rooted in words, rather than in materiality – and in words that exist independently from human memory, in subjectified words.

Given Conrad's manifesto is the credo of an impressionist, here we must deal with impressionism from back to front: it is not that bundles of sensations direct you to think of an idea, but rather that an idea denoted with a combination of words 'radiates' across the memory and the imagination in cascades of associations, which, in part and on some level, can be illustrated by images, sounds and feelings.

The third: the function and tradition of text as an abstraction of form.

These texts are by definition impossible to elevate beyond the realm of letters or speech sounds: their meaning and value lies in the auditory properties of these sounds, the visual composition of the letters on paper, the rhythms of the sentences, the aesthetics of the phrases. Occasionally they become completely divorced from what they are denoting and cannot be translated into other sensory impressions, because they appeal to the very sense of the beauty of text (or speech).

Besides these functions, in the 20th century yet another, fourth, tradition developed, the beloved child of analysts and ideologues of literature: causative function.

Here a literary text serves to alter extratextual, and in particular social and economic, reality. It is an act, an event, a deed – just like a work in another artistic discipline. It operates not through individual empathies, emotions, or logics – but by pure force of fact effected in intersubjective reality.

Hence the success of what we might call 'a literature of provocation' (literature which is not to be read, but *read about*), celebrity authors (distorting the space of culture with the mass of their personalities), as well as the progressive blurring of the line between fiction and non-fiction (if a text has changed the reality you live in, is it fiction or non-fiction?).

It no longer sounds like a Woody Allen joke to say that buying a book is just as good as reading it. The act of purchasing – online or in a material bookstore – engages you intellectually and emotionally. You purchase a book along with all the cultural trappings which have urged you to do so: the aesthetic and emotional aura from advertisements, reviews, write-ups, taglines, graphic (multimedia) covers, information you've gathered about the book, information you haven't gathered but which has osmotically penetrated your conscious and unconscious mind, conversations with acquaintances – who have also not read the book but in a higher sense have *acquired* it, for they carry it in their minds just as you do – the book already *acts upon* you all.

The environment around a book can provide a richer reading experience than the book itself. *The New York Review of Books* and similar periodicals of the healthily snobbish lettered classes have developed a curious form of essay-review: a long write-up, frequently lacking a clear artistic assessment of the book, but so satisfying in content that it actually renders reading the book superfluous; you have already absorbed the book, in the form of a high-calorie extract with appetizers, aperitifs and desserts served up on the fine china of newspaper columns.

Celebrity status is not a side effect of a writer's fame; in the case of authors of highbrow literature it is increasingly an authorial act in the strictest sense. Is it not the highest value and goal of the ambitious humanities to reflect the truth of the human condition? Authors no longer write using themselves, but write themselves. When was Knausgaard's *My Struggle* truly created: when he was writing down memories of previous events, or when he was *living* them?

Conrad, by contrast, appears to be a forerunner of a use of literature which dominated popular readership throughout the 20th century and which 21st-century neuroscience has elevated to an objective mechanism of the psyche: literature as a story in which words are used to drive the reader into the internal state the author intends.

This state cannot simply be transplanted from one person to another. But how has a given member of *Homo sapiens* ended up at precisely the point of existence where they are? By having the subjective experiences they have had, of course. Therefore, if you had the same exact subjective experiences, most likely you would find yourself in the same internal state, or at least a state so similar as to feel 'the subtle conviction of solidarity that knits together the loneliness of innumerable hearts'.

But! Not I, nor Conrad, nor any other writer can lead you through *the same* subjective experiences. The best I can achieve is to present you sequences of sensations analogous to those which the original experience provoked.

How can I do this? 'By the power of the written word'.

WORLD → SENSATIONS → MIND → INTERNAL STATE

Authors must use half-measures, tricks, associative shortcuts. They suggest word-keys you can use to unlock the right door of your imagination, so that instead of a view of the jungle, you receive an imagined view of the jungle; instead of the sound of drums in the night – the imagined sound of drums in the night.

And if both of the following conditions are met – on the author's part: a talent for the evocative use of words, and on the reader's part: a rich imagination – the difference between the sight of heads on sticks and the imagined sight of heads on sticks turns out to be so minor that you effectively have the same inner experience as Marlow did when he was struck by this sight in Africa and, at least for a moment, you will be Marlow: a person with Marlow's subjective experience.

'As people comprehend a text, they construct simulations to represent its perceptual, motor, and affective content.

Simulations appear central to the representation of meaning'.[9] Similarly, as we hear, read, or think about more abstract subjects, we leverage a system of metaphors grounded in memories of concrete subjective experiences; by simulating the body's movement or our own internal states, we comprehend elevated philosophical theories.[10]

And if these sensations themselves are indistinguishable, what difference does their origin make? An image may be artificial, false – yet the emotion it evokes in you is nevertheless real.

WORDS → MIND → IMAGINED SENSATIONS → INTERNAL STATE

This is not a matter of telling a story – the story is a tool, the plot is a trick – it's a matter of *living another person*.

In the history of literature, we may find many other examples of impressionism used intentionally to induce existential shock. *Heart of Darkness* presents this mechanism first and foremost within the story itself, making it into a subject, a focus of the story. It speaks of it and speaks through it.

Between the reader and Kurtz, in a scheme written across several characters and levels of narrative, at least three such *transfers of life* occur:

(1) Marlow lives Kurtz.

As he sets off for the Congo, Marlow knows nothing about Kurtz, yet after returning to Europe, he carries Kurtz within him: Kurtz and the existential discovery of Kurtz become as much a part of Marlow as his childhood or his maritime adventures.

'I thought his memory was like the other memories of the dead that accumulate in every man's life – a vague impress on the brain of shadows that had fallen on it in their swift and final passage; but before the high and ponderous door [...] I had a vision of him on the stretcher, opening his mouth voraciously, as if to devour all the earth with all its mankind. He lived then before me; he lived as much as he had ever lived.'

(2) The narrator lives Marlow living Kurtz.

After entering a state of sensory deprivation on the Thames, after superimposing the virtual reality of Marlow's story onto his senses, the unnamed narrator lives the voyage towards the heart of Africa, lives Marlow's successive encounters, adventures, and emotions, his transformations – and does not notice when he has in fact begun living Kurtz.

(3) The reader lives the narrator living Marlow living Kurtz.

The entire history of how *Heart of Darkness* has been received, the longevity of this text, its countless adaptations, interpretations, subversions, and the ideological-literary disputes that have raged around it prove that Conrad's artistic intentions were successful. We live Marlow, we live Kurtz.

Yet while the first two transfers remain under the author's control, the third is more of a roll of the dice, a leap of faith. Not only because of the random nature of the author's contemporary readership, but because we cannot predict the conditions shaping the experiential database of all future readers, one hundred, two hundred, a thousand, a million years from now – as long as any conscious being is able to use letters to *live themselves into* others.

But how precisely does Marlow live himself into Kurtz? What paths does he take to reach peaks and troughs of fate sufficiently similar to Kurtz's that he takes Kurtz away with him, incorporates Kurtz into his own 'self'?

Kurtz does not reveal a single detail of his own biography to Marlow. The matter-of-fact conversations between the two men are fractured echoes of consciousness, enigmatic missives from the depths. From these shreds of dialogue you might compose thousands of different, consistent life stories and psychological profiles.

Even after his return to Europe, as he meets Kurtz's prior acquaintances and his fiancée, Marlow gets lost among the variegated and equally obvious truths about Kurtz. He does not know the facts, does not possess the knowledge; he is not acting from reason. 'The artist appeals to that part of our being which is not dependent on wisdom'.

So how, how exactly, does Marlow live himself into Kurtz?

Above all, Marlow retraces the path of people, places, and things along which Kurtz himself travelled. Of course, what happens to him on this path is not precisely what happened to Kurtz in the past. Yet since what played the key role in Kurtz's transgression was the very confrontation of an educated European with the realities of Sub-Saharan Africa – its political-economic wilds and natural wilds – we are therefore given long, dense descriptions of Africa, overwhelming in their hypnotic intensity. And why, on the Thames, does Marlow rattle off litanies of sensations of the monotony of the coast, the savannahs, the rivers; of the monumental colonnades of trees; of the texture of the darkness, the symphonic secretions of exotic flora? Because it is precisely through this siege on the senses that he was driven to a state analogous to Kurtz's – nourishing his soul with the same images, sounds, smells, touches, bodily torments – and which he subsequently induces in his listeners by drawing them into the 19th-century VR of literature – so that in their minds, their imaginations, they repeat to themselves what he has repeated, they replay what he has replayed.

At the same time, a mysterious pre-perceived Kurtz emerges from Marlow's unlit interior like a silhouette of someone at once strange and familiar standing in the half-light of a foyer. How do we build models of others' personalities in our minds? What mechanism is responsible for predicting others' behaviour, the capacity to successfully deceive others (and for multi-layered deception, i.e. for deception by telling the truth), for feeling along with them? Here, we turn to the category of 'empathy', ἐμπάθεια, which literally means 'in-feeling', *Einfühlung*.

Empathy in animals and young children does not extend beyond the range of feelings displayed to them directly. This is how 'emotional contagion' works: one baby in a room begins crying and before long they all are. Dogs and humans find yawning equally infectious. 'Pupillary contagion' occurs entirely outside of our control and awareness. It is not until they are older that people (people and some apes) can feel themselves into figures from their imagination. A necessary condition for empathy is being able to fully distinguish between oneself and the other – the in-felt – as well as being aware of the very act of empathising.

The scene of Marlow eavesdropping on the manager and his uncle is a demonstration of the author's prestidigitational virtuosity: watch me do this – you'll see, you can understand the mechanics of the trick and yet it will work on you again – and again – and again. Look!

Marlow finds himself in a state of half-sleep (theta rhythm). He hears snippets of sentences, descriptions repeated, incomplete stories of events – in lieu of other sources of information, these penetrate his imagination and he begins living them, meaning once he realises the conversation is not about him, Marlow constructs within himself a hypothetical subject, feeling, thinking, living the experiences the manager and his uncle attribute to this figure. Does Marlow understand him? 'I did not know the motive.' He was already on his way back from the Inner Station to Europe to collect the requisite profits, awards, honours; there was nothing left for him at the Station, even goods to trade, even people to help. Then abruptly – he turns back. In a mere husk of a canoe, bereft of possessions and bereft of hope he slinks his way back to the heart of darkness. Does Marlow understand him? We cannot truly understand the motivation even for our own actions; empathy is not a tool of psychoanalysis, psychoanalysis is not a temple of empathy. But – 'I seemed to see Kurtz for the first time'.

What alchemy of words brought about this act of Marlow living himself into another human being? Yes, sensory deprivation - the senses feeding on imagined sensations. But is that enough? Yes, words – the insinuations, vulgarisms, curses and exclamations of the manager and his uncle call to mind mysteries above and beyond the senses and the material. Is that enough?

Nonetheless, this is how Marlow beheld a Kurtz of his own creation. And it is hard not to presume that Kurtz-in-Marlow is more than simply a reflection – imperfect, incomplete – of an original in a different mind, but that it is (also) a product of that other mind.

To live someone else, they need not exist at all.

A psychoanalytical digression:

Let us assume that Kurtz does not exist and never existed as an element of Marlow's reality. (Within the text-world of *Heart of Darkness* it is impossible to verify the truth of Marlow's words.) In that case, we must interpret Marlow's entire story on the boat as a psychoanalyst interprets the couchbound confessions of their patients, who frequently do not recount their trauma in the first person, but go to great lengths to transpose their inner experiences and states into other people's stories or into utter fiction. 'You know, doctor, something happened to a friend of mine...' – all the while honestly believing this friend exists. Various schools of deciphering these stories – the Freudian, the Lacanian – provide tools to reconstruct the underlying source material.

What then might Marlow's 'true story' look like? Well, that it was Marlow, sucked into the myth of the 'emissary of light' and 'of pity, and science, and progress', who travelled to the Belgian Congo, leaving behind in Europe an unfulfilled career and a lovesick fiancée from a higher social class; driven by noble intentions as well as personal ambitions, he descended into a caricature of colonial brutality and plunder, until, coming to rest at the very heart of darkness and there having tasted man's terrifyingly easy power over values, meanings and lives, ravaged by this power until he was little more than a skeleton, succumbing to spiritual and bodily illness and symbolically burying his 'old self' (henceforth known as 'Kurtz'), he returned to Europe as the younger, purer, more naïve Marlow. 'No, they did not bury me, though there is a period of time which I remember mistily, with a shuddering wonder, like a passage through some inconceivable world that had no hope in it and no desire.' No wonder Kurtz's 'shade' trails Marlow down the streets of Brussels and London, no wonder at key moments images from the hell of Africa emerge from his memory – it is his past, his memory, his Africa and his own hell. Now how profoundly significant is Marlow's account, intercut with feverish visions and exclamations, of the meeting with Kurtz's Intended! How ambiguous are Marlow's digressions!

'All that had been Kurtz's had passed out of my hands: his soul, his body, his station, his plans, his ivory, his career. There remained only his memory and his Intended – and I wanted to give that up, too, to the past, in a way – to surrender personally all that remained of him with me to that oblivion which is the last word of our common fate.'

And how should we now interpret the Intended's behaviour? Marlow comes to her to break off their engagement – this is how we must decode their entire conversation:

Marlow returns Kurtz's letters, that is *renounces Kurtz's words*, i.e. frees his Intended from her pledge. Marlow breaks with his Intended because he has broken with 'Kurtz', his ambitions, his plans, his life – and in this place, his Intended is their avatar, if not their ultimate cause and driving force. 'I believed in him more than any one on earth – more than his own mother, more than – himself. He needed me! Me!' The story ends at the moment of purification from ambition – Marlow flees this crumbling house of higher cravings and we know it was no lie when he said the last word spoken by Marlow-who-was-Kurtz was the name of his Intended – the name of what she personifies for him in the repressed knowledge of his own actions – 'The horror! The horror!'

Once we have entered this hermeneutic, the text will only continue to confirm it for us. 'Ever any madness in your family?' And then – the conversations with the journalist, the cousin, the Company official after his return, the people who knew Marlow-when-he-was-Kurtz – how do they now sound to us? Of course these people were demanding complete, clear answers! It was Marlow who was behaving oddly, as though he was meeting them for the first time in his life; of course they grew cross. And beyond that – Marlow's sequence of encounters with Company representatives on his way to the Inner Station. It was not in the least Marlow's miracle-working aunt who got him wrapped up in the legend of the Company's golden boy - she was invented for the purposes of the story on the Thames. These men were entirely correct to greet him with such reverence and make such effort – because they were greeting Kurtz.

And when in this second level of reading, now in the psychoanalytic mode, we reach the conversation between the manager and his uncle, overheard in half-sleep – what now do we hear? Both of them giving Marlow scraps and echoes of Kurtz, which he uses to weave together a person in his mind? – or rather voices from Marlow–Kurtz's own subconscious, bringing the first signs of this painful self-awareness to the surface?

'And it is not my own extremity I remember best – a vision of greyness without form filled with physical pain, and a careless contempt for the evanescence of all things – even of this pain itself. No! It is his extremity that I seem to have lived through.'

Moving this way or that, this literary experiential transference ultimately comes full circle.

III. THE HERMENEUTIC CIRCLE OF FACEBOOK

'I don't want to bother you much with what happened to me personally [...] yet to understand the effect of it on me you ought to know how I got out there, what I saw, how I went up that river to the place where I first met the poor chap. It was the farthest point of navigation and the culminating point of my experience. It seemed somehow to throw a kind of light on everything about me – and into my thoughts. It was sombre enough, too – and pitiful – not extraordinary in any way – not very clear either. No, not very clear. And yet it seemed to throw a kind of light.'

You must know the end to understand the beginning.

But none of you will understand what the end means if you have not experienced the path which has led to it.

Yet without this dim light emanating from the future – what will you see along that path? What will you understand?

Heidegger's hermeneutic circle turns from part to whole, and from whole to part, and from part to whole, and from whole, etc., etc... A piece of a story can only be understood in the context of the whole; and not until we come to know it piece by piece can we understand the whole.

But with each turn of the circle our understanding alters – expands, deepens, sublimates, problematises – and the number of subsequent interpretations necessary to comprehend it 'correctly' reaches infinity. The circle never ceases turning.

Gadamer's hermeneutic circle is driven by the course of readers' lives as embedded in history: each reader is different and each differs from the author in a different way, therefore the same word-symbols open up different mental experiences. The keys do not change, but the contents of the vaults of the soul originate not in the Platonic world of ideas, but the flickering, impermanent reality of matter. We build up these repertoires of sensations – images, sounds, emotions, complex networks of associations – for ourselves from childhood, gathering up some life events and not others, linking meanings and occurrences in our brains in one way but not in another.

Therefore even readers coming from the same culture, from the same language, will understand the same sentences differently after decoding them using sensations and associations taken from a decade, a generation, a century later.

TEXT + EXPERIENTIAL DATABASE = MEANING

A theological digression:

This problem becomes elevated to one of the fundamental principles of the world and morality when the author of the text in question is God. Readers are immersed in history; the Word of God constitutes superhistorical Truth.

We are left with two choices:

(A) The Truth contained in the text (its meaning) nevertheless changes over time and with each culturally different reading;

(B) God did not speak (or write) to people of all cultures and times, but to one concrete subset of humankind, and all others' interpretations are mistaken, i.e. they produce a meaning incommensurate with Truth.

(The hypothesis that God did not foresee that human interpretations would change we reject as internally contradictory, i.e. denying the omniscience of God.)

One solution to the above paradox is to accept the concept of a so-called 'textual core'. Peripheral meanings, incidental to the 'core', may be subject to change, re-interpretation, or falsification, but nonetheless the core meaning will forever remain correctly interpreted.

Yet since even with sacred texts there is no agreement among exegetes as to what this 'core meaning' ought to be, how are we meant to establish it for human-made literature?

Gadamer proposed a different solution — accepting this variability and rejecting the very strategy of feeling oneself into the original meanings of the text, the intentions of the author, and the situation of the text's first readers.

A text accumulates meanings as it moves through history — and it is precisely thanks to this increasing richness of interpretations that we are able to understand it. There is no question of 'in-feeling', of empathy — it is specifically a question of understanding. 'It is the task of hermeneutics to illuminate this miracle of understanding, which is not a mysterious communication of souls, but rather a participation in shared meaning'.[11] It would be hard to find a more direct antithesis to Conrad's 'appeal to that part of our being which is not dependent on wisdom'.

Undistorted transference is therefore impossible as long as it is dependent on language. Each of Marlow's listeners on the Thames holds within them an experience of a different journey to the heart of darkness, and meeting a different Kurtz, and returning to Europe with a different darkness. The readers of A.D. 1899 experienced these same words differently to the readers of A.D. 2017. There is not even a theoretical possibility of implanting in our minds the 'experiential database' shared by Conrad and his contemporary readers.

Instead, following the advice of Giuseppe Tomasi di Lampedusa, it would be necessary to change everything so what is most important might stay the same. This means giving today's readers completely different word-keys – a different text – to provoke the same motions of the spirit that Conrad intended in his own time. (I undertook precisely such a hopeless attempt at authoritatively reconstructing the meaning of *Heart of Darkness* by making my own pseudo-translation.)

But! What if we could successfully fulfil Conrad's ideal of existential impressionism while completely bypassing, 'skipping over' the words in this transfer, taking the internal experiences the author has thought up and imposing them on ourselves directly?

A philosophical digression:

Let us attempt to step into the radical subjectivism of Thomas Nagel: just as a person cannot feel themselves into a bat, in the same way one representative of *Homo sapiens* cannot feel themselves into another representative of *Homo sapiens*. After all, the only difference is the scale of the gap dividing them – the logic of the argument itself still applies. (Today, gender studies provides hundreds of pieces of evidence that 'being a woman' is not translatable into 'being a man'.)

Therefore every subject whose *Umwelt*[12] is not precisely identical to the *Umwelt* of the recipient of this transference, and whose history of life events (i.e. experiential database) is not precisely the same as the recipient's history, remains eternally locked into a cage of untranslatable qualities of *being*.

I see this as a peculiar kind of *reductio ad absolutum*, very useful for the world of mathematics, though not for creatures fashioned of mud and saliva. Empathy presumes far-reaching differences between the subject and object of in-feeling –

actually, these differences are a necessary condition for empathy! We resolve to make a conscious *effort*. We settle for an imprecise in-feeling whose value lies in the very fact of one heart inching closer to another, of taking even a half-step against an onslaught of concentrated nothingness.

This is not pleasant. It disrupts our childish egotism. It hurts. Sometimes it demands a complete ontological revolution. 'The earth seemed unearthly [...] and the men were – No, they were not inhuman.'

Heart of Darkness is as much a treatise on and exercise in low-tech experiential transference as a journey to the outer limits of translation. For Marlow, for Europe – from the Greeks with their definition of *barbaroi*[13] to Wittgenstein – these were the limits of humanity.

Here, I am striving for a basis for a hermeneutic project transcending the theoretical limits of Gadamer and Nagel.

'And why not? The mind of man is capable of anything – because everything is in it, all the past as well as all the future.'

This is not a declaration of some gnostic divinity of the human mind, but – as is obvious from reading *Heart of Darkness* through the lens of his Foreword to *The Nigger of the 'Narcissus'* – a statement of belief in the mind's infinite elasticity, meaning the elasticity of human beings themselves. This lies in their power to shape and reshape themselves from the content of transferred inner experiences – with effort, with pain, in spite of the inertia of tradition and cultural delusion, yes, in spite of all that, it is possible – I read you, you read me – 'I have a voice, too, and for good or evil mine is the speech that cannot be silenced' – and in this way, living one another and building towards one another in a positive feedback loop, we overcome that curse of life-idioms: that 'we live, as we dream – alone'.

Nagel: 'Fundamentally an organism has conscious mental states if and only if there is something that it is like to be that organism – something it is like for the organism.'[14]

Can we be conscious of this quality of 'being ourselves' without being able to experience 'being someone else'? And in that case, will this very quality not inevitably change, the more so as our methods of experiential transference become more effective?

The hermeneutic circle of Facebook intertwines the very lives of the site's users in an ouroboric plait. Ever since the introduction of Facebook Live, social media has been breaking away from the tradition of texts and narratives created *ex post* – filtered through reason, encoded in words – to set off down the path of ultimately perfecting the technology of experiential transference.

Facebook wagers that in four years, text will be completely supplanted by transmissions (a) from mobile devices, (b) live and (c) in video. 'The best way to tell stories in this world – where so much information is coming at us – actually is video.'[15] The phenomenon of television series assuming the role of prose, particularly of novels, has already been well documented. But let us examine this fact in historical perspective, meaning as one component of a vector of civilisational change that is stretching ever further. We will not stop with TV series. Mark Zuckerberg is in no doubt as to the result of the spread of such experiential technology: 'It frees people up to be themselves. [...] Somewhat counterintuitively, it's a great medium for sharing raw and visceral content.'[16]

How much more 'raw and visceral' can it get? We are inevitably heading for complete, full-sensory participation which eventually bypasses the external sense organs, so that *a story about life would be lived as life itself.*

In absolute categories Nagel is still correct: I will not understand John Smith without being John Smith – even if I no longer need to match inner experiences from my own repertoire to his words, since I am receiving them in wordless sensory batches just as they reached John Smith's senses, and at the same time as he is living them himself, with the same sense of agency; even then I will not understand. For these new inner experiences will fall onto the soil of prior experiences – unique and mine alone – and therefore grow differently and bear different fruit.

Still, Facebook Live is not an accident of civilisation; it is a natural consequence of the universal aspiration of a *Homo sapiens* straining under a Sisyphean load of self-consciousness. After all, how many essays, poems, and scientific works have been dedicated to the phenomenon of Japanese tourists living the world through their camera lenses! The trend has advanced, via ever more pervasive mass media and social media, via the digital universes of YouTubes, Instagrams, Snapchats, and Periscopes, in the high-speed race of countless businesses, technologies, and lifestyles, all straining towards one goal: to be able to better and better, deeper and deeper, and more and more universally live other people and so that others can live me.

You still retain a private corner of your soul, lived only by you and no one else. But your children? Generations of descendants after them? Those who since infancy will have lived other people and have been lived by millions?

Here is the hermeneutic circle of Facebook: John lives Frank living Pierre living Svetlana living Mariko living Li living John.

We are finally approaching salvation from the Purgatory of 'the loneliness of innumerable hearts'.

'Imposter syndrome' as a sociological phenomenon arose in the 1970s in the context of the emancipation of women and, later, of ethnic, cultural, and sexual minorities. Members of these groups confessed to an intense feeling of 'success by deception':

I've been successful, but I can't believe that 'on the inside' – in my mind, in my heart, in my character – I possess the requisite qualities, skills, or knowledge. I'm only *pretending*. And because I'm pretending, I try twice as hard, so my success increases, so I feel even more like a fraud, so I work even harder...

Over time, research has shown the majority of exceptional individuals suffer from 'imposter syndrome'; indeed, rare are those who have not harboured such convictions. The 'softer' the discipline, meaning the more it lacks objective measures of quality, the easier to become convinced that you are 'faking it'.

For as long as I can remember, I have been tormented more or less intensely by a variant of 'imposter syndrome' – not in the least related to a discipline of art or knowledge, but to something significantly more fundamental. This blossomed along with the growth of technology for transmitting privacy and intimacy and obsessively comparing lifestyles; in the era of the epidemic of Asperger's and autisms tied to traits and talents essential for the digital economy. It is the syndrome of feigned humanity.

Everyone around me knows how people speak, think, behave, feel, live – more than that, they *intuit* it, they know it instinctively, like an effortless awareness deep in their reflexes, their genes, the bones of their souls. Only I, I alone, I, the fraud in a human mask, am forced to devote hundreds, thousands of hours to painstaking, humiliating observation and study and analysis and algorithmisation of *true humanity* so that later I can imitate it successfully – successfully act out being human.

So, you haven't even glimpsed the shadow, the reflection of that feeling? But you've grown out of it; it used to be so easy, so natural to grow out of adolescent wonderments and epiphanies.

And is this not how culture matures, little by little shedding convictions about a 'nature' that lies hidden beneath geologic layers of the products of consciousness? Is there not a liberating wisdom in all this, where we finally understand that *everyone* is an imposter?

We live ourselves into each other in an endless chain of desperate empathising. We imitate imitators of imitators of imitators of imitators of imitators –

Kurtz is a voice. Marlow does not write, Marlow speaks. *Heart of Darkness* does not treat its text as a form of imagistic transmission, befitting the 20th century's culture of visualisers; it is an unmodulated recording of a voice reverberating in silence and darkness.

This symbolic Facebook Live and other 21st-century media are bringing to fruition a post-writing civilisation. For tens of thousands of years *Homo sapiens* lived in a culture of oral informational transfer – writing was not invented until about 3000 B.C. And after this five-millennium interval of the domination of the written word, we are now confronting the third incarnation of humanity – which is neither an oral culture nor a written one. It is the cultural superstructure of the technology of symbol-free recording, processing and transmitting ideas and experiences. We have already acquired the tools we need to no longer restrict the exchange of thoughts and feelings to words, whether listened to or read.

When he published *The Origin of Consciousness in the Breakdown of the Bicameral Mind* in 1976, Julian Jaynes introduced into the intellectual arsenal a theory that self-consciousness arose as a construct of a civilisation of writing. Pre-writing peoples, in antiquity, in Neolithic cultures and hunter-gatherer groups, in an environment of low complexity and stable structures, before the agricultural revolution, lived, conversed, reasoned, worked, planned and fought – without being self-conscious as we understand it. They were incapable of introspection; the 'inner voices' driving them were the voices of deities, demons, spirits, or nature; no 'self' existed comparable to ours. Relics of narrative art from their times allow us to reconstruct the existential limits of these almost-people, from myths, from *Gilgameshes* and *Iliads*. In these, we will search in vain for descriptions of inner lives and multi-layered self-reflection; a person was whatever imprint they left on their exterior.

Whereupon humankind passed from a word- and sound-based operating system to a word- and picture-based one – and in the same way we are now passing from a word- and picture-based system into a culture of experiential transference.

Jaynes's theses did not fit into the scientific mainstream. Most anthropologists and cognitive scientists approach them with scepticism, instead admiring the totality of his iconoclastic hypothesis and the persuasive appeal of *The Origin of Consciousness*. At the same time, they recognise that during the process of anthropogenesis some tectonic shift did indeed take place very recently – thousands, not hundreds of thousands of years ago – and that it was related to language, to a qualitative leap in methods of communication. Daniel Dennett seeks to pinpoint this moment, deducing it from differences between animals and modern people: 'There is such a difference between the consciousness of a chimpanzee and human consciousness that it requires a special explanation, an explanation that heavily invokes the human distinction of natural language'.[17]

With increasing frequency, new theories of the brain are upending the traditional hierarchy that says experiential data goes *from* the world, through sensory stimuli, to a representation *of* that world created in the brain. Instead, the theory of 'predictive processing', as developed by Andy Clark and others, shows how the brain itself generates sensory impressions on the basis of internal models of the body, the world, and other people, which are only afterwards matched to divergent external stimuli. These internal data streams refract across a whole spectrum of hypotheses about reality, and the hypothesis which wins out – this is the final act of perception.[18]

Let us set aside the genesis of human consciousness and consider the very historical course of this change. It inevitably took place not only over an extended period, but also sequentially and selectively – i.e. consciousness did not arise at the same second in all members of *Homo sapiens*, nor even in everyone of a given generation, neither is there any logical reason it couldn't have 'faded away', e.g. in the descendants of mixed populations, at the intersections of genetic lines and cultures.

Therefore at the dawn of humankind the condition of the 'imposter' – the fraud in the human mask – was natural and inevitable. This fraud slowly, by degrees, story after story, transfer after transfer, naturalness after artificiality – internalised *true humanity*. Until the mask became a face. Until from a story about a human – the first human came into being. Until the sequence of 'selves' living 'selves' came full circle.

And was there, at the start of this chain of mirrors reflecting mirrors, any kind of 'non-fiction human'? What difference does it make?

How exactly does Marlow live himself into Kurtz?

VI. Darkness in Europe

'His intelligence was perfectly clear – concentrated, it is true, upon himself with horrible intensity, yet clear [...]. Being alone in the wilderness, it had looked within itself, and, by heavens! I tell you, it had gone mad. [...] He struggled with himself, too. I saw it – I heard it. I saw the inconceivable mystery of a soul that knew no restraint, no faith, and no fear, yet struggling blindly with itself.'

Now replace Kurtz here with – Europe. Europe, European civilisation, Western culture. 'All Europe contributed to the making of Kurtz'.

Its intelligence is perfectly clear...

Kurtz is Europe's consciousness at its furthest extremes. Europe armed with the entire tradition of Enlightenment rationalism, Europe which turned its murderous intelligence and the instruments of knowledge it had honed conquering the globe back on itself, and saw through itself, and imperceptibly sank into madness, solitary in a land barren of morals and truths.

It still strains. It still wrestles – with itself, with reason. We see, we hear. Zero faith. No scruples. Nothing above, nothing below. It thrashes blindly in the darkness – 'a being to which one could not appeal in the name of anything high or low'. All round are rotting heads on stakes and idolatrous howls. The barbarians' drums are pounding. Unspeakable dread is growing.

If only we still had our burning ambition for power, money, honours! That, too, is extinguished.

If only we still had brute force, the power to bend reality to our ambitions, dreams, visions.

The strength is gone. The vision is gone.

Marlow had to journey beyond the boundaries of the world of his time, beyond encyclopaedias and cartographies – to reach that heart of darkness. We, children and grandchildren of the 20th-century engineers of nihilism, heirs to Disneylands of the Holocaust, to revolution as *haute couture*, consoled in our city-worlds with ever-improving experiential technologies, don't have to slog off anywhere – the darkness has come to us.

I am not very interested in post-colonial discourse and the phantom pain of amputated empires. It is not my pride, not my burden. Other fearful symmetries have chained me to this reliquary of age-yellowed fiction. Just as Nietzsche foresaw and diagnosed the existential convulsions that followed the death of God, in *Heart of Darkness* Conrad used Kurtz's shade to project – the fate of the post-European.

'Sick! Sick! Not so sick as you would like to believe. Never mind. I'll carry my ideas out yet – I will return. I'll show you what can be done.'

You step onto the streets of a metropolis of the euro or dollar – Kurtz lurks behind you, a flickering shade.

The people running about for the sake of their businesses, gobbling down fast-food or having brilliant workouts, and fiddling with gadgets and bodies and fashions and politics – look – isn't it hilarious? What a circus of cliché!

The people sermonising to you in the name of the Idea, Goodness, Duty – you can't even be surprised anymore at their impudence, their yearning for a mass plague of naïveté.

And once again – that pompousness; once again – that hypocrisy surrounding you, the hypocrisy of the propaganda of *life*. A life that's better, longer, nobler, more colourful, someone else's. Live, live, live them.

Kurtz smoulders behind you as a black fever, 'opening his mouth voraciously. He lived then before [you]; he lives as much as he had ever lived'.

And do they make even the slightest effort to conceal the totality of this commodification of experience? Cultural capitalism is your natural ecosystem; you were born into it.

You don't pay for food – you pay to live the experience of ingesting elixirs of Health and Luxury, drinking the coffee of Youth and Success, sipping the wine of the Educated and Progressive, and for the satisfaction of later being lived by others as someone living it all.

You think you're driving a car? You're driving a construct of the experience of living big-city life, masculinity, modernity, risk, sexual attractiveness and disdain for those who can't afford to live this way.

You buy your spiritual life – at concerts, lectures, meditation sessions. You buy your sensitivity and compassion – with micro-donations to wonderful charities, with fair trade and eco-friendly products, by spending time sorting the recycling.

You think an iPhone is for talking and texting and taking pictures and using apps and the internet? An iPhone is to live the experience of being an iPhone owner.

You think you bought this book on Joseph Conrad? You bought the feeling of being a reader of a book on Joseph Conrad.

You buy yourself by living.

You buy yourself by living others.

You buy yourself by living others living you. (Oh, this is the greatest delight!)

Darkness in Brussels. Darkness in Europe.

Economists are calculating the level of a guaranteed income, a universal basic income for all citizens. Everyone is entitled to it – by the mere fact of existing. You do not have to work in order to survive. You do not have to want in order to have. You do not have to do anything.

Universities strain the last muscles of knowledge and reason to generate irrefutable proof that there is no such thing as knowledge or reason.

Dehumanised businesses supply you with better and better tools to manage your life, which not only do you good, but are better at choosing what is good for you than you are yourself.

Parliaments debate the right to freely select your gender, body, grammar, consciousness, identity. You are free to be whoever you want. You are free to be whatever you want. You are free not to be. 'I had taken him for a painter who wrote for the papers, or else for a journalist who could paint – but even the cousin could not tell me what he had been – exactly.

He was a universal genius.'

Soon this won't be the crowning achievement of humanity - to be a universal genius will be the fundamental right of every citizen.

And your individual subjective experiences – these are the foundations of all politics and the cornerstone of all realities. By what right can someone here, within the realm of your own interaction with the world, say something you don't wish to hear? By what right can something happen here that you don't wish to know about, or something exist without your permission?

At the end of Europe's civilisational journey, at the culminating point of self-knowledge and self-rule, where every individual is an entirely free, entirely independent and entirely self-sufficient creator and object of creation – what community of 'all the hearts that beat in the darkness' could there possibly be?

You have the right and the obligation to make of yourself who you want, what you want. You do not need society to live, to be safe, to flourish. You do not need a family to reproduce. You do not need another person to fulfil your emotional, sexual, or religious needs. You can change your emotionality, sexual identity, values. Once, twice, thrice, any number of times; you and altered you, and you altered by altered you. You are the absolute master of your universe. And there are billions of you.

Behold the triumph of humanity liberated from nature and culture, from need and duty, from law and biology: absolute rule in a kingdom of one, cut off from all others by never-ending darkness.

'I am lying here in the dark waiting for death.'

You can be anyone, anyone can be you.

Reason has seen right through itself. We live in a time of experimental ethics. A subject is placed in an MRI scanner and we see what is really going on in their brain; a subject undergoes extreme testing and their emotional reactions are objectively measured. In this way, it has been shown that exercising empathy results in negative responses later on, when we truly confront another person's suffering: the brain activates the same regions and neural connections as if we were suffering ourselves. Often this leads to increased aggression,[19] prompting hypotheses that empathy is a relic of hunter-gatherer cultures, harmful in a world of 21st-century mega-cities and the internet, just as the mechanisms for stocking up on fat we've inherited from eternally famished hunters now only do us harm. Doctors, hospice workers and similar professionals forced to empathise show exceptionally high levels of burnout and increased risk of suicide.[20] Our defence mechanisms activate against this 'vicarious traumatisation'; we crave insensitivity; we fraternise by alienation.

Beyond a certain point, further increases in empathy do not bring us closer to others but rather drive us further away. It seems the *sine qua non* of empathetic experience is a 'self' so expansive and separate that others' inner experiences have something on which to imprint.

However, if there is no one to take these feelings in – since we've so efficiently dissolved, de-subjectified and deconstructed ourselves – we return to the very beginning of the cycle of inner experience, to this half-animal 'empathy' of simple copying, imitation, pretending – an empty echo chamber of humanity.

How exactly does Marlow live himself into Kurtz?

Once they've finally met, after bearing Kurtz on a stretcher to the riverbank and then onto the steamship, Kurtz and Marlow do not open up effusively to one another. Kurtz has received the package of delayed correspondence, in which Marlow is purportedly recommended to him. After flicking through the stack of papers, Kurtz lifts his gaze to Marlow (they have not so far exchanged a single word) and remarks, looking him straight in the eye: 'I am glad.'

How exactly has Kurtz *recognised* Marlow?

Immediately afterwards Marlow refers to himself as Kurtz's friend, 'in a way'. They have not exchanged a single word more. In the middle of the night Kurtz sneaks from the ship out onto the shore; Marlow catches up with him, and there follows their key conversation – though once again they barely exchange a few sentences – in which it transpires Marlow already knows Kurtz so well, has so seen through and comprehended him, that he is able to instinctively find the one and only argument that will dissuade Kurtz.

There was no need at all to meet him in real life. Marlow had already lived himself into Kurtz before.

Would this have been possible if Kurtz's story had not been told to Marlow, if Marlow had not woven himself a Kurtz out of words, out of literary fiction? If not for all those tales about Kurtz – the accountant's, the manager's, the brickmaker's, the harlequin's – out of which Kurtz-in-Marlow-in-the-narrator was conceived?

If we approach *Heart of Darkness* using the method laid out in the Foreword to *The Nigger of the 'Narcissus'*, distilling out everything which can induce the transference of sensory experience – what crystal of 'pure literature' precipitates on the surface of the text?

Ideas which cannot be removed from the material world – the grand words from Kurtz's writings, the contents of his diatribe about Humanism, Progress, Civilisation – is it this?

The sound of phrases, the melody of language – Kurtz's 'magnificent folds of eloquence' – is it this?

Or is it instead that, in a culture of living one another,

what is lost is what emerges in the reader's mind from the superimposition of these fractured layers of meaning, possible only in the very incompleteness and imperfection of the transfer, when the mind must resort to its own simulations to fill in that gap 'between the senses and ideas' – and *reconstruct a non-existent original*?

What is literature in an era of ideal transfer of inner experience?

Will this 'remnant' precipitated from it not be precisely humanity? The 'self' created by a culture of imposters from written stories about the life of *Homo sapiens*?

John lives Frank living Pierre living Svetlana living Mariko living Li living John.

We are overcoming, we have overcome the limitations of written humanity.

Now you see: language leads us astray, grammar is deceptive – we must invert the subjects and predicates. Whatever is conveyed in this flawed transference along chains of lonely souls, whatever *experience* - this is the subject here, this is what comes into being and is active; the Johns Franks Pierres Svetlanas are empty organs for living experiences, imposter-tools for feigning a non-existent original. Masks to mask their own maskedness.

Fictions of humanity merging ever more smoothly into real life.

Lived by thousands, millions, billions.

All that lasts, all that is of value, is the power to create them and impose them.

Their content – does not matter. Their truthfulness – does not matter. Their source –

'He electrified large meetings. He had faith – don't

you see? – he had the faith. He could get himself to believe anything – anything. He would have been a splendid leader of an extreme party.'

'What party?'

'Any party'.'

Notes

1. All unattributed quotes come from *Heart of Darkness* by Joseph Conrad.

2. Mason, O.J. and F. Brady 'The Psychometric Effects of Short-Term Sensory Deprivation', *The Journal of Nervous and Mental Disease*, Oct 2009.

3. *Ibid.*

4. Fletcher, Paul quoted in Hadley Leggett, 'Out of LSD? Just 15 minutes of sensory deprivation triggers halllucinations', *Wired*, 21 October 2009: https://www.wired.com/2009/10/hallucinations/

5. Stephens, G. J., L.J. Silbert, U. Hasson, 'Speaker-listener Neural Coupling Underlies Successful Communication', *Procedings of the Natural Academy of the Sciences of the United States of America*, 2010.

6. Banakou, Domna and Mel Slater, 'Body Ownership Causes Illusory Self-Attribution of Speaking and Influences Subsequent Real Speaking', *Proceedings of the Natural Academy of Sciences of the United States of America*, vol. 111, no. 44, 2014.

7. Conrad, Joseph, Preface to *The Nigger of the 'Narcissus'*, 1897.

8. '[W]herever psychologists and neuroscientists have looked, they have found neural systems that evolved for one purpose (e.g. action, perception, emotion) being used for language comprehension.' – Glenberg, Arthur M, 'Language and Action: Creating Sensible Combinations of Ideas', *The Oxford Handbook of Pyscholinguistics*, 2007

9. Barsalou, Lawrence W., 'Grounded Cognition', *Annual Review of Psychology*, 2008

10. Wiemer-Hastings, K., J. Krug, X. Xu, 'Imagery, Context Availability, Contextual Constraint, and Abstractness', *Proceedings of the Annual Conference – Cognitive Science Society*, 2001

11. Gadamer, H.G. quoted in John M. Connolly and Thomas

Keutner, *On the Circle of Understanding: Hermeneutics versus Science?*, University of Notre Dame Press, Notre Dame, Indidana 1988.

12. *Umwelt* – the physical environment of an animal, as perceived and represented internally by the animal, given it's unique biological constitution and semiotic range.

13. *barbaroi* – Greek for 'barbarians', who in ancient Hellenic culture were defined by the inability to speak Greek.

14. Nagel, Thomas, 'What Is It Like to Be a Bat?', *The Philosophical Review*, October 1974

15. Nicola Mendelsohn, Vice-President of Facebook for Europe, the Middle East and Africa, at Fortune's Most Powerful Women International Summit in London, 2016, quoted in: http://fortune.com/2016/06/14/facebook-video-live/

16. Honan, Matt, 'Why Facebook And Mark Zuckerberg Went All In On Live Video', *Buzzfeed News*, April 6, 2016, https://www.buzzfeed.com/mathonan/why-facebook-and-mark-zuckerberg-went-all-in-on-live-video

17. Greenwood, Veronique, 'Consciousness Began When the Gods Stopped Speaking', *Nautilus*, 28 May 2015, http://nautil.us/issue/24/error/consciousness-began-when-the-gods-stopped-speaking

18. Clark, Andy, *Surfing Uncertainty: Prediction, Action, and the Embodied Mind*, Oxford University Press, 2016

19. Buffone, Anneke E.K. and Michael J. Poulin, 'Empathy, Target Distress, and Neurohormone Genes Interact to Predict Aggression for Others – Even Without Provocation', *Personality & Social Psychology Bulletin*, vol. 40, no. 11, November 2014

20. Klimecki, O.M. et al., 'Differential pattern of functional brain plasticity after compassion and empathy training', *Social, Cognitive and Affective Neuroscience*, vol. 9, no. 6, June 2014

About the Authors

Farah Ahamed is a short fiction writer. She was highly commended in the 2016 London Short Story Prize, joint winner of the inaugural Gerald Kraak Award and has been nominated for The Caine and The Pushcart prizes. Her stories have been published in *The Massachusetts Review, Thresholds, Kwani?, The Missing Slate, Out of Print,* among others.

SJ Bradley is a writer from Leeds. Her short fiction has appeared in various journals and anthologies including *New Willesden Short Stories 7, Queen Mobs, Litro* magazine, and *Untitled Books.* Her first novel, *Brick Mother,* and her second novel, *Guest,* are both published by Dead Ink. She is the editor of the Saboteur Award-winning anthology *Remembering Oluwale,* which is available from Valley Press.

Agnieszka Dale (née Surażyńska) is a Polish-born, London-based author conceived in Chile. Her short stories have been selected for BBC Radio 4, Liars' League London, *Tales of the Decongested* and *The Fine Line Short Story Collection.* Her feature articles have been published by *Stylist* magazine, and her song lyrics performed on BBC Radio 3's *In Tune Live from Tate Modern.* In 2013, Dale was awarded the Arts Council England TLC Free Reads Award. In 2014, her story 'The Afterlife of Trees' was shortlisted for the Carve Magazine Esoteric Short Story Contest and longlisted for the Fish Short Story Prize. *Fox Season,* her debut collection of 21 short stories, was published in October 2017 by Jantar.

Jacek Dukaj is one of Poland's most important writers of science fiction and fantasy. In 2009 he was winner of the inaugural European Literary Prize, and has also received the Koscielski Award and the Janusz A. Zajdel Award for his writing. His books include *In the Land of the Infidels*, *The Black Seas* and the bestselling *Ice*. In 2003 filmmaker Tomasz Baginski adapted his short story 'The Cathedral' into a short animation that was nominated for an Oscar.

Giles Foden was born in Warwickshire in 1967. His family moved to Malawi in 1972 where he was brought up. He returned to England at the age of 13 and was educated at Malvern College and Cambridge University where he read English. He worked as a journalist for *Media Week* magazine and became an assistant editor on the *Times Literary Supplement*, then deputy literary editor of *The Guardian*. He contributes regularly to the *The Guardian* and is books review editor for *Condé Nast Traveller* magazine. His first novel, the acclaimed *The Last King of Scotland* (1998), is set during Idi Amin's rule of Uganda in the 1970s and won the Whitbread First Novel Award, a Somerset Maugham Award, a Betty Trask Award and the Winifred Holtby Memorial Prize.

Zoe Gilbert's short stories have appeared in anthologies and journals in the UK and internationally. Her first novel, *Folk*, is published in 2018, and she is completing a PhD in creative writing at the University of Chichester. Her story 'Fishskin, Hareskin' won the Costa Short Story Award 2014.

Professor Robert Hampson FEA, FRSA was Professor of Modern Literature at Royal Holloway, University of London, until 2016. He is currently Distinguished Teaching and Research Fellow at Royal Holloway. He has an international reputation as a Conrad scholar and critic. His books on Conrad include *Joseph Conrad: Betrayal and Identity* (Macmillan,

1992), *Cross-Cultural Encounters in Joseph Conrad's Malay Fiction* (Palgrave, 2000) and *Conrad's Secrets* (Palgrave, 2013). He has also edited various works by Conrad (including *Heart of Darkness, Lord Jim* and *Victory*) and was the editor of *The Conradian*. He recently co-edited *Conrad and Language* (Edinburgh, 2016) with Katherine Baxter. He has also co-edited two collections of essays on Ford Madox Ford.

Jan Krasnowolski is a writer, essayist, translator. He is the author of four books - *9 łatwych kawałków, Klatka* and *Afrykańska elektronika* – and is the winner of three Machina Magazine creative writing awards. In 2017, his book *Syreny z Broadmoor*, which translates as *The Sirens of Broadmoor*, was published by Swiat ksiazki.

Dr Richard Niland is Lecturer in English at the University of Strathclyde in Glasgow. His research and reading is mostly in nineteenth and twentieth-century literature and history. He is the author of *Conrad and History* (OUP 2010) and has recently published work on the Marx Brothers, R. B. Cunninghame Graham, and Joseph Roth. In 2013 he was the recipient of the Adam Gillon Award for Best Book on Conrad published 2009-2012 from the Joseph Conrad Society USA.

Wojciech Orliński (born 1969 in Warsaw) trained as a chemist but has devoted most of his professional life to writing about science fiction, as a journalist, writer, and blogger. Since 1997, he has been a regular columnist for *Gazeta Wyborcza*. He has published science fiction stories and opinion pieces in *Nowa Fantastyka*, and his books include *What Are Sepulki?, All About Lem* (2010) and *America Does Not Exist* (2010).

Grażyna Plebanek is a novelist, columnist and a playwriter, author of bestselling novels *Illegal Liaisons* (WAB 2010, English edition of Stork Press 2012 and American New Europe Books 2013), *Portofino Girls* (WAB 2005), and *Box with Pins* (2002). She also wrote 'Girl called Przystupa' (WAB 2007), *The Boxer* (WAB 2014) and 'Madame Fury' (Znak 2016) as well as *The Robbermaid's Daughters*, a series of literary essays and many short stories. Her play 'Madame Fury' won two prizes and will be on stage in 2018. Plebanek is a Golden Owl winner for promoting Poland abroad. www.grazynaplebanek.com

Sarah Schofield's prizes include the Writers Inc Short Story Competition and the Calderdale Short Story Competition. She was shortlisted for the Bridport Prize in 2010 and was runner up in The Guardian Travel Writing Competition, and currently teaches Creative Writing at Edgehill University. Her stories have appeared in several Comma anthologies: *Lemistry*, *Bio-Punk*, *Beta-Life*, *Spindles*, and *Thought X*. She is currently working on her first collection.

Kamila Shamsie is the author of seven novels, which have been translated into over 20 languages. *Home Fire* was longlisted for the Man Booker Prize, *Burnt Shadows* was shortlisted for the Orange Prize for Fiction, and *A God in Every Stone* was shortlisted for the Bailey's Women's Prize for Fiction. A Fellow of the Royal Society of Literature, and one of Granta's 'Best of Young British Novelists', she grew up in Karachi, and now lives in London.

Paul Theroux is an American travel writer and novelist, and short story writer, who over the past fifty years has published more than fifty books, some of which have been made into feature films.

About the Translators

Sean Gasper Bye is a translator of Polish, French and Russian. His translations of *Watercolours* by Lidia Ostałowska and *History of a Disappearance* by Filip Springer were published in 2017. His translations of fiction, reportage, and drama have appeared in *Words Without Borders*, *Catapult*, *Continents*, and elsewhere, and he is a winner of the 2016 *Asymptote* Close Approximations Prize. He studied modern languages at University College London and international studies at the School of Oriental and African Studies. Since 2014, he has been Literature and Humanities Curator at the Polish Cultural Institute New York.

Scotia Gilroy is a literary translator from Vancouver, now based in Kraków. She graduated with First Class Honours from the English Literature department of Simon Fraser University, and in 2010 received a Kościuszko Scholarship to study Polish language and literature at the Jagiellonian University (Kraków). In 2016-2017 she completed the Emerging Translator Mentorship Program at Writers Centre Norwich. She currently translates for many Polish cultural institutions and publishing houses.

Eliza Marciniak is an editor and a literary translator. Her translations include *Swallowing Mercury* by Wioletta Greg, published by Portobello Books and longlisted for the Man Booker International Prize 2017, and a series of classic Polish children's books by Marian Orłoń, with illustrations by Jerzy Flisak, published by Pushkin Press: *Detective Nosegoode and the Music Box Mystery*, *Detective Nosegoode and the Kidnappers* and *Detective Nosegoode and the Museum Robbery*.